VOICES DANGER

'Do you know what a war is?' he suddenly found himself asking. It was one of his questions that expected no answer. He slotted careful thoughts into place. He needed to tell them something important. A flare soared over the British lines, close by; the barn roof and the three of them were tinged briefly with pale blue-white. 'Old Men killing Young Men. That's what war is.'

C. Woods

Please Return

If Found

VOICES of DANGER

ALICK ROWE

MAMMOTH

*This book is dedicated to the boys of Hereford
Cathedral Choir for their singing and
friendship.*

Author's Note

In 1916 the voices of young men broke
generally at sixteen or seventeen – the same
age at which very many volunteered to fight
in the war, though officially underage.
Apologies for accidental inaccuracies and for
issuing a recording of Elgar's 'Serenade for
Strings' seventeen years early. Gratitude and
admiration to Lyn Macdonald for her
magnificent books on The Great War

First published in Great Britain 1990
by Methuen Children's Books Ltd
Published 1992 by Mammoth
an imprint of Reed Consumer Books Limited
Michelin House, 81 Fulham Road, London SW3 6RB
and Auckland, Melbourne, Singapore and Toronto

Reprinted 1992 (three times)

ISBN 0 7497 0412 8

A CIP catalogue record for this title
is available from the British Library

Printed in Great Britain
by Cox & Wyman Ltd, Reading, Berkshire

VOICES of DANGER

PART ONE

Archenford, England:
Spring 1916

1

In Time of War

The boy pressed back in the side-chapel and let the scare thrill through him. His breathing jerked; his stomach ached. All round him the brassy beats of the organ hammered and snarled in the dark. He shut his eyes and felt dizzy. He heard the men pass the chapel door – quiet voices and clicking boots on flagstones – then counted to ten and darted out: three quick steps across the passage and four more up into the choirstalls. He glanced up to the organ loft but the player's eyes were steady on his music. He ran almost silently down to the cathedral nave. He felt safer. This part of the building was massive with thick pillars of stone, rows of pews, monuments to hide behind. He paused at the first pillar. The dizziness had gone; now he felt light-footed, light-headed. He waited briefly to catch his breath.

Two dim pools of light glowed in the darkness. Far across the nave he saw the men leave the north porch and the verger lock the door. As the gas-lamp there dimmed and died, he moved from shadow to shadow towards the central south pillar where the remaining lantern glimmered. This was the moment he longed for and feared the most. He stood motionless on the one side of the thick column of stone knowing the verger would already be crossing the nave directly towards him. The ache and the thrill returned and he tried to force his fear up into the soaring echoes of music. He felt the thrill grow. Then the organ stopped and the sudden silence was like light flooding down.

Alex was shocked. He was immediately aware of his fast, shallow breathing; he could easily hear his heart-beats. He flattened himself against the stone as Gwynne, the verger, reached noisily up to the lamp on the other side of the pillar and brought an almost total blackness to the nave.

New sounds slid into the dangerous silence. From the street came the muffled rattle of a cart, a girl's voice shouting, plodding hooves and the raucous splutter and backfire of a motor car. Inside the cathedral, Martin Cleeve thumped down the organ loft staircase, Gwynne wheezed away to his next duty and Alexander Davies felt his way to the collecting-box on the central south pillar to steal the coins inside it.

Tired and anxious to be dismissed to supper, the rest of the boys looked hopefully up as Alex came through the Robing Room door. Chatterton, the head chorister, glanced over.

'Where's Cleeve?'

Alex knew his breathing was still unsteady. Heaviness was creeping into him and he felt sick. He had been away from the room for no more than three minutes. He forced himself to grin brightly.

'He's coming, Chatterton.'

'Where's your hymn book?'

'Here.' Alex waved it.

'You forget things too much.'

'Yes, I know. Sorry.'

Seb Carpenter reached out to take his best friend's hymn book and stack it with the others but the door opened and all the boys stood as Martin Cleeve, the assistant organist, walked in to dismiss them. The Choir's two processional lines hurried out into a cold March night. Gusts of wind bounced round the huge cathedral, buffeting the boys as they made for School House in the north-west corner of the Close.

Dusk was early tonight. In a corner of the Close the lamplighter was beginning work. The Choir was almost at the gate when two men called from a bench.

10

'Left right left right.'

'Get them arms swinging.'

The young soldiers laughed as if a great joke had been made. 'King and Country, lads,' one added and the laughter grew again. The boys passed through the gate keeping their eyes straight ahead. There was something terrible about two crippled soldiers joking this way, even though people were getting used to such things. It was March 1916 and the war was eighteen months old.

Alex suddenly turned aside and was sick. Seb hung about near him kicking at the gravel as the laughing from the bench dwindled to silence. Seb knew Alex would say nothing but needed to know what was troubling him. Over the next few weeks Alex would not talk and Seb gave up trying.

Martin Cleeve and the boys of the Choir crowded into the summerhouse at the centre of the bishop's immaculate lawn as two hundred spectators, from every walk of Archenford life, wildly cheered the end of a marching display by the band and cadets of the Cathedral School.

It was a chilly afternoon at the beginning of April but everyone was eager to raise money to provide comfort and memories of home to the local men fighting far away for King and Country in France. Martin Cleeve had selected six patriotic songs and hoped the boys would cope well enough, since Doctor Brinsop, Cathedral Organist and Master of Choristers, had, of course, allowed him no time for practice.

'Mind you sing good now.'

A smiling girl passed the summerhouse on her way to a white First Aid tent among the trees. Boys grinned back. 'Hello, Winnie.'

'Bet you're skiving off.'

'Don't let Flo see you.'

Winifred Price made for the VAD tent. She was small

and dark, popular with those of the Choir not scared off by her fierce Welsh temper. She was undermaid in the Brinsop household and had come to know the choristers during those strange weeks when the school was on holiday but the Choir was not. At such times, 'Keeping-the-boys-out-of-mischief' between practices and services was a major obsession and the boys worked long unpaid, unthanked hours weeding, mowing and rolling a succession of gardens in the Close. Sometimes they were allowed to polish Mrs Brinsop's furniture or paint the servants' part of the house. The older boys saw at once that Winnie was at everyone's beck and call and admired her spirit and energy. Hard work was natural to her. Like Seb, she came from a farming background but there the similarity ceased. Winnie's father was a sullen slow-witted labourer who strongly disapproved of his daughter leaving home and (worse) crossing into England from his ramshackle cottage near Knighton in Central Wales. Fortunately, Winnie's mother had understood her need for a better life and had smuggled her away. Her father had sent word she need never return and she knew better than to try. Twice a year, her mother risked her husband's anger to travel to Archenford and see Winnie – during her free time, of course – in the kitchen of Brinsop's house.

This spring afternoon, Winnie felt good; she enjoyed helping her new friends of the VAD unit and took pleasure in the knowledge that Mrs Brinsop – Flo – strongly objected to granting her time from household duties but could find no way of preventing her without seeming to undermine the war effort. Winnie was fifteen, ambitious and keen to learn whatever she could wherever she could.

'Hello, Winnie.' A young woman, only a few years older than the Welsh girl, grinned up at her from a table spread with linen. Fiona Templeton was the daughter of Archenford's chief constable. Winnie smiled back and nodded. 'Good afternoon, ladies,' she called to the rest of the workers who bobbed and clucked round the table like a perch of busy hens. Winnie rolled up her sleeves and took the empty chair next to her friend. The linen was being cut and rolled into bandages and dressings for field-wounds and Winnie's strong, rough hands worked fast. There was a spatter of applause as the boys finished 'The British Grenadiers' and, hearing the piano strike up the first chords of 'Hearts of Oak', Fiona joined in. Winnie began to sing too and soon the entire First Aid tent was clucking, trilling and singing wonderfully well as bandages and field-dressings steadily mounted on the table. Winnie hoped this work would lead her where she really wanted to be and tried not to think of the wounds the linen would cover.

Cold. It was cold. His feet were cold. He tried to stamp them but his boots were heavy as lead. He heard whistles and bugles and tried desperately to sing 'Hearts of Oak' as bullets cracked and zipped all round him. Then Seb jolted awake in the dark dormitory, gasping and scared. It was the third night of sharp, late frost and it was bitterly cold. His breath plumed in the chill air and his feet were numb. As he hauled his blankets from the floor he glanced at the next bed where Alex slept. He screwed up his eyes and peered into the dark. He could just see that the bed was empty.

Seb was still worried about Alex. They were close friends perhaps because they had joined the Choir the same day, six years ago, when they were ten. Each looked upon the Cathedral Close as home and loved the music they sang.

Seb's family, the Carpenters, were tenant-farmers in Herefordshire, who had been first disbelieving then pleased when the rector of their isolated village had suggested that Seb undergo a voice trial for a Choir scholarship at Archenford. Mr and Mrs Carpenter farmed poor land with a large family and were grateful to have one major responsibility honourably taken from their hard-working shoulders. Because the Choir followed the church year, holidays were few – a week at Christmas, four days at Easter – and it was only during the four weeks of the summer break that Seb returned to the overcrowded farmhouse to help bring in the harvest. He always tried hard but always felt an outsider, ashamed that he looked forward to his return to the Close. For a few days afterwards there would be some mockery – not all of it cruel – about the strong stench of sheep but Seb Carpenter stayed calm and smiled gently. He had narrowly escaped grinding poverty and knew it. His secret fear was that the war would take his older brothers and force him back.

The war had killed Alex's father. Company Sergeant-Major Davies had been shot by a sniper during the battle for Le Cateau in the first weeks of fighting in 1914. Alexander was an only child, brought up in Bristol by his father and aunt. Enquiries about his mother had always brought easy lies or disapproving silence from aunt and the promise from his father to tell the whole story when he was older. Now he would never know, though, in fact, Alex had long given up trying and had buried the faint memories of his mother in some deep place where they could not hurt him. He had swiftly done the same over his father. Six years earlier, Alex had come to the cathedral for much the same reasons as Seb. Mr Davies' wage as a printer's assistant could not give his son the education – the start in life as he called it – that he wished, so he encouraged Alex to try for the Choir scholarship which he had won. Alex had seemed happy until recently.

Seb could not find Alex in the bathroom where a single gas jet burned against the freezing of pipes. He walked past empty rows of lavatory cubicles and opened the bootroom door. It was slightly less cold here; the pipes were still lukewarm. He heard brushing, scraping. A dim glow edged the bottom of the door to the boilerhouse.

Alex was close to the massive stove which heated School House and wore an army greatcoat over his pyjamas. He looked up anxiously as Seb opened the door. He seemed embarrassed at being found. Seb's eyes strayed to a clean belt and shining cap badge with one bright boot. 'It's Tarrington's kit,' murmured Alex.

'Why not do it tomorrow?'

'No time.'

Alex gave a final rub to a gleaming boot and laid it beside the other. He reached for a fire-iron to flick the stove door open. A glow of heat reached out and both boys leaned gratefully into it. Seb glanced across at Alex. Even in the warm orange light he looked pale and the hollows around his eyes seemed deeper than usual.

'What's wrong?' he asked softly.

Alex swung angry eyes at him. 'It's nothing,' he snapped. 'I don't sleep well. That's all.'

Alex turned back towards the square of warmth; his face glowing a little in his annoyance and he held out both hands to the dull fire. After a while, Seb laid an arm across his shoulders and they stayed like that until the cathedral bell-tower gave out three-quarters. When Alex spoke, it was little more than a whisper.

'I don't know what to do about myself, Seb.'

Seb waited for more, not understanding.

'Too many mistakes.' Alex seemed to decide he had said enough. He stood and replaced the rags and polish on a shelf. He swung the stove-door shut, picked up cap-badge, belt and boots before blowing out the candle. The dark was tinged with grey; it would soon be dawn.

In Tarrington's study Alex put away the belt and boots while Seb slid open the curtains. This was the sheltered side of the house and there was a light covering of frost upon the glass. Out in the Close gaslamps gleamed but there was no sign of life.

Seb looked at his friend. 'What mistakes? In choir?'

Alex raked the tiny grate and sent ash cascading into the tray beneath. He paused. For several seconds he didn't move. He knelt before the fireplace.

'Not only the Choir,' he said slowly. Before he could explain, a fine cloud of dust came to his nose and he sneezed. He sneezed again. Seb was immediately worried; the noise was enormous. 'Sssh.' Alex sneezed again. 'I can't stop it.' He began to grin as he muffled another explosion in the greatcoat. Alex began to laugh. Although nothing was funny, Seb found himself smiling foolishly. He opened the study door and listened carefully as Alex struggled giggling from the coat and hung it behind the door. He sneezed again, and again.

In the dormitory it was colder than ever but the other six boys were sleeping soundly. It was lighter. The whirls and fossils of frost grudgingly admitted the light at the window. Alex slipped into his bed and gasped.

'It's cold. O God, it's like ice.'

Seb pulled the blanket from his shoulders and spread it back upon his bed.

'Alex?' he asked carefully. 'Do you go down there often at nights?'

But Alex was already burrowing deep into his bedclothes. Seb didn't know if he had even heard. In any case, Seb was shivering now and, teeth chattering, he made for the tangled centre of his bed. He was tired now but couldn't sleep again. He dozed fitfully until the first bell was rung in the room at half-past six. Alex was already dressed and making his bed. He grinned and shouted for Seb to get up. Seb struggled into the sharp morning, wondering if his visit to the bootroom and study had been just another dream.

2

Daily Orders

At much the same time as Seb and Alex tunnelled between cold sheets in School House, Winnie counted to ten and bravely launched herself into the freezing air of her attic room. She cracked the crust of ice across her wash-basin and plunged her hands in, gasping, to pat her face awake. By the time she had pulled on her under-maid's heavy uniform she was shivering and glad to run quietly down the back stairs into what was left of the kitchen's warmth. Making sure the pipes were unfrozen she filled two iron kettles and heaved them on to the hob of the long black range. Winnie unlocked the back door and hurried into the crystal ice-garden where the silence was as deep as the frost and each breath drew the cold deep down to her lungs. She unbolted the coalshed and found the full scuttles, one of coal and one of coke. The metal handles bit and numbed her hands as she dragged them inside. She opened the fire door of the range and carefully dropped in small chunks of coal, encouraging flames, and when they suddenly flapped up she built coke round them and closed the door.

For the first time since leaving her bed, Winnie paused and sat down. The most important job of the day was done: the kitchen range was the heart of the house, summer or winter, and without it there would be no hot water, no hot food. She checked the flames, then took newspaper and kindling to lay the dining-room fire which would give comfort to Doctor and Mrs Brinsop when they sat down to breakfast at eight o'clock. Eight o'clock? She glanced at the clock above the mantelpiece: plenty of time. She heaved a scuttle of coal across the hall to Brinsop's Study where, after breakfast, he would read the newspaper and glance though the morning's post. (She noticed a light film of dust on his piano; she must remember to polish it as soon as she had the fire burning in the grate.) She straightened up and briefly considered fires – the dining-room fire to be lit the moment Brinsop and Flo were awake, the study fire to be lit as soon as they began breakfast. Back in the kitchen, Cook was slumped in her chair, grieving for tea as she waited for a kettle to boil. There was time to lay the fire in Flo's sitting-room.

As the girl gathered the empty scuttles she thought how strange it seemed – rooms for the doctor, rooms for his wife; she recalled the grubby rough-and-tumble of the three-roomed cottage near Knighton. Winnie made for the back door, beginning to tire; in spite of her almost nonstop activity, the sharp chill of the morning was having its effect. She took a determined breath and battled out once more into the garden. Cook shouted at her. 'Close that door, you. Don't you know there's a frost?' Winnie did know there was a frost as she cracked lumps from the frozen mass of coal in the shed. The cathedral bell struck three-quarters. A quarter to seven, she thought automatically – Brinsops must have tea in their bedroom at half-past seven sharp; Brinsop's bath must be run for him at exactly a quarter to eight.

And at much the same time as the Master of the Choristers coated his hot buttered toast with marmalade and his wife tinkled the bell to summon Winnie, his choirboys were jumping up and down in the Close, flapping arms, snorting like horses and running hard on the spot while Chatterton hammered for admittance on the Choir Cloister door. During this cold snap the boys had permission to add gloves, scarves and sweaters to their everyday school uniform since the Song School had no efficient heating. The frantic activity stopped as Martin Cleeve appeared, so wrapped up against the cold in hat, coat and long scarf that his pebbled spectacles peering out gave him the apearance of an owl. He tried an ex-perimental knock on the door himself before fumbling with numb fingers for the spare key he carried.

As they all stamped, gasped and flapped their freezing way to their ice-box of a Song School, Martin Cleeve thought of Brinsop stretched at ease before a roaring fire and felt a twinge of disloyalty. He blinked in surprise at the sharpness of it. This was not the first time rebellious thoughts had struck Doctor Brinsop's quiet-mannered assistant. It would definitely not be the last.

Lewis swiftly and expertly swept the study floor, making sure not to raise too much dust.

'Excuse me, Tarrington.'

Tarrington drew in his legs. He was in Officer Training Corps uniform; there were parades and training three times a week after school. At the table beneath the window Alex buffed the senior boy's boots. Lewis was keen to get away; he had a lesson to prepare before school began again at two o'clock. He tapped the bristles of the broom into the fireplace and leaned it behind the door.

'Is that all, please, Tarrington?'

Tarrington stretched back his legs and nodded.

'Thank you, Tarrington.'

Lewis left at once, pleased to escape Tarrington's strange mood. At the small table Alex gave each toecap a careful burnishing and laid the boots side by side on a sheet of newspaper.

'Is that all, please, Tarrington?'

He was keen to be away; the Geography test would start promptly at two. Tarrington saw his anxiety.

'No. See to the fire.'

Alex went swiftly to the hearth. There was very little coal in the battered bucket but he had no intention of telling Tarrington, who would send him to forage for

19

more in the other studies. He tidied the already tidy hearth, broke a large lump of coal into three and laid the pieces carefully round the dull flame. He stood, shaking coaldust from his hands into the grate.

'Can I go now, please?'

The noise from the passage had almost stopped. Alex needed to leave soon.

'No. Check the French exercise you did for me. I've copied it in my book.'

'I've already checked it once.'

'Then check it again.'

'It must be nearly two, Tarrington. I haven't got my things ready yet.'

'That's not my fault. Check the exercise.'

Briefly Alex considered a refusal but crossed quickly to the small desk in the corner and flipped open an exercise book. He found the page and began scanning the work. Tarrington watched. From the rest of the House there was almost silence. A few shouts in the Close could be heard and suddenly the warning bell clanged from the neighbouring schoolyard. Alex was alarmed. 'Please, Tarrington.'

Tarrington scrutinised the pale, nervous face and, without switching his gaze, deliberately swung an arm to rock and topple an empty cup at his side. It smashed in the hearth.

'Clear it up.'

Alex knew he must come to a decision.

'I've got to go, Tarrington.' He moved determinedly towards the door.

'Clear it up.' The voice was quiet, threatening.

Alex turned, frightened and exasperated.

'I told you. I can't. I'm already late. We've got a test.'

'Then the sooner you begin, the better.'

Alex felt his eyes moisten with the helpless frustration of the moment. He was angry; he didn't want Tarrington to see this.

'Why exactly are you doing this, Tarrington?' He tried to keep his voice calm but the words jerked out high and fearful.

Tarrington smiled. 'Because you're a thief,' he replied, smooth as silk.

The shock hit Alex like a physical blow. 'What are you talking about?' he whispered.

Tarrington flicked at the saucer. It fell among the fragments of the cup and cracked in two.

'Clear this up.' There was no smile at all now.

Alex fought his panic and just managed to win. He moved, trembling, to gather the smashed cup and saucer. Tarrington reached for one of his boots and slipped it on.

'We'll talk about it later. After supper.'

Alex stood before Tarrington, holding the fragments. He knew he was in danger of crying. A muffled handbell was rung, inside the school, to mark the beginning of classes. He begged.

'Please, Tarrington.' His voice shook; it was little more than breathing. Tarrington stared into the younger boy's face.

'You disgust me,' he snapped. 'Put that down. Get out.'

Alex dropped the broken earthenware in the bin and darted from the room. Tarrington examined and approved the sheen of his boots as he began carefully lacing up.

Lionel Tarrington was eighteen, a senior member of School House, and entitled to have a first-year boy run his errands, keep his study tidy and act generally as his servant, his fag. Lewis performed his duties efficiently but without enthusiasm. However, Tarrington knew Alex to be short of cash – shorter still since the army pension due at Sergeant-Major Davies' death had been granted to his absent wife, much to Aunt's disgust. So,

21

for five shillings a term, Alex worked for Tarrington in his rare free time. Tarrington enjoyed having two boys at his beck and call. It reminded him of the servants at home and made him feel almost equal to the head of house who was permitted two fags by right.

Everybody admitted Tarrington had 'spirit'. He was a fearless sportsman who represented the school in rugby, hockey, cross-country running and cricket. He swam and boxed bravely too. His nature was overkeenly competitive and he could not bear to lose; above all he hated the humiliation of putting on the brave face and pretending to a successful opponent that it didn't matter and that the best man or team had won.

Tarrington's dislike for Alex was complicated. The younger boy shared none of his interests and saw no sense in any of the activities which gave his employer importance. He and Tarrington were opposites. Alex was not particularly strong; Tarrington despised weaklings. Alex was intelligent; Tarrington was not – for his five shillings Alex was expected to do a certain amount of the older boy's schoolwork. Alex was also, of course, a member of the Cathedral Choir and Tarrington enjoyed owning a tame representative of this élite. But Tarrington found Alex intriguing, too. On the last night of the previous term, hiding in the cathedral nave to put a bowler hat on the statue of a bishop, for a wager, Tarrington had seen his servant step neatly from the shadows and expertly rob an almsbox. He had told nobody. He had preferred to store it away for his own future use.

3

Under Attack

Alex ran from Tarrington. Along the Study passages and into the dayroom snatching books from his locker, down the six steps and out of the house by the trunkroom door. Alex ran. Over the gravel, across the grass, through the gate in the wall and into the Schoolyard. Alex ran. Inside the building he scaled stone steps, passed three rooms of verb-chanting classes and came to his own formroom door.

Alex stopped.

Since the headlong flight from Tarrington he had not used his brain; fear had driven him. Now, outside his classroom door, he found himself beginning to think. The extent of Tarrington's power over him begin to sink in. How did Tarrington know?

Panic gave way to anxiety. He was in no state for a lesson. As his breathing levelled, he heard Mister Collett's clipped and deliberate voice posing test questions. 'Question number six . . .'

The words came clearly through the heavy door. Alex supposed he must be at least five minutes late. He gazed helplessly at the door. It would have to be Collett, he thought; another replacement teacher pulled from retirement: a leathery old man of peppery temper, a disciplinarian. The man's voice grew suddenly louder; he must be the other side of the door. Alex stepped back involuntarily and noticed coal dust on his hands, black smears on his books. He had the habit of rubbing his forehead when worried and guessed his face would be smudged too.

'Question number seven . . .'

Alex took another step backwards. Better to sneak

back into School House and work out the next move there. He would probably go to Matron's room and lie that he'd been in the lavatories feeling sick since first bell. Yes. He took a quiet step back, about to turn.

'Boy.'

Alex's heart missed a beat then seemed to beat in double-time. He swung round to see Kemp, the house-master, watching him from the other end of the corridor.

'What are you doing, Davies?'

'Class, sir.'

Alex gabbled the words and did the only thing poss-ible to avoid further questions. He knocked on Collett's door and walked straight in.

He walked straight into Collett. The door brushed the teacher's back as Alex pushed it open and, as the man turned in surprise, Alex walked straight into him. The untidy collision might have been funny if it had been with any other member of staff. Even those in the class, who had no liking for Alex, felt sympathy and alarm. There was total silence and stillness.

Collett was outraged. For several seconds he stared at Alex in disbelief. Seb and Matthew exchanged apprehensive glances.

'How dare you?'

Alex had difficulty with his words. 'Sorry, I'm . . . Sir. Sorry.'

Collett scrutinised him with distaste.

'Have you any idea what you look like?'

Alex felt his stomach turn and grip in fear; he actually felt his legs begin to shake. Collett's scrutiny passed to his grimy hands clutching the books.

'Monitor?' Collett rapped, and a boy came swiftly from a desk at the front. 'Basket,' the man said. The boy moved quickly to bring the wicker waste-paper basket from the corner of the room. Collett pointed at Alex's books and then to the basket. Alex carefully laid them in and the Class Monitor returned the basket to its corner and hurried back to his place. Collett's eyes had never left Alex from the moment the boy had come so abruptly into the room.

'You know the time, boy?'

Alex could only nod wretchedly.

'Why are you late?' It was the impossible question. Silence stretched. 'Are you dumb, boy? Are you stupid?'

Silence. The whole class held its breath. Collett eased back the flowing sleeve of his gown to free his arm and strike out. Alex bit his lips and Seb deliberately knocked his books and ruler to the floor. The sudden noise was thunderous and Collett turned angrily from Alex.

'I'm sorry, sir.' Seb stood; he spoke clearly and politely.

'I'm very sorry, sir. May I pick up the books, please, sir?' Collett examined Seb's open face for any hint of misbehaviour but could find none. He nodded. Seb thanked him and collected his things from the floor. Collett's attention moved back to Alex but the tension had been broken. The man was aware that time was passing and he had questions to put to his class. The class felt the release also; there was a quiet shifting and a boy coughed. 'Go and wash your hands and face, boy. When you return, be sure to knock and wait.' Collett half-turned back to the class. He looked down at his list of questions.

'Collect brown paper from your housemaster and recover your books. I shall inspect them tomorrow,' he added as an afterthought. Alex made for the door. He felt terrible.

Outside, safe in the corridor, Alex leaned back against the wall. He felt tired, drained – the way he felt back in the Robing Room after . . .

He suddenly remembered Tarrington and caught his breath. He rubbed his eyes and forehead and walked quickly away in the direction of the washroom.

There was no chance for Seb to find out what had made Alex so late. As the handbell clanged in the corridors, the boys of Collett's class sneaked hopeful looks towards the old man at his desk and pretended to carry on shading their maps of Australia. The test was over and done with. Seb had done well – 25 out of 30 – but by the time Alex had knocked gently at the door and waited for permission to come in, the test had been halfway over and of the fourteen questions that Alex had answered only six were answered correctly. His mind had simply refused to turn to the empire's climates and economies; it had more important and disturbing facts to make sense of.

At last Collett carefully folded the newspaper he was reading and looked levelly around the room before dismissing the dozen boys who began rummaging in desks and gathering books with great speed – though nobody dared speak. Seb glanced at Alex who shared a double desk with him. Boys began to leave.

'Davies?' Collett beckoned him to his desk on the low platform. By now, Seb was the only other boy in the room and tried to dawdle, to be with his friend, but it was no good.

'You, boy. Close the door behind you.'

Seb reluctantly did as he was told. Outside, he listened hard at the door but the echoing din of a hundred and twenty boys leaving lessons for the day defeated him and he wandered to a window which overlooked the Close. A watery sun was about to be locked in again by leaden cloud. A group of younger boys trotted towards the River Gate, beginning a run round the upstream and downstream bridges, their breath steaming. Once the sun was down, the frost would sharpen again. Seb moved back to the door but could hear nothing. He was worried for Alex. Between the end of school and the beginning of afternoon practice in the Song School there were only fifteen minutes.

26

Collett would not listen. Collett was not interested. It was nothing to do with him. Like most of his colleagues, the old man had only a hazy idea of Choir duties and responsibilities. He knew the choristers as a yawning, under-educated gaggle who frequently interrupted his lessons by arriving late or leaving early. Alex's case was simple. Afternoon school consisted of two hours' work and since the boy had finally joined the class in a clean and fit state some twenty minutes late, he must make up those twenty minutes now – and they would not begin until Alex stopped arguing and sat at his desk to copy the list of questions and answers in which he had done so badly.

Outside, Seb listened again at the door. Nothing. At Evensong that night Alex would sing the treble solo in Stanford's setting of the Magnificat in G. It was tricky and very exact. Brinsop would want to practise it the moment the boys were assembled in the Song School. But Alex would not be there, and Brinsop, like Collett, would not be interested in excuses. Seb came to a swift decision.

'Come in.'

Seb opened the door, determined not to show his nervousness. Alex looked up surprised and Collett peered in Seb's direction.

'Yes?'

'Can Davies come to the choir cloister for practice, please, sir?'

Seb managed to keep his voice level, trying to give the request some authority, as if he were the messenger of Brinsop. Collett glanced at the watch open on his desk.

'Davies may come to the choir cloister for practice in precisely thirteen minutes.' He waved Seb away as if brushing away an annoying fly. Seb stood his ground.

'Davies is needed now, sir.'

Collett was irritated and glared at Seb. 'Thirteen minutes. Did you not hear what I said, boy?'

Seb gulped. 'Please, Mister Collett. Doctor Brinsop requires him immediately.'

'Be so kind as to inform Doctor Brinsop that Davies will be available for his practice in precisely . . .' (He examined his watch) '. . . twelve and one quarter minutes.'

He snapped the watch shut and bent over his paper. Seb tried to give as much reassurance to his friend as he could in one quick glance but Alex felt even more doomed, thinking that Brinsop was demanding him and he could not go.

The bells in the tower sounded the quarter hour as Seb sprinted to the choir cloister door. There was no sign of the rest. As he reached for the handle, the door opened and Martin Cleeve appeared. Seb pulled to a halt and stood back for the man to pass. He was about to move on when the sub-organist called, 'Carpenter?'

Seb turned in the doorway.

'Is something the matter?'

Seb examined Martin Cleeve's round face and saw a genuine concern. He panted out the problem. Martin Cleeve listened without interrupting.

'Go to practice,' Cleeve said. 'Leave this to me.'

Seb opened his mouth to thank him.

'And go very soon,' Martin Cleeve added. 'The Doctor is twenty yards ahead of you.'

Seb went.

Martin Cleeve marched on Collett. Today he had had enough of the privilege and insolence of old men who clung to their authority like a raft. As he stamped beneath the schoolyard gate his thick glasses began to mist and he paused briefly to clear them with his scarf. Then he was in the school buildings and heading for Collett's classroom like an avenging angel. He refused to allow himself to imagine the possible results of this mission. His friends at home on leave from the battle front told

28

him the same story – of arrogant old men, secure in their authority and too proud to listen or learn who sent young soldiers to their deaths by the thousand. Lions led by donkeys. Martin Cleeve was not in France; he was climbing the school stairs. But he was about to do his bit.

'Where is Davies?'

Nobody answered. Doctor Brinsop turned to Chatterton. 'Where is Davies?'

Chatterton cleared his throat and hoarsely confessed he did not know. Perhaps Carpenter might.

'Where is Davies?'

'Mister Collett kept him behind, sir.'

'For what reason?'

'I don't know, sir.'

Brinsop straightened his music on his piano and looked hard at Chatterton who was coughing.

'Do you have a cold?'

The head chorister admitted that he did. Brinsop gazed at the uneasy boy thoughtfully and struck a chord. 'Scales.'

The boys accurately climbed and descended two easy octaves in company with the piano.

'Now Chatterton on his own.'

Chatterton clearly climbed the first octave, clambered throatily up half the second, rasped through the next two notes, croaked on the last and finally arrived at the end of his nine-year career as a boy treble.

Martin Cleeve rapped on the door and walked directly in. 'I am removing this boy from your detention. He is needed in the Cathedral.'

Collett peered disbelievingly and Alex gaped. Collett and Cleeve had never met.

'Who are you?'

'My name is Cleeve. I am assistant to Doctor Brinsop.'

29

Collett glared angrily down at his watch; he glared even more angrily up at Martin Cleeve.

'This boy will be available in eight minutes. Good day, sir.' Martin was already at Alex's desk.

'Come along, Davies.'

No such thing had ever happened to Collett before. He was white with anger. He slapped the desk hard like a spoiled child. Martin Cleeve pretended not to have heard. Alex moved with him towards the door.

'Mister Cleeve, sir?'

'What is it?'

'My books are in the waste-paper basket.'

Cleeve laid a protective arm across Alex's shoulders and steered him towards the basket, close to Collett's desk. Collett clambered down from his platform.

'This is an unwarranted impudence,' he spluttered. He powerlessly followed Martin Cleeve and Alex to the door.

'Go straight to the Song School, Davies.'

Alex ran and Martin Cleeve turned to face Collett who stood inches higher, despite his age. They heard Alex's hurrying steps stamping downstairs and clicking into the yard. Collett's lower lip trembled.

'I will not tolerate interference. I shall inform the headmaster.' To his delight, Martin Cleeve found himself beginning to smile which infuriated Collett even more.

'No laughing matter, sir,' he shouted furiously.

Martin Cleeve removed his spectacles and polished them with the end of his scarf. He raised his pale, dim eyes to Collett's gimlet glare. The hint of a smile vanished.

'You are correct, Mister Collett,' he said mildly. 'It is no laughing matter that Alexander Davies and the other choristers sing fourteen services a week during forty-six weeks of the year in your cathedral but instead of appreciation and co-operation find only pettymindedness and obstruction.'

30

He set his glasses upon his nose and looked up mildly.

'It is no laughing matter that these young musicians perform exacting work under uncomfortable conditions but are treated without sympathy or respect. It is no laughing matter that allowances are never made for the twelve lessons a week that they are forced to miss. No laughing matter, Mister Collett, that the boy Davies is the cathedral's finest soloist who, on the Sunday after half-term, will sing before the bishop, the dean and chapter, the lord lieutenant, the mayor and all Archenford's worthies, but instead of allowing him his practice you sit on him here like some broody, offended hen. God protect me, sir, from elderly schoolmasters.'

He turned on his heel and left the classroom delicately closing the door behind him. Fool, he thought. Fool. Where will I go if they boot me from here? Martin Cleeve had not quite regretted his actions by the time he came to the River Gatehouse where he lodged, but it was a close-run thing.

Brinsop saw Alex creep into the Song School and lifted his hands from the keyboard. Everyone in the room, boys and men, was silenced.

'What hour do you call this?'

'Mister Collett kept me behind, sir.'

Brinsop turned back to the piano dismissively.

'See me after Evensong.'

Alex pushed his way past Victor and Quinn to come to his place. Instead of Chatterton, he now had Matthew Freeman as neighbour. He looked round for Chatterton but he was gone. 'Stanford in G. Magnificat,' the doctor said. The Choir found its copies and set them on the practice desks. 'I expect the solo to be immaculate, Davies,' he warned.

Across the room, Seb grinned and nodded encouragingly but Alex couldn't respond. He felt weighed down, his eyes itched with tiredness and he knew that his concentration and will-power were shattered and scattered between Tarrington, Collett and Brinsop. There was not enough left for Stanford, too. The practice was bad but not as disastrous for Alex as the service. He missed the first solo entry, faltered on the second and virtually gave up on the rest. Nothing felt real. Brinsop was furious. After Evensong, he led Alex into the small music library next to the Song School. He lectured him on his responsibility to the Choir and to the Master of Choristers, as well as his duty to the Dean and chapter. Then he took the cane from behind the door and told Alex to remove his woollen gloves before hitting his chapped hands four times. The two ugly welts across his left hand were for arriving late at an important practice and the two across his right were for stopping during the solo. The doctor warned Alex about his future conduct. He would be watching him carefully. No more mistakes.

4

Cracks in the Defence

'All right, Lewis. You can go now.'

Lewis brushed the final mud from Tarrington's OTC tunic and hung it near the fire. He said goodnight and closed the door behind him. Alex got up from the table where he had been working at the senior boy's mathematics and picked up his belt and boots, wet and dirty from the afternoon's training.

'Leave them.'

Alex listlessly obeyed and waited for instructions but Tarrington's eyes widened; he had suddenly noticed the results of Brinsop's caning.

'Sit down, Davies,' he said softly.

Alex dropped to the chair at the table. Tarrington came and stood over him.

'Is that what you got for being late for school?'

Alex shook his head.

'What then?'

Tarrington sat on the corner of the table looking down at the boy. Alex could see he was genuinely interested and would badger him until he got what he wanted, so, in a dull voice and without once unfolding his hands or raising his eyes from the table, he told him.

Tarrington was impressed and delighted – to have all that happen because he had delayed the boy five short minutes. His eyes glowed and he returned to his chair by the fire.

'Why did you do it, Davies? Steal from the God-shop, I mean.'

Alex shrugged.

'Did you need the money? What about your father's army pension? That must be worth a bit?'

Alex shrugged.

'Doesn't your mother see you right from that?'

'I don't live with my mother.'

'Why not?'

Alex shrugged.

'Stop doing that,' Tarrington snapped. Alex's eyes fell again to the table.

His voice was scarcely more than a whisper.

'I don't do it for the money,' he added, unwilling to be seen as a simple robber. 'Not just for the money.'

Tarrington thought it over; this was more intriguing than ever. 'You mean you do it regularly? How often?'

'Every two weeks.' Alex felt the beginning of an unlikely sense of relief. How strange to be telling somebody of this thing he was driven to do; how strange that it should be Tarrington.

'They empty the box once a fortnight, on the Friday morning. I take about the same every time. That way

33

they don't notice any difference when it's counted. I don't take all the money in the box. That would be stupid.'

Tarrington nodded in agreement. 'How much do you generally get?' he asked.

'Two or three shillings.'

Tarrington roared with disbelieving laughter. 'You take a risk like this for just a few bob?' Tarrington looked at him briefly with something like admiration. 'What do you do with the money?'

'Just keep it. Sometimes I buy cakes or chocolate for me and Carpenter.'

'Does Carpenter know about this?'

Alex looked up sharply.

'No.'

'Does anybody else?'

'No.'

'How long have you been thieving from the God-shop?'

Alex said nothing. He remembered it well: ten days after he had heard of his father's death at Le Cateau.

The handbell began its noisy journey along the corridors warning of the end of free time: five minutes left before work in the dayroom. Alex stood and Tarrington came quickly to him and seized his hands. He looked at the damage in silence. Boys were noisy in the passages of the House.

'Go on,' he said quietly. 'You've been late enough for one day.'

Alex turned to the door. He was suddenly anxious. 'But I won't ever do it again, Tarrington. I promise.'

Tarrington looked levelly at him; the crooked smile came to his lips. 'Yes you will,' he said simply. 'Whenever I tell you.' Alex gaped at him.

'Tomorrow is Thursday, isn't it?'

Alex said quickly: 'But I musn't . . . not until next week.'

'Yes, you must. Tomorrow. And I'll double it.'

'I told you: I don't do it for the money. I don't want you to double it. Why are you doing this, Tarrington?'

'Sport. Excitement. Risks. If you played games or hunted instead of spending all your time dibbing on your knees and singing, you'd understand.' Tarrington moved from the door. 'You keep quiet and I'll keep quiet. All right?'

Alex nodded.

Tarrington dropped a hand on his shoulder and gripped it tightly. 'You're mine, Davies.' He said it casually, matter-of-fact. 'Because you don't belong to anybody else.' He released his painful grip and walked back to the fire. Alex left, scared.

While Seb forced history dates into his mind and the other boys worked in silence at other subjects, Alex tried to bring the day's events into focus but failed. His mind skeetered and slipped. He could not concentrate on the History Kemp had set. For several seconds panic bloomed in the pit of his stomach like some huge freak flower. For the first time in his life, Alex faced the possibility that he simply couldn't cope with the events that seemed to be crowding him in.

At the uncurtained windows, the pricking of sleet became a shower, then a deluge of rain. The cold snap was over. A more unsettled period had arrived. Alex shivered.

Alex pressed back in the side-chapel and waited to feel the danger. Martin Cleeve was playing a Handel voluntary but the music danced and did not threaten. The pitch blackness of winter in the nave had given way to the dim darkness of spring. His breathing was fast but the thrill was not there. Tarrington had taken that from him. He felt he was here for Tarrington's sake; not for his own.

He stepped swiftly round the column to where the box stood on its small table. The lid was never locked but was tightly fitted. Alex expertly levered it open and reached in. It was empty.

Alex gasped and felt round the box again. Nothing. He tried to work out what exactly this meant. He jammed the lid shut just as the voluntary began to wind grandly to its conclusion. What had happened to the box? Who had emptied it? Was somebody watching him now? That very minute? Alex ran for the choir cloister, panicked. It was lucky Gwynne was nowhere near for anyone could see the boy's clumsy retreat across the nave, back into the choirstalls and down the tiny stairway between the tombs. The final grand chords hung in the air as Alex arrived outside the Robing Room door and tried to make a casual entry.

'Why do you always forget books on Thursdays?' Seb asked as they ambled across the Close. He smiled at his friend. Alex would not meet his eyes, and snapped, 'Just because you're deputy head chorister now doesn't mean anything.' Seb was hurt; he threw a glance to Alex's strained face and wondered what was wrong. The march continued. Matthew Freeman was an easy-going head of the Choir and talking broke out in the two lines. Matthew was kinder than Chatterton, too. 'Say hello,' he quietly commanded as they came close to the bench where the two disabled soldiers smoked away the early evening. The boys obeyed shyly and the man with the deformed hand looked pointedly away but the other called out: 'Eyes Right – that's the way' and took a mock salute as they passed.

'You bring me nothing so I give nothing to you,' Tarrington said. Alex tried to make the older boy appreciate the seriousness of what had happened.

'Tarrington – somebody has emptied the box. It could mean – I don't know . . .'

Lewis put his head round the door and Tarrington shouted at him to go.

'It could mean somebody's checking,' Alex concluded. He looked up into the other's face, eyes big with worry.

Tarrington suddenly laughed. He lifted his OTC cap from the table. Underneath, in neat piles, stood about two poundsworth of small change. Alex felt sick. Without a word he turned and moved to the door.

'Come back.'

Alex took no notice; the door closed behind him.

'Don't be a fool. I'm going to put it back tomorrow. No one will know it was ever gone.'

As he walked the study corridor, Alex began to shake. Lewis watched him curiously as he forced himself to walk normally round the corner and into the dayroom. Alex heard Tarrington call for Lewis and the fag's prompt response, then he turned aside, up a twisting staircase to Matron's room where he waited with three other boys. When his turn came, he told Matron he felt ill and asked if he could go early to bed. She thought he looked sick enough to have a temperature but, though the thermometer proved her wrong, she agreed he should drink hot milk and get a good night's sleep. He asked if he could move to Sick Bay for the night and Matron thought that was a good idea, too. But Alex did not get good sleep. His mind raced round and round the danger he was in. He longed for half-term and a long weekend without Tarrington. He tossed and turned. His worries pressed down on him.

5

News from Home

Alex and Seb looked down from the tower and watched the world go by. Bathed in early summer sun, the boys gazed lazily down on the Archenford afternoon.

They had been lucky. As part of the 'War Work', Kemp had donated six choristers to the head verger for whatever use he could put them to during the long weekend, but Seb was a favourite of Norman Wickstead, who was about to make his weekly climb to wind the clock mechanism in the tower. Norman had commandeered Seb and Alex to keep him company and sweep up after the bell-ringers who had practised the previous evening and always left the belfry in a mess.

Now the boys looked out over the countryside while Norman patiently cranked machinery somewhere below them. Alex bent back his head and followed the sandstone spire eighty feet to the copper spike at its tip. The speed of the hazy cloud driving past made him sway. He turned to join Seb, gazing out.

'That's my road home,' Seb murmured. 'Just where the sun's dropping down. They'll be cutting grass now, for winter feed.' Alex nodded solemnly and leaned back against the warm stones of the spire.

'Do you miss home?' he asked.

'I miss some things,' Seb said carefully.

Alex closed his eyes against the fullness of the setting sun.

'I don't miss home,' he said. 'This is my home. I love the music,' said Alex suddenly. 'Or I used to.'

Seb wondered why Alex had raised this subject. He turned to look at him.

'You're our best soloist.'

Eyes tight shut, Alex swung his head from side to side in violent denial.

'You are.'

The forceful movement of the head ceased. Alex took a deep breath; held it and released it.

'I'm afraid most of the time and that makes my throat and chest tight. I don't like solos any more. I just try not to make mistakes.'

Seb turned back towards the west.

'I know what you mean.'

Alex opened his eyes, straightened and stretched. He began ambling round to the south where he could peer down into the Bishop's Cloister.

'Anyway, it doesn't matter much,' he said quietly as he moved from sight. 'Nothing matters much.'

A voice rose through a tiny open door in the base of the spire.

'You two,' called Norman Wickstead from the foot of the staircase inside. 'Come on, you two. I'm done here.'

Seb hurried to the opening.

'You go on down, Mister Wickstead, I'll lock the doors.'

The darkness inside the tower was total after the bright sunlight as Seb locked the spire door. He backed carefully down the steep wooden steps to where Alex was waiting near the belfry with a sack of bell-ringers' rubbish. They moved along a walkway of planking, stooped beneath a stone arch and found themselves in the strangest place the cathedral had to offer – a vast, gloomy cavern, musky with bird droppings and dust. Light nudged in through a series of dirty, round windows, like portholes. At one of them a pigeon was flapping, exhausted and hopeless. There was nothing the boys could do to help it and they were glad to come to the narrow door which opened upon a descending circular stone stairway.

Forty-nine steps spiralled down the north-west corner

of the tower. Dusty stripes of light shone through slits in the walls, angled sharply against bad weather. Both boys began counting aloud. Around the halfway stair, Alex passed the sack of rubbish to Seb and took the bunch of keys in exchange.

At the foot of the steps was a small landing. The steep stairway continued down but the boys turned left through a low arch where Alex shouldered a grudging door open and they came into the higher of the two galleries running along all four sides of the tower. For a second or two, they stood dazzled as light flooded upon them – coloured light from the sheer banks of stained glass all round them. Sounds rushed up at them too, from the nave crossing and choirstalls two hundred feet below. At this height it was hard to make out figures but Norman was unmistakeable in his overalls.

Seb had a head for heights but hated this gallery. In spite of a thick, waist-high stone balustrade he always felt panic when he looked down the sheer interior walls of the tower, past the fluid confusion of stained glass, past the lower gallery and into the gaping space below. Long ago, a head chorister, it was said, had balanced on this balustrade for a full minute, with his hands clasped above his head. Seb shuddered.

'Come on, Alex. We've got to give the keys back.'

Alex did not respond immediately. Where Seb felt panic, Alex felt fascination. He was leaning over as far as he could.

'I like this place,' he said dreamily. 'Everything's different here.'

'I'm going,' said Seb. And went.

They were circling down another staircase in the tower when the organ began playing. Angles of stone bounced the music awkwardly to them, spoiling time, ruining pitch. On the fiftieth step, Seb called a halt and handed the sack back to Alex and Alex graciously surrendered the keys.

They came out on the lower gallery where they were not much higher than the organ loft and could see the player. It was a young blind man to whom Martin Cleeve gave lessons. He had lost his sight in one of the first gas attacks of the war. The boys idled their way towards the final set of fifty-six steps which would bring them out at ground level in the corner of the North Transept. Dragging the rubbish sack behind him, with more than half his attention still on the blind organist, Alex walked hard into Seb. His friend was stockstill, staring down into the Nave. Alex peered over the balustrade. A young soldier was directly below, looking round anxiously. Seb turned and thrust the keys at Alex.

'Here. Lock up.'

He ran to the stairway at the end of the gallery.

'What's wrong? What's the matter?'

'That's my brother,' Seb shouted back as he swung down the stairway and clattered out of sight.

Luke was the second eldest of the four brothers – three years younger than the oldest, John – and the brother most missed by Seb. There was only a year between them and they had always been good friends.

They relaxed in the last of the sun on a bench in a quiet angle of the Close. Nine months had passed since Seb was last at Broxwood Farm and the last letter, in the careful, cramped hand of his mother, had been three months ago. Now Luke gave him the latest news. Mother was well. Father's back was playing him up and he had visited a famous bonesetter at Lyonshall. Both sisters were thriving: the elder was walking out with a neighbour's son. A silence fell between them. The youngest choristers – the Babes – ran from the Dean's garden towards the Choir Cloister. Seb picked up Luke's cap from the bench and polished the badge with his sleeve.

'Why all this?' he asked gently.

Luke was almost embarrassed.

'I'll tell you truly, Seb. I'm not sure. It's a man's duty to defend his country; you've seen that picture – Lord Kitchener glaring and pointing you out. There's six of us together. You know them all, Seb. All lads from Broxwood and Pembridge.'

'How did you join up? You're too young.'

'We lied how old we are.' He kept his eyes straight ahead. 'There's none of us ever going to take over a farm so what's to lose? That's what I say. See the world, Seb, eh?' He looked across, imploring his younger brother to agree. 'You got away from Broxwood by your singing,' he added quietly. 'Now I've got the chance to make something of myself. And I can't let the other lads down; not now. You see it, don't you, Seb?'

Seb nodded and Luke was relieved. He laid an awkward arm across the boy's shoulder.

'You and me – we always knew each other best.'

The tower clock struck five times. 'I've got to go to practice, Luke.'

Luke nodded and stood, taking his cap from Seb who suddenly needed him to stay.

'Come to Evensong. I can maybe see you afterwards.'

Luke smiled, embarrassed.

'Can't, Seb. The train leaves at six and you know me – I'm not much of a one for church.'

Other choristers were gathering at the Choir Cloister door.

'One thing –' The young man looked steadily into Seb's eyes.

'John's liable to go for calling-up, under the new laws. Dad says he won't have to go – he's more use on the farm. But if they go ahead and call him up . . .'

Luke's eyes stayed on Seb as he gazed at the Choir knocking for admission across the Close.

'If John goes, Dad'll send for me to work at home in

in his place.' Seb's voice was low and calm. Luke nodded.

Gwynne appeared at the Choir Cloister door and let in the laughing boys. Alex waited for Seb.

'I've got to go, Luke.'

The brothers embraced for the first time in their lives, holding on tightly. Then they moved slowly apart and Luke lifted a hand to ruffle his brother's hair. Seb felt his eyes moisten.

Luke suddenly put on his cap and walked quickly away without looking back.

Alex came quietly to Seb's side and they watched Luke leave the Close. Seb spoke at last, quietly and clearly.

'You were right – about nothing mattering much.'

He turned and hurried towards the choir cloister door. Alex kept to his side.

'Everything's changing,' said Seb as they walked into the cool of the cathedral. 'Better make the most of what we've got.'

6

A Change of Plans

On Saturday afternoon, Winnie hurried to the Town Hall for a lecture on 'Gas Gangrene and Trench Foot'. She had an important question for Fiona Templeton. Winnie turned from Old School Lane into Dean Street, rehearsing what she would say.

Lady Dormington, Fiona's Aunt Gemma, was forming The Lady Dormington Ambulance Unit. With the financial assistance of her husband (who owned two coalmines in Kent), of Fiona's father and several other wealthy friends, Gemma Dormington had bought two grocers' delivery vans which were at that moment being converted into well-equipped ambulances. She was also about to buy a small lorry which would carry medical supplies and members of her unit; others would ride in the two cars provided by her long-suffering husband. Since most able-bodied men were already serving in the forces, she had recruited a team of women drivers, though she herself would be driven by her chauffeur, Hollingworth. There were to be two trained nurses in the Unit and four VADs, one of which was Fiona, and they were due to leave for France in a month's time.

Winnie had felt so jealous when her excited friend had told her the news that she had snapped back aggressively.

'You can't go. They won't let you. You're not old enough.'

Fiona had looked at her coolly, surprised at the depth of feeling in the Welsh girl.

'Too young for an official organisation, Winnie, yes. But not for a private unit like Aunt Gemma's.'

Winnie dodged a group of cyclists as she crossed Saint Owen Street to the Town Hall. It's so unfair, she thought as she ran up the steps. If you've got money, you can do anything; if you haven't, you can't do nothing.

Winnie showed her ticket to a fierce lady in sister's uniform and hurried up the ornate staircase to the long gallery where Fiona was waiting.

'Come on, Winnie. The lecturer's already inside. You're late.'

They made their way to the Assembly Room and squeezed past a cluster of well-dressed ladies at the door. They looked round for two seats together.

'What a crowd,' murmured Fiona. 'It's only because the bishop's wife is here. Come on. I can see a place.'

But Winnie suddenly gripped Fiona's arm, forgetting her well-practised speech.

'Fiona,' she said urgently. 'You've got to take me with you. To France.'

Fiona looked sadly at her friend.

'I spoke to Aunt Gemma about you, Winnie. But she says she's got to fill the unit up with people whose families have stumped up cash for ambulances and stuff. I'm sorry.'

Winnie nodded gloomily and they pressed into the third row to wait for the lecturer to be introduced. I should have known, thought Winnie. Very English; it's what-you-have and who-you-know. Nobody wants a nobody-with-nothing. She made a big effort to shake off her deep disappointment. Fiona tried too. 'Gas Gangrene and Trench Foot,' she said brightly. 'Give me other names, Miss Price.'

'Also known as bacterial infection and frostbite,' Winnie replied quietly.

'Correct, Winifred Price. My friend Toby Tate who's on leave says some of his men have got trench mouth, not trench foot. Have you ever heard of that?' Winnie had never heard of trench mouth.

'It's from not brushing your teeth and eating revolting food,' explained Fiona. 'They paint the mouth and lips with a bright blue sort of disinfectant. Toby says it doesn't seem to cure anything but at least you know whose breath to avoid.'

To make up for having wasted the afternoon on the tower (as Kemp put it) Seb and Alex were sent after Evensong to pull the last weeds from Brinsop's gravel path. After half an hour, with sore fingers and grazed knees, they slipped into the kitchen in search of Winnie. They were lucky: Cook was visiting friends and Winnie was glad to make them tea. They talked of her disappointment about the ambulance unit and Seb's meeting with Luke. Winnie approved of their decision to make the best of things – to try to do something worth doing each day.

'This old war could go on for ever, never mind what they say.'

The boys nodded seriously.

'That's what we think.'

'It'll get us all, one way or another,' she said.

They sipped in silence from the thick kitchen cups.

'What's your big adventure for tomorrow then?'

'We're rowing up the river to swim at Sarson Bridge.'

'That's right,' confirmed Alex, though this was the first he'd heard of it. 'Come with us.'

'Good idea,' agreed Seb.

'I can't, no, really I can't,' Winnie said, already deciding that she'd sneak sandwiches for three from the larder while Cook was having her afternoon nap.

The Sunday adventure had no surprises but was good enough on its own. With Kemp's grudging permission (he had not forgotten their idleness, the previous day) the boys collected a boat from the school boathouse near the River Gate and set off inexpertly – Seb was hopeless – upstream past the twenty or so other pleasure boats parading up and down the popular half-mile of river alongside the town walls.

They collected Winnie, as arranged, from the ferry steps on the outskirts of Archenford. They all regretted the secrecy but knew that to openly invite aboard a school boat somebody who was not only a non-pupil but (worse) a servant and (worse still) a girl was asking for trouble, even though Winnie proved to be the most efficient rower of the three and replaced Seb for the last mile of the voyage.

Near Sarson village the weather was kind and the Linnow bearably cold as it flowed slowly beneath the railway bridge. After they had swum and dived from the pontoon of the bridge, Winnie produced the sandwiches and they sprawled on the banks to munch and chat in content.

This was the first time all three had been alone for any length of time but it felt as if they had known each other for much longer. The more they talked, the more they found they had in common.

Winnie told them, hesitantly at first, of life in the broken-down cottage near Knighton and Seb compared it with life at Broxwood Farm. Both listened in sympathetic silence while Alex spoke quietly and stumblingly of the brief home life he remembered. In growing confidence, they related their hopes and fears.

Winnie's iron determination surprised the boys. She intended to make a good career for herself in which her abilities were valued and respected. Seb and Alex began to understand the frustration she felt at the many opportunities which were open only to those with money. She believed things would be different after the war. There would be chances to pull herself from the servant class to which her upbringing seemed to condemn her.

'I seen your matron and housekeeper. I can do what they do – no bother.'

Seb and Alex agreed. Everything would be different. It would be a time to take chances – after the war.

'If there's any of us left,' said Seb quietly, fearing for Luke and bringing the talk to silence.

Then, luckily, the Sunday afternoon stopping train from Worcester to Hereford could be heard pulling into Sarson Halt and the three friends dashed thrashing into the water to cower beneath the bridge as engine and coaches thundered deafeningly overhead. As they waded back to the bank, Winnie suggested an adventure for the following day that would be the most unusual and daring of all.

7

Walking Wounded

The moment Martin Cleeve had dismissed the choir after the morning service Seb and Alex raced across the close to the smallest of the gates – Verger's Gate – and out into Capuchin Lane.

Winnie was waiting in the front passenger seat of a gleaming Wolsley 6 h.p. sports car whose engine was already turning. Behind the wheel sat Fiona, a loose raincoat over the white starched apron of her VAD uniform. The boys scrambled into the rear seats and barely had time to be introduced before they were off. The Wolsley was open-topped and it was a breezy whirl-wind of a journey, not helped by the occasional diversion to the right-hand side of the road 'to see what it would be like driving in France'.

Their destination, Blatchfords, was a small mansion which had been converted into a convalescent hospital for Archenford's wounded soldiers. It was at Blatchfords that the men in blue suits, white shirts and red ties stayed until they were fit to be returned to their homes and families. Winnie had Flo's grudging permission to help at the hospital two hours a week. As the car drew up to the front steps, Alex and Seb exchanged apprehensive glances – they knew how unpredictable the men in blue could be.

They need not have worried; they felt at home and of use from the moment they stepped inside. The girls left to find Sister Robbins while a friendly medical orderly called Harry took willing charge of the boys. They were surprised to find the nursing staff and volunteers so young. Even Sister Robbins was only in her twenties and Harry, at forty, was the oldest person there.

Before setting them to work, he showed them round. In a light, spacious ward a few of the beds were occupied by sleeping men but most patients sat in armchairs playing cards or listening to a scratchy record on the wind-up gramophone.

'The boys in here are on the mend,' Harry explained as they left. 'I'll show you the other ward.'

They turned into what had once been the dining room. It was darker, quieter. Harry lowered his voice as he gently opened the door.

'All the men in here have internal wounds,' he whispered. 'They recover slowly.'

There were a dozen beds and each contained a soldier. In contrast to the larger ward hardly a word was spoken. Most of the men were asleep. There was a sense of pain, and quiet concentration against it.

'Harry?'

A soldier called weakly from a nearby bed and Harry walked over.

'Morning, Terry,' he smiled. 'What can I do for you?'

Terry seemed to lack the strength to reply. He held a letter in his hand.

'You want me to read your letter to you, Terry?'

There was no answer.

'I'll come back later,' Harry promised. 'Just now, I'm to show these two the ropes, then it'll be time for my stores inspection.'

Terry closed his eyes.

'I'll read your letter to you.'

The dull eyes opened and moved slowly to Alex.

'If you'll let me.'

The eyes stayed on Alex's face and Terry's head nodded very slightly. Harry grinned and patted Alex on the shoulder. As he and Seb left, Alex was drawing a chair near Terry's bed and explaining who he was. They closed the door behind them with care.

'Your mate's got the easy job,' grinned Harry. 'You

can give me a hand getting the dirty linen baskets over to the laundry.' As they walked through the courtyard, Seb told Harry of the soldiers in their blues who gathered each day in the Close.

'That'll be Frank Brown – the one that's lost his fingers, poor chap – and Rex Hickey. On crutches right?'

Seb agreed.

'Frank was a carpenter,' Harry said softly. 'A real craftsman. Promising cricketer too. Famous round the villages.'

Seb found he could say nothing for a while but Harry was a sensitive man and understood how Blatchfords affected newcomers.

Back in the routine of School House nothing seemed the same. Seb and Alex had fitted into Blatchfords wonderfully well. They had written and read and re-read letters for a surprisingly large number of patients who couldn't themselves read or write. Moreover, they were close to the ages of the young wounded men and filled the roles of younger brothers to be teased or impressed in the same way that Harry provided a father-figure. The boys looked forward to their next visit. It would have to be a secret, of course. Kemp would never allow his pupils to mix with rough soldiers, wounded or not.

The long weekend of the half-term holiday drew to its end and bit by bit School House straggled back. When the Choir returned from Monday Evensong there were carriages in the Close and, although the break didn't end officially until the following morning, the dining room was already half-full. Tarrington and Chatterton had not returned. While Tarrington's absence was no surprise – he lived close to Archenford and could be counted on to enjoy his considerable home comforts up to the last minute – Chatterton's decision to leave school and train for entry into the Army was a shock.

The Tarringtons always dined at nine.

Swithenbank Hall, six miles west of Archenford, had been built in 1849 by Tarrington's great-grandfather as home for his wife and children. Now only one of those children – Harry, Tarrington's grandfather – lived there. With him lived his son, Giles, and Mollie, his son's wife, and of course Lionel Tarrington himself when home from school. Harry Tarrington's wife had been killed in a hunting accident and friends noted that the old man had lost much of his bounce and good humour as a result of that fatal New Year's Day in 1914.

Giles sat at the head of a table far too large for the four diners, with his wife at the other end and Lionel opposite his grandfather. Since it was the last night of Tarrington's long weekend, the family was dining informally, attended only by two serving-maids and the Swithenbank head butler, Wilkins. Tarrington was an only child, which possibly accounted for his anger when he failed to get what he wanted.

Most of the talk during the meal was of recent events – the continuing siege of Verdun, the Republican uprising in Dublin, the capture of the British garrison town of Kut by the Turks. The discussion was gloomy.

Wilkins, immaculate and impassive as he poured the claret, believed much of it was also inaccurate or highly coloured by the politics of the Tarrington family. With his high forehead, bald dome and round spectacles, Wilkins looked precisely what he was – a formidably intelligent man. Only Lionel was stupid enough not to recognise the fact, and all but the boy knew – though never admitted – that if knowledge and ability were more influential than wealth, Wilkins would be at the head of the table instead of his master. The butler replaced the claret jug on the sideboard and took up his discreet place near the door.

Harry Tarrington moved the discussion to the recent act of Parliament which had widened the call-up to include married men. This was a worrying matter for Swithenbank; the number of available workers would be much reduced and Giles might even lose his efficient estate manager. Although this would throw extra weight on Giles, Harry Tarrington refused point-blank to involve himself in the running of the farms or pedigree herd of cattle. He was too old; he had done his bit. In any case, the world was going mad in its furious fast change – cars, tractors, even airplanes for God's sake. In his view, it was up to the youngest generation.

'What's the point?' asked Lionel airily. 'I shall soon have to join up, myself.'

'The point is,' growled his grandfather, 'that you could leave school now – you need never go back – and help your father run this damn estate until you're called to the colours.'

Giles nodded and pushed away his dinner plate which was immediately removed by one of the maids.

'It would help me over these coming months while things are rearranged,' he said.

Mollie smiled at her son.

'Good practice too,' she added. 'The day will come when you'll have to cope with the estate single-handed.'

(God forbid, thought Wilkins from the door.)

'God forbid,' murmured Harry beneath his breath. Lionel took no notice; he was quite clear about his future plans.

'When I leave for the war,' he said casually, 'I'll join the Archenford Militia, I suppose.'

'Certainly,' said Harry. It was his own old regiment.

'As a junior officer of an infantry company in France I shall be unlikely to survive. It's improbable I shall come back and almost impossible it'll be in one piece even if I do.' Lionel Tarrington kept his voice level and without any trace of fear or self-pity. 'So I'm going to enjoy myself while I can and that means going back to school. I don't want to miss the cricket.'

He took a swig of wine.

(Cunning, thought Wilkins. And impressive. There's no reasonable argument against that.)

Old Harry coughed.

'There's no reasonable argument against that, of course,' he said.

A brief silence descended. Mollie Tarrington stretched a hand towards her son but was defeated by the length of the table between them. Giles pointed at a fruit bowl which a maid hurried to place before him.

'I would, however, appreciate your assistance, Lionel. Since you only have seven weeks or so of school ahead, why not leave now?'

He selected one of last autumn's russet apples and began to peel it carefully.

'If it's such a short time,' Tarrington countered, 'why can't Swithenbank wait 'til it's over?' He beckoned the maid with the fruit, chose an apple and handed it to her for peeling.

'No, I'll enjoy the last of school, thank you, Father. Unless you insist.'

'I don't, of course, insist,' murmured Giles politely. 'I dare say we shall muddle through.'

Harry quietly tapped his wine glass which Wilkins came forward to fill.

'Good drop of claret, Wilkins,' muttered the old man.

'Thank you, Colonel.'

Tarrington gulped down his wine and rapped the elegant glass sharply on the table to draw Wilkins' attention.

'If it's that good I'd better drink as much as I can while I've got the chance.'

Wilkins walked the longer way round the table to serve him.

'It all tastes the same to me anyway. I prefer beer,' added Tarrington.

Wilkins took care to fill Tarrington's glass no more

than one-quarter full which Harry noticed and approved as the butler smoothly returned to his position near the door and waited, his white-gloved hands behind his back. He had a terrible suspicion that the youngest Tarrington's ignorance and arrogance might make him a hero in battle. That was Lionel's own intention, too, at any cost.

8

Skirmishing

A finger of intense sunlight slanted across Seb's face and pillow. He blinked and began to wake. He yawned, shut his eyes firmly and curled into a ball but could not slip back into sleep. He hauled the bedclothes over his head in the hope of a good doze: no use. He yawned once more and flicked his eyes open. It was quiet in the dormitory; Seb guessed it must be early – about six. The bright light irritated his eyes. He twisted over upon his stomach and jammed the pillow over his head but it was still no good. Nobody else in the room was awake. Only three of the beds had sleepers; the others had not yet returned. As Seb swung his legs to the floor he noticed Alex' bed was empty, too.

Seb found Alex cleaning Tarrington's study and stood in the doorway watching. He was surprised to find himself annoyed.

'Why are you doing this?'

Alex carried on with his dusting. He would not look at Seb.

'Tarrington's coming back this morning,' he mumbled.

'Let Tarrington clean his own study.'

'You don't understand.'

Seb moved and sat at the table. This is all wrong, he thought; I musn't fall out with my best friend over Tarrington.

'I thought we agreed things had changed,' he said quietly.

'It's all right for you. You don't need the money.'

'But this isn't what Tarrington pays you for. This is his fag's job; you should leave it for Lewis.'

Alex came to the open window and flapped the duster outside. He said nothing. Seb grew exasperated.

'I don't understand. The long weekend changed everything – my brother coming, then Sarson Bridge and Blatchfords. Now you're looking scared and fussing round Tarrington again.'

'I'm not scared.'

Alex put the duster away and took the broom from behind the door. He began brushing dust into the hearth.

'What's wrong? You won't even look at me. You're my friend; not Tarrington's.'

Alex paused in his sweeping as if he had run out of energy. He kept his head down and his eyes away from Seb though Seb knew he was paying full attention.

'Why are you doing this?' Seb asked again, softly.

So Alex told him. He straightened up slowly, turned to look Seb full in the face and told him. He told his shocked friend how he stole regularly from one of the charity boxes in the cathedral and how Tarrington had discovered this. He tried to give the full picture. In a low voice he told Seb that the first time had been an impulse.

'I just found myself doing it.'

Seb could hardly believe it.

'Did Tarrington report you?'

'No.'

Alex explained how Tarrington continued to blackmail him into repeating the thefts though he was desperate to stop. He told Seb how this was breaking him up, how he was jumpy and ill, how he couldn't concentrate on singing which only brought him more problems. Alex was honest. He told Seb what a thrill it had been, those first few times.

'Thrill?'

Alex tried to explain the excitement and danger, the feeling of spending ten minutes on the edge of panic; the power of outwitting Gwynne, Brinsop, everybody.

'What reason does Tarrington give for making you steal?'

Seb found this sudden flood of information difficult to manage.

Alex smiled bitterly.

'Sport. He says it's good sport. He says if I were a sportsman, I'd understand.'

Alex took a sudden step towards Seb.

'It was a relief, Seb. To be able to speak to somebody openly about it. Even Tarrington.'

'You could have spoken to me.'

Alex swung his head violently from side to side.

'No. It matters what *you* think of me. Tarrington hates me, so it's not important.'

'But you don't have to become his slave,' Seb protested.

'That's a relief too. It's my punishment on myself for what I've done.'

In the silence footsteps clattered down creaking stairs and the clanking of the milkman's churns came from the Close.

Seb took the broom from Alex' hands and propped it in the corner, behind the door.

'Have you still got the money?' he asked.

'Most of it. Sometimes I bought us chocolate. It's in the boiler-room behind a loose brick.'

'We'll put it back after early practice.'

'What about Tarrington?'

'Your word against his. The extra money he forced you to take will make up for what you spent.' Seb searched for the right words and fell back on the language of sermons.

'You'll still be a thief, but you'll be a repentant thief – and that makes it all right.'

'What shall I tell him if he tries to make me do it again?'

'No stealing; no slaving.'

Alex was nervous.

'He won't like it,' he said doubtfully.

First bell rang upstairs in the dormitories and Seb put his hands on Alex's shoulders.

'Think of Rex and Frank. Think of Blatchfords. Tarrington's nothing in comparison.'

They moved to the door.

'And there's three of us, remember.'

'Three?'

Seb grinned.

'If there's any trouble, we'll set Winnie on him.'

They were still debating how long it would take young Lewis to sweep up the pieces after Winnie had been unleashed upon his fag-master while they made their beds, and by the time they crossed the Close for early practice – each with heavy pockets – they had worked out what should be said to Tarrington and what might have to be done.

As the Choir concentrated on the difficult sections of Croft's impressive setting of the *Jubilate*, to be sung at the approaching Service of Thanksgiving, Tarrington returned from Swithenbank. Ten minutes before the bell for morning school he clattered into the Close astride his spectacular black horse with Wilkin's friend, the groom, riding quietly and politely ten paces behind.

The clash, when it came, was like the war: nobody wanted it but everyone contributed. At the time it seemed simple – black and white: nobody could have

57

looked into the future and seen the long-term effects. The clash, like the war, was a storm that built up gradually.

At four minutes to eleven, Lewis came running to the dayroom to tell Alex that Tarrington was demanding his presence – his riding boots were filthy. Alex asked Lewis to tell Tarrington there was too little time before lessons.

When Seb and Alex walked back to School House after morning school, Lewis was waiting anxiously. Tarrington wanted Alex to complete and check an arithmetic exercise. Alex asked Lewis to tell Tarrington that he would come to the study after lunch. There was no time now.

'Do I really have to say that?'

'Yes.'

The boy shuffled apprehensively towards the study where Tarrington was already in a foul mood.

During lunch Tarrington kept a cold, angry glance on the middle table where Alex was careful to avoid his eye. Matthew and Dobbin sat either side of him and Seb, opposite, kept the atmosphere loud and funny which annoyed Tarrington even more. Others were noticing Tarrington's scowls. Lewis explained the situation to the Junior Table while, on the Senior Table, Tarrington's contemporaries secretly enjoyed his displeasure.

'Why didn't you come when I sent for you?'

Tarrington sat very still in his study armchair, taut as a spring. Alex stood before him. In his corner making coffee, Lewis hardly dared breathe or move for fear of drawing attention.

'There wasn't time.'

Tarrington studied Alex carefully, noting the nervousness but also aware of an obstinacy he had not found before. He was pleased. He would enjoy destroying it.

'My boots need cleaning.'

'I'll take them to the boot room now.'

'I've got work for you to check.'

'I won't be doing your exercises any more, Tarring-ton.'

Lewis hadn't noticed how long he'd been holding his breath and hiccuped loudly.

'Sorry, Tarrington.'

Tarrington paid his fag no attention. He kept his eyes on Alex, probing for weakness. Alex continued, fighting to keep his voice level and unafraid.

'I'll clean your sports kit and uniform but it's Lewis' job to clear up after you, run your messages and keep this place tidy, and it's not fair that I do your schoolwork.'

Alex licked his lips. Tarrington seemed to be about to smile. Lewis strained the coffee into a cup and brought it carefully to Tarrington – then he hiccuped so violently he spilled some into the saucer.

'Sorry, Tarrington.'

He hiccuped again.

'Get out.'

Lewis went fast. Tarrington sipped his coffee. Lewis' quick footsteps were cut off by the slam of a door.

'You think you're being brave.'

Alex stayed silent.

'What is it? Do you want more money?'

'It's not a question of money, Tarrington.'

Tarrington took another sip from his cup. He looked up, a thin smile on his lips.

'All right. No schoolwork; no fagging.'

Alex caught his breath; he hadn't expected this.

'Can I go now, please?'

The thin smile again.

'But we haven't talked about the other thing. Your adventures over in the God-shop.

'That's all over, Tarrington.'

'No.'

'Yes.'

Tarrington was not used to worms turning. On the other hand, his hunting experiences had shown him that

59

cornered animals tend to snap back before the kill, maybe even worms.

'Don't be a fool, Davies,' he sneered. 'Do you want me to tell Kemp what you've been up to?'

'Why should he believe you more than me?'

Tarrington laughed.

'I know where you keep the money.'

'Not any more. I've put it back.'

Tarrington leaned forward beginning to feel his prey slipping away.

'Kemp would make enquiries. Remember: I saw you.'

'He'd want to know why you hadn't reported me before.'

Tarrington made himself lean back casually and play for time by sipping coffee. He was not a good debater and sensed Alex's confidence hardening. He suddenly put down his cup and reached for the boots by his chair. He flung them into Alex's arms.

'Clean these boots,' he shouted. 'Come back here after supper. I'll deal with you then.'

Alex took the boots from the study, making sure he walked unhurriedly.

Tarrington was furiously angry – not only with Alex but with himself for losing the advantage and letting the boy have his own way. It was unthinkable he should dictate to Lionel Tarrington what he should or should not do. He must decide on something really frightening for Davies.

Alex felt faint with reaction as Seb patted his back outside the study door. They made for the boot room.

'It was easier than you thought, wasn't it?'

Alex still felt terrible. Seb opened the boot-room door.

'It's habit. The more you stand up to him, the easier it gets.'

Alex forced himself to smile. After all, he had come through in one piece.

Nothing happened after supper. A list on the notice

board from the Captain of Cricket named Tarrington among those who were to report at the gamesfield for fielding practice.

Alex and Seb hung about in their dayroom waiting for Lewis to bring a message during the last free time of the evening but their good fortune continued; Tarrington had not returned to the House.

Cleaning his teeth in the bare, echoing bathroom, Alex began to feel that Seb might be right. Perhaps Tarrington was an empty vessel after all, unable to have his bluff called. Six weeks of Tarrington left. Alex spat into the basin and turned on the tap.

9

Battle

The May night was surprisingly warm and still. Sleep was difficult to come by.

Winnie lay gazing through the attic window at the soft darkness of the sky. Her thoughts were with Seb. Back home in Mid-Wales people of their age would be walking out together, even setting up home. Soft ideas, Winnie thought: too soft. No good to think like that. She had higher ambitions, no matter how much she liked him. She put him firmly from her mind.

Seb slipped out of Winnie's mind and into his own. He was gripped in a dream. He and Luke were harnessed together, dragging a heavy plough over a rocky field as his father and Brinsop – each in German uniform – shouted and threatened. Seb called out to them.

'Give us peace.'

Alex turned his head as Seb called out in the dormitory. Matthew, from the other side, called 'What?' but

Seb slid easily back into sleep. Alex envied him. He had been going over and over Tarrington's threats. Now he tried to snatch his thoughts away. He needed to think about Blatchfords and how Seb and he could escape there for a few hours at the weekend. He had promised to write home for sad, silent Terry.

Too late. Sad, silent Terry had slipped quietly away from life an hour earlier. In the stuffy dining room where rich and famous people once fed and joked, the boy with the broken stomach and lung had given up the struggle against pain. The night sister had encouraged him to fight on and Harry had added soft support but Terry had already fought long and hard enough.

At some time Alex got up, taking care to be quiet, anxious not to wake Seb. Alex wanted to take pressure from himself. The coming day would be heavy with choir work for the Service of Thanksgiving. It would be crazy to give Tarrington any excuse to harass him. If Tarrington had been playing cricket, Alex knew the kit would be, as usual, scattered over the study floor. Since Alex could not sleep he might as well collect it, sponge away the grass stains and whiten the boots. He pulled his grey shirt over his head and climbed into his trousers. The cathedral clock struck three-quarters past something and there was just enough moonlight to show him the door. Nobody else was awake.

Alex came quietly into the dark study and felt his way to the box of matches dangling from its string on the gas bracket. He felt his foot catch something soft and heavy; a cricket sweater or towel. He struck a match and laid it close to the mantle as he turned the gas key. The soft rush of gas popped and hissed and the room grew lighter, dimmed, grew light again. Alex bent for the garment on the floor – it was a sweater – and his heart hammered and jumped.

Dull eyes gazed at him. Tarrington was sprawled in the armchair, a bottle, three-quarters empty, in a hand across his chest. Alex noticed for the first time the strong, stale smell of whisky. Tarrington was not drunk. He was half-drunk; more dangerous.

'Alexander Davies.'

Tarrington's voice was low and menacing, and his face expressionless. This was not a greeting but the acknowledgement of one adversary to another. Alex should have turned – now – and left. Instead he heard himself reply.

'Yes.'

Nothing moved in the room. The gas hissed and popped.

'You think you're being brave.'

'No.'

'You and your little friends.'

'What little friends?'

'Carpenter. Steed. Matthew and all the other pathetic Godbotherers.'

He lifted the bottle to his lips and swigged noisily, then, with a hand that shook very slightly, he held out the bottle towards Alex.

'No thanks.'

Alex was nervous. Tarrington shook the bottle. He hissed out his words.

'If I say drink, you drink.'

The bottle swayed before Alex's face and the dark, dull eyes were almost hypnotic.

'No thanks.'

Tarrington's body tensed in the chair and snapped forwards. The bottle in his hand hit Alex's chest and aggression contorted his features. Alex gasped as he felt the start of panic. Unwillingly he reached and took the bottle. Tarrington laughed without humour as the boy lifted it and tilted a little whisky between his lips. The sour spirit burned his mouth but before he could react

Tarrington had sprung at him. So quick that he seemed to fly, he moved behind Alex. While his left arm pinioned the boy, his right tipped the bottle up and rammed it down. Alex felt it hit his teeth sickeningly and the next moment was choking for breath, as the whisky hit his throat.

Tarrington let him go as he doubled up, coughing and gagging. There was a smear of blood on his hand from his split gum. Tarrington closed the door and turned to focus full attention on Alex. Eyes watering, nose running, he felt humiliated and Tarrington knew it. The joyless smile came back to Tarrington's lips.

'Not so brave.'

He drained the bottle and stood it carefully on the bookshelf, never taking his eyes from Alex and waiting patiently as the boy pulled air into his lungs and wiped his nose on a sleeve. At last he stood painfully upright, rubbing his eyes and staring at Tarrington apprehensively.

'Look at you,' continued Tarrington mildly. 'Just look at you. Blubbing snotty Alexander Davies who thinks he's somebody.'

'What are you talking about?' Alex whispered.

'About Alexander Davies who has nothing.' He spat out the word. 'Nothing. Yet acts so superior.'

'I don't, Tarrington.'

'Just because you do my maths and just because you do my French you think you're better. You are nothing and you have nothing.'

He stabbed a sudden finger at Alex. The smile had gone; so had the dullness in his eyes. They glowed now, large with the whisky. And they were cruel – like an animal's. Alex forced himself to speak.

'I want to go now.'

'To run away? To tell your little friends I've been drinking? So they can laugh?'

'Don't be stupid.'

Tarrington's open hand cracked Alex hard across his face, catching him off balance.

'Don't call me stupid.'

The boy straightened carefully. A sharp pain jabbed in his side where he had hit the table and his cheek flamed. His anxious eyes stayed on Tarrington; he must be ready for another attack. Tarrington's mood swung as he noticed his cricket team picture slanted on the wall. He moved to adjust the frame. 'They don't want me in the team. Can you believe that? I've been put out of the Eleven.'

He and the 1915 School Cricket Team stared at each other. He nodded very slowly.

'A bad day.'

Tarrington turned to Alex again. His voice grew more menacing.

'Today I got put down a class. Big laugh for everybody. Do you know why?'

He hardly waited for an answer though Alex briefly shook his head.

'You wouldn't do that exercise for me. That's why. Crowhurst said it was the last straw. He's been waiting for an excuse and you gave it him.'

Alex shook his head again.

'You try to make me look a fool in front of Lewis.'

Alex shook his head more determinedly.

'Yes, you do.' Tarrington rapped out the words. His jabbing finger hit Alex's chest.

'So I have everybody laughing at me behind my back and it's all down to you.'

The venom in Tarrington was so vicious that Alex panicked. His mouth opened to shout but suddenly the jabbing finger became a hand which clamped over his mouth.

'Call out and I'll kill you.'

There was complete silence. Tarrington felt the trembling begin in his adversary's body and was pleased. He dropped his hand and stooped to pick up his sweater on which he wiped his fingers. He smiled as he moved back.

'Look at you.'

He leaned against the door. 'You're so scared you could wet yourself. Alexander Davies – errand boy, poor man, beggarman, thief.'

Alex felt anger but forced it away. That was what Tarrington wanted. If blind temper made Alex lash out, he could be badly hurt. There was nobody to help him. Alex began at last to use his brain. Even so, he found he was so scared he could not speak above a whisper.

'It's not like you think.'

Tarrington's eyes narrowed, waiting for an opportunity but Alex hurried on.

'Not really like that. Everything's different. And everyone. It's the war, Tarrington. It's changing everything.'

Tarrington didn't move. Alex pushed quickly on.

'Crowhurst's just an old man like the rest of them. All the decent teachers – they're away at the war. It's the same with the cricket.' (He saw Tarrington tense a little.) Careful. 'If Silverthorn was still at the school . . . I mean, you were his top scorer.'

Tarrington nodded. Robin Silverthorn had been last year's cricket coach. Alex pressed home his advantage.

'If you think I've been showing off, then I'm sorry. I get tired. That's all. And sometimes I don't think. The war means a lot of extra practices and services.'

Tarrington said nothing and his eyes were heavy. Alex hoped he was feeling tired. His cheek and side still throbbed; his cut mouth stung. He said, very quietly, 'Please, Tarrington, can I go?'

In fact, Tarrington was confused. He was not really listening to Alex. He had a sudden lack of interest in the whole affair and found this strange. Alex took one tentative step towards the door.

'Stay still.'

Tarrington moved quickly forward to within a few inches of Alex. His eyes sharpened and locked on Alex's nervous gaze.

'You don't fool me, Davies.'

Tarrington found the answer to his problem and was relieved. By refusing to fight back it was obvious that Davies was trying to fool him – and anybody who thought he could fool Lionel Tarrington clearly believed himself superior. Yes. Davies was as good as calling him second-best, was sneering at him, mocking him, thinking he was stupid. Tarrington's eyes gleamed. His stance became balanced. He was more like an animal than ever.

'Who do you think you are?' he jeered, moving sharply forward, forcing Alex back.

'I'm nobody,' gasped Alex, desperate at this new turn. Tarrington's finger came jabbing and stabbing to his face. His voice suddenly lifted; it was high now and excited. 'You sing like a girl and you can't play games. You're a thief and a freak. Your mother ran off with another man and your father was so stupid he couldn't even last the first week of the war.'

Alex spat in Tarrington's face and felt a fist club his left cheek, then another his right; his head snapped one way, then the other. He cried out quietly as he staggered back, thrashing out, swinging hopeless blows towards Tarrington who came on, grinning.

10

Defeat

In his third dream that night, Seb dreamed that Lewis was shaking him violently and woke up to find that he was.

'What's wrong?'

'Quickly,' said Lewis. 'You've got to come. Quickly.'

The night porter of the Red Dragon Hotel was not pleased to be serving coffee at two-fifteen. The young gentleman in cricket whites had clearly drunk too much during the evening but young gentlemen were expected to go on the spree now and then – so long as they could behave themselves, pay the bill and tip well.

'Everything in order, sir?'

Tarrington nodded and leaned back in the chair.

'I'll find you a room immediately, sir. When you're ready to use the telephone you'll find me at the desk in the hall.' There was no reaction from Tarrington. The porter closed the door behind him. Tarrington drank hot coffee and shivered.

Alex had managed to prop himself against an arm of the chair but was beginning to hurt. He had lost track of time since Tarrington had slammed the door. He gingerly raised an arm to finger his ribs; not too bad. He began breathing properly again – in through the nose, out through the mouth – filling the lungs. It was uncomfortable but not painful. Part of him wanted to sleep and part of him wanted to find out what damage had been done. None of him wanted to stand up or walk – it had been difficult enough to crawl to the side of the chair. His cheek was aching and the inside of his mouth was numb. He dared not think what Brinsop would say and shut his eyes, not hearing Seb and Lewis hurrying along the corridor.

Tarrington lay flat on his bed in the Red Dragon feeling tired and depressed. He had just been very sick. He did not waste time thinking of Alex – what was done, was done; he guessed the boy would keep things to himself, not wanting his cathedral adventures to come to light. Tarrington sighed at this sudden end to his schooldays. He had not wasted time. He had telephoned Swithenbank and woken Wilkins with instructions. He had written a brief letter for Kemp explaining he had decided after all to return home where his father was anxious for his help on the Estate during the few months before he joined the army. The letter also told Kemp to have Matron and Lewis pack up his belongings which would be sent for at the weekend. Kemp could expect a formal letter from his father. He had now merely to await the call to an early breakfast and hoped he would not need another trip to the bathroom.

He did – but afterwards slept soundly and without dreams.

Alex was perched on the edge of a bath as Matthew, Dobbin and Seb brought cold, wet flannels for his face and ribs. He was grateful for their care, and for their lack of impossible questions.

'How do you feel now?' Matthew asked.

'Better.'

'You should tell Kemp.'

'Or Brinsop.'

Alex shook his head gently. Matthew and Dobbin were indignant.

'Don't let Tarrington get away with it, man.'

Seb knew why Alex could take the matter no further.

'You don't want the fuss or bother, I expect,' he said mildly. 'Not with the service tomorrow and Blatchfords at the weekend.'

'That's right,' replied Alex gratefully.

Matthew soaked a flannel in the wash-basin.

'What are you going to do about Choir?' he whispered.

'How do I look?'

Dobbin reached for a small mirror on the wall and

handed it to Alex who examined his face in silence. Matthew brought the flannel.

'Not bad, considering.'

There was a bruise high on his left cheekbone which was merging with a darkening eye. Alex handed back the mirror and pressed the flannel to his cheek.

'I'll say I slipped and fell here, on the tiles. All right?'

Matthew was still angry.

'But why?'

Alex was very tired. He yawned.

'I want to get some sleep now.'

He stood delicately. His ribs and stomach were patched with red bruising. Seb draped Alex's shirt gently across his shoulders. Alex looked at his three worried friends. He made himself grin. 'Thanks, Matt. Thanks, Dobbin. Thanks, Seb.'

They wrung out the flannels and left. There were three and a half hours before first bell.

At six – half an hour before first bell – the Swithenbank groom left the horses in the Red Dragon stables and was shown into the dining-room where Tarrington sat alone wolfing a huge breakfast. The groom had followed all his instructions. Carrying a case of clean clothes and a wallet of cash, he stood inside the doorway and waited patiently until Tarrington pushed away his plate and beckoned him over. He gave him new orders, handing over two letters, of which one was the one for Kemp.

When the young man had taken the suitcase upstairs to change, the groom was invited into the staff sitting-room and offered a cup of tea. He kept his eye on the clock. He was to deliver the first letter at half-past six. He was then to pay the hotel bill and deal with the second before riding out to the estate.

The groom was glad for the tea. He did not like this flurry of early-morning orders any more than Wilkins, who had packed Tarrington's bag and wallet. They had guessed they were getting the boy out of trouble. The groom had noted Tarrington's swollen lip and wondered who his opponent had been.

Ten minutes later Tarrington was on his way home through the quiet streets.

Brinsop was in full swing. His music surged round the columns and arches and his pedal-notes were like hammerblows. Alex almost felt part of the performance as he waited for the men to pass the side-chapel, almost felt controlled by the organist's fingers and feet. He crossed the passage and climbed to the choirstalls. He could see Brinsop's eyes reflected in the slanting mirror fixed upon the music before him.

'I hate you,' he hissed softly as he edged between the desks and benches.

Brinsop had shown no sympathy for his bruised and blackened face, the day before. He had made sarcastic remarks during the practice and, in the end, had given his solo to Birdy Wren, unwilling to make allowances for the sharpness in Alex's chest when he filled his lungs.

'I hate you,' he hissed again as he made his way forward. He did not realise he had spoken.

There was soft evening light in the nave; a few shadows for hiding. Alex did not care. He moved into a gap between two massive tombs and listened for Norman Wickstead. He wished Gwynne were on duty; there was no joy in outwitting somebody he liked. His fingers touched the cap badge in his pocket, then closed gently round it. Four bolts slammed into place, jolting the boy's attention to the north porch. Now he knew where Norman was and padded softly from cover.

He felt no thrill: those days were over. Tarrington had ruined the excitement and even though he was free of Tarrington he felt nothing. Only the need.

Alex leaned against the cool stone of the first pillar. The music was violent, beating through the air. Alex

71

walked calmly to the second and the music died in echoes. Voices came to him from far away; there was laughter before a heavy door boomed shut, probably in the Ladye Chapel. Brinsop began the next movement of his voluntary; a different mood – slower, sadder. Alex came to the pews. There was a service sheet on the floor. He picked it up. The Service of Thanksgiving. He opened the pamphlet and his mind slipped back eight hours to the moment when time had stood still.

The Choir had been crossing the Close when Harry had called him to a group of patients and staff from Blatchfords gathering to make a quiet entrance for the Service of Thanksgiving. Harry had a cap badge for Alex – a gift, he said, from Terry. Alex recalled Harry's glance of sympathy before he had broken away, running hard to take his place in the two lines of choristers. There had been no need for other words.

Alex closed the service sheet and dropped it on the nearest pew as Brinsop crashed into the final section of his voluntary. Alex was annoyed at himself for losing concentration. He looked quickly round the nave and gathered his thoughts. Brinsop was playing a grand march and the swelling sound made his head swim but there was no thrill, no excitement. There was only the need. The need to do this. To overcome. To overcome? Overcome who? Overcome what?

The boy edged round the south central pillar and forced the lid open. There was money there. Suddenly there was also Gwynne behind him and Kemp and the archdeacon moving from the shadows. It was another moment for time to stand still. Alex – who had always known it would come to this – slowly withdrew his hand from the box as the head verger gripped his shoulder and shoved him forward. Brinsop's closing chords slammed triumphantly down on his solo chorister who dug into his pocket to hold tight to Terry's gift, for strength, for courage and for the real world.

11

The Shock

Brinsop was excited with the drama of it all but hid his feelings beneath a good show of disgust and contempt. Mrs Brinsop found the matter of much less interest but knew better than to come between a man and his righteous indignation. She nodded and sighed at the appropriate moments as the Master of Choristers brandished knife and fork and let his dinner grow cold.

The doctor shovelled the last of the chops into his mouth and pointed to the bell at his wife's side – which she obediently rang even though she had not yet finished her own meal.

Winnie tapped on the door and came in to clear the table. As she deftly shifted the plates and dishes to the tray on the sideboard, the Doctor continued to enjoy his scandal, lowering his voice which meant that servants were not supposed to listen.

'Somebody knew what the boy was up to, though.'

'Yes, dear?'

'A real mystery.'

'Oh?'

'You know the prayer-board in the Ladye Chapel? Yes, you do. You write your prayer and fold it and pin it on the board; the archdeacon or somebody collects the notes at the end of the day and prays for everybody who's asked. It seems somebody wrote and tipped off the dean. Stuck it on the prayer-board. Unsigned. Told him to look out for a thief at such and such a place tonight after Evensong.'

'Well, well.'

'And that's how they caught him,' concluded the man

with smug satisfaction. He remembered suddenly to be disgusted.

'One of my own Choristers too – and a senior one at that.'

'What will happen to him, dear?'

'Punishment. Expulsion. Sent home in disgrace. I've given the headmaster my advice on the matter.'

'Oh dear.'

'Oh dear nothing,' corrected the good doctor sternly. 'Serve him right. Alexander Davies must have known the risk he ran.'

Before Flo could mouth more meaningless words they were both able to shout at Winnie who dropped an expensive cut-glass tumbler which exploded in fragments at her feet.

Martin Cleeve breathed on his spectacles and polished them carefully as Winnie and Seb leaned forward for his advice. He slotted the glasses into place and gazed out over the Linnow and its coal wharf below the gatehouse. In truth, he did not want to do battle on their behalf and half-wished they had not told him this depressing story.

'What do you expect of me?'

They were puzzled.

'How do you mean?'

'You've got to tell Doctor Brinsop.'

Martin Cleeve turned to face them.

'Tell him what?'

They looked at each other and back to the man.

'The truth.'

Martin groaned to himself. They expected him to go to a superior who mistrusted and disliked him and plead the case of a nervous and unreliable self-confessed young thief. They wanted him to challenge the reputation of a dashing son of local gentry who had dutifully returned home to help his father before joining His Majesty's Forces.

'Why me?'

It was another question they did not understand.

'Who else?'

Martin rose slowly and sat at his piano. For a minute or so his hands found slow, quiet chords. He was thinking through his fingers. He came to a resolution and swivelled the music stool towards them.

'Tell me again. And be sure you tell me everything.'

Martin waited nervously in Brinsop's study, wondering what he should say. He had as many facts as Seb had been able to give him and fervently hoped they were as accurate as the boy claimed.

Brinsop strode in, shut the door and moved straight to the tall chair behind his desk from where he looked up without curiosity at his assistant. Martin coughed nervously. Brinsop spread his fingers and lowered them delicately to the surface of the desk.

'I am told you insist upon seeing me.'

'Yes. It's about Alexander Davies.'

'What is your interest in this matter?'

'The boy's friends are concerned for him.'

'And they have come to you?'

'Yes.'

Brinsop's blank mask continued. Martin Cleeve coughed again.

'There are facts which should be put in Davies' defence.'

'You should be speaking with the headmaster or the dean or the police.'

'Davies is a member of your Choir, I assume you would wish to help him.'

Brinsop permitted the mask to show surprise at this novel idea. 'And why, sir, should I wish to help a wretched boy who confesses to have robbed the cathedral over a period of some eighteen months?'

'I'm told he returned the money he took.'

The cold mask tightened again. Silence. Martin Cleeve tried another track.

'There is an older boy. Tarrington.'

'I am aware of the Tarrington family.'

'Much of the blame would seem to lie with him.'

Martin Cleeve's misgivings were justified. In an indignant onslaught Brinsop compared Alex's unhappy background to the stability of ten generations of Tarringtons. He weighed the motives of a penniless moaner against those of a rich, confident sportsman. Even Alex's cleverness in class somehow counted for less than Tarrington's dependable dullness and when Martin Cleeve began to raise Seb's account of the blackmailing, Brinsop angrily waved him to silence.

'I cannot any longer listen to tittle-tattle against a young man who is not here to defend himself.'

'But that is exactly why Tarrington left so hurriedly. He needed to avoid having to reply to harsh questions.'

Martin Cleeve told Brinsop of Tarrington's attack on Alex.

Brinsop suddenly thumped the desk with his fist and glared up at the younger man with distaste.

'What possible proof is there of this?'

'The boy's face.'

'The boy himself told me he slipped and fell against a wash-basin.'

'He was afraid to tell the truth.'

Brinsop pulled a pad of notepaper towards him. He took up a pen and flipped open an inkwell. 'Who are your informants? Who are these friends of the wretched boy who have brought you this fantastic fable?'

'They would prefer not to be named.'

Brinsop was scornful. 'Do not indulge in schoolboy attitudes, Mister Cleeve. You and I are adults; with responsibilities. We are not boys sneaking upon their companions.'

Martin thought quickly and decided that Seb and

Winnie must be prepared to accept responsibility for their beliefs. He thought they would agree.

'Sebastian Carpenter told me of Tarrington's part in the affair.'

'And how did Carpenter come to know Davies had been caught?'

'Winifred Price told him.'

Brinsop threw down his pen and stood, angry to have his servant involved and aghast that she should relay private talk at his table.

'She acted bravely and in good faith,' Martin added hurriedly but Brinsop was on his way to the door which he swung open.

'You listen to servants' gossip. You accept boys' rumour as truth. You must grow up, Mister Cleeve. Davies has stolen from the House of God which he served. He has admitted it and there is nothing more to say. He is now in charge of his housemaster and tomorrow will be punished and expelled. His treatment has been just and right; to do less would encourage others. Goodnight, sir.'

Martin Cleeve turned back to Brinsop as he passed into the hall. 'Davies lost his father in the war.'

'So did others.'

'He has been under pressure.'

'So have others.'

'Much of that pressure has come from you, Doctor Brinsop.'

Brinsop smiled thinly. 'So I am to blame? Or the boy Tarrington is to blame? Or the Germans are to blame? Everybody is to blame but Davies himself.'

'Doctor Brinsop – only Tarrington could have pinned that note on the prayer-board.'

The choirmaster was suddenly angry. 'Then we owe him our thanks. Goodnight, Mister Cleeve.'

The study door slammed shut and Martin turned wearily to leave. Cook was standing frostily at the front

77

door to let him out. He wondered how much she had heard. He nodded thanks and passed from the house, guessing Winnie would soon be in trouble whether Cook had eavesdropped or not. He walked into the warm Close, knowing himself a total failure.

From his sitting-room in the gatehouse, Norman Wickstead saw Martin Cleeve's miserable approach and went at once to the kitchen where Seb and Winnie were quietly eating scrambled egg which his wife Betty had insisted on cooking.

'Here he comes,' said Norman. 'And he's not a happy man.'

Martin Cleeve's account of his discussion in Brinsop's study allowed nobody else to feel happy either. After an hour's urgent talk their meeting broke up. Martin wrote an excuse note for Seb whose bedtime was well past, and while the boy returned to School House, Martin and Winnie slipped from the River Gate taking the narrow streets to the Castle Hotel and its telephone. Winnie then took a deep breath and headed pluckily for the vengeance of the Brinsop household while Martin stayed in the hotel and bolstered his courage with a large brandy. Seb was hurrying up to his dormitory to find Matthew when Kemp saw him but was forced to accept Martin's note. Back in the gatehouse, Betty set about her task while Norman padded listlessly round her like a caged animal, distressed for Seb and Seb's friend Alex and for Mister Cleeve – even if he did play the piano at all hours and wake the kids up.

'It's not right,' he kept saying to his busy wife. 'It's never right. Not right at all.'

12

Escape

As the cathedral bell was striking three-quarters past midnight, urgent knocking on her bedroom door woke Matron with a start.

'Yes, yes. I'm coming.'

After ten years in School House, matron was used to emergencies and woke clearly from deep sleep. She pulled her dressing-gown round her and hurried to the door.

'Quinn? What on earth is the matter?'

'Please, Matron, Ruscoe's fallen down the Junior Dorm stairs.'

'Ruscoe?'

'He must have slipped. He's not moving. Please, Matron.'

Quinn's agitation worried her. They both passed quickly through her sitting-room.

'Is he bleeding, Quinn?'

'Yes, I think so – no, he's not. Please, Matron, I can't remember.'

They moved speedily along the creaking corridor towards the junior dormitory. When their whispering had died away, Seb slipped from the shadows and entered Matron's rooms. He was fully dressed and carried a bundle. Matron's sitting-room had three doors. One led out to the corridor and one to her bedroom. It was to the third that Seb went. He turned the key in the door.

Alex was not asleep. Quinn's knocking had woken him, too, and he had wondered what was happening. He had not expected to hear the sickroom door unlocked and see Seb come grinning to him.

'Seb. What are you doing here?' He actually threw his arms round Seb. Since Evensong he had spoken only to aggressive or cold adults. Both boys were happy to see each other.

'I've got clothes from your cupboard. I didn't know if you'd have any up here.'

'They took them away.'

Alex scrambled from his bed and began dressing. 'How did you know I was here?'

'Tod saw you at the window. He thought you were just ill.'

Seb stood in the doorway, listening for Matron's return. Alex did up his bootlaces. 'What's happening, Seb?'

'The first thing is to get you out of here. When Matron comes back she might check you're still asleep, so when you're dressed get back into bed and pull the bedclothes right up to your neck.'

Alex obeyed. Seb came over and made final adjustments to the blankets. He picked up Alex's pyjamas from the floor.

'Where did Matron go?'

Seb briefly explained as he shut the sickroom door and made for the bed furthest from Alex. He crawled beneath it. There was silence for a while as they waited.

'I suppose it was Tarrington.'

Alex's voice was a whisper. Seb spoke softly back. 'He put a warning on the prayer-board.'

They waited. Seb spoke again. 'Was it terrible?'

Alex replied after some thought. 'I don't know. Yes, probably.'

A door closed somewhere in the house. 'She's coming back,' whispered Alex. He arranged the bedclothes.

'Alex? Why did you do it?' I thought it was all finished.'

The footsteps were undeniable now and heavy with annoyance.

'I don't know,' Alex finally answered. 'Tarrington knew me well, didn't he? Better than I knew myself.'

Matron was not sure if she had been tricked or not. They had eventually found little Ruscoe, not unconscious at the foot of the stairs but in a lavatory cubicle, and when at last he had emerged he was entirely normal, if a little sleepy. Yes – he seemed to remember slipping some-where; no – he felt fine; yes – it might have been something to do with a staircase but perhaps he'd been dreaming. Matron felt it was more likely that the unusually silent Quinn might have been the dreamer and sent both to bed after a swift examination of Ruscoe.

She was about to pass into her bedroom when her glance fell on the sickroom key. It was not turned. She gently opened the door and saw her prisoner fast asleep in the nearest bed. She retired and closed the door, turning the key and removing it. It was not like her to make mistakes: she was sure she remembered having locked the door as Mister Kemp had instructed. Or perhaps not. She yawned and passed into her bedroom, eager to resume sleep. She would discuss Quinn's emergency with the two boys in the morning. The cathedral clock struck one: it was morning now. Matron groaned and sank into her bed.

Seb and Alex waited until the clock struck the quarter-hour before moving or speaking. Alex was fearful. 'She's locked us in.'

Seb slid the window open.

'What now?' asked Alex anxiously.

As if in answer, the tip of a ladder wavered and probed immediately below the window. Seb leaned down to grab it. Alex climbed down carefully. It was a long climb, past other windows, before he came shakily to the ground where he found Norman Wickstead and Matthew firmly anchoring the ladder. Matthew grinned and thumped his back in greeting; Norman smiled and shook his hand before calling Matthew to hold the long ladder firm for Seb's descent.

When Seb, too, was safely on Kemp's private lawn, Matt whistled three times and almost at once Birdy loomed out of the patchy moonlight, followed shortly by Dobbin and Tod. They greeted Alex warmly.

'Anyone about?' whispered Matt.

They all reported no. Matthew took a bag from beneath a bush and handed it to Alex. 'I packed all your things I could find. You know – your private things,' he explained.

Norman handed over a neat package wrapped in greaseproof paper. 'Sandwiches, from the wife. Just in case.' He reached into his jacket pocket. 'And this bottle's from me,' he shrugged apologetically. 'It's beer. The only drink I had in the house.'

There were anxious moments as they all balanced and propped the Vergers' longest ladder as it came wobbling down from the sickroom window, waving wildly outside Kemp's room and noisily scraping the wall at one side of the Senior Dormitory window, but at last it was safely flat on the lawn and in a flurry of farewells, Dobbin, Tod, Birdy and Matthew picked it up and carried it quietly across the Close to the workyard whose gate had been unlocked by Norman.

Norman led the way to a gate which he also intended unlocking. Seb picked up his own battered suitcase from the bush.

'Come on,' he whispered to Alex. But Alex was confused. He had total faith in Seb but the happenings of the last ten hours had taken their toll. He suddenly stopped. 'Seb?'

Seb turned. 'What is it?'

'I don't know what's happening.'

Seb saw the tense anxiety and put an arm round his friend's shoulders. 'Norman's unlocking Verger's Gate for us. Everything's all right,' he explained reassuringly.

Alex nodded and they caught up with the man as he swung open the narrow door. 'All clear,' he whispered as the boys passed through. They turned to thank him and shake hands.

'Good luck, lads,' Norman called softly.

He watched the figures merge into the shadows of Capuchin Lane.

'It's not right,' he told himself as he closed the studded wooden door. 'Never in a million years.'

Alex and Seb had a nervous wait at the corner of Capuchin Lane and Paternoster Row until footsteps could be heard hurrying towards them. They pressed back into a deep doorway as a shadow fell across the road: too small for a patrolling policeman.

'Seb?' called Winnie softly. 'Alex?' She gasped with alarm as they suddenly materialised. Then she laughed in relief. Seeing Alex's tight and bewildered face, she put her arms round him and held him tight for a long time.

They could hear the Wolsley snarling through distant streets for so long before it actually arrived that the noise grew alarming and they could not believe others would ignore it. They pressed back into the doorway once more and listened apprehensively to its roaring approach. With all their concentration on the car, they were suddenly aware of the panting presence of Martin Cleeve, which made all of them jump, and then Fiona had spotted them and soon they were clambering aboard the small machine. Ignoring pleas for caution Fiona careered round the twisting backstreets, the plucky Wolsley swaying under its heavy load.

When they came at last to Blatchfords, Martin, who loathed all evil-smelling combustion engines, had been sick twice and was glad that they had come to rest outside a hospital where a man was hurrying to meet them with a lantern.

13

Regrouping

The next six weeks saw an old way of life end and a new one begin.

Twelve hours after the late-night meeting in Harry's room, Fiona, as she had promised, collected Seb from Blatchfords and drove him home. As they pressed through the counties of Archenford and Hereford towards the blue-black outlines of the Radnor Hills, Seb carefully worked out his questions – and replies he might be called on to give. In the event, they were not needed. From the hill road overlooking Broxwood Farm they had seen Seb's grimfaced parents emerge and shake hands with Kemp and an unknown police sergeant. Fiona was willing to go down, herself, to the farm and sound out Mister Carpenter and his wife when the men had left but Seb shook his head and asked to return to Blatchfords. He had seen Broxwood Farm go over to the enemy and that made decisions easier.

Seb and Alex stayed a week at Blatchfords, hidden and protected by the handful of patients and nurses in the secret. However, when the catering officer noticed he seemed to be feeding extra mouths, Sister Robbins thought it was time she and Harry had a firm but friendly chat. The result of this was that Harry himself accompanied the boys to Ludlow and smoothed any difficulties that threatened their recruitment. Seb and Alex spent that night in the Shrewsbury Barracks, frightened and excited. They agreed it reminded them of their first night as boarders in School House.

The dean and Kemp received brief notes from the boys informing them that they had decided to enter the army as a way of avoiding disgrace. Alex's aunt and the

Carpenters received longer letters with much the same news. Everyone was relieved that the boys were at least safe and it was felt that they had done the honourable thing in joining up. No further action was taken. They became the army's responsibility and the army was pleased to turn a blind eye to the question of age since a major new offensive was to begin later in the year. Major offensives meant major casualties which had to be replaced.

Winnie had a miserable time. Her small part in the escapade became known to other servants and she was severely lectured, not only by the Brinsops, but by Cook, the dailies and even the gardener. They had always resented her hard work and feared her Welsh temper but now had something solid to which they could pin their dislike. After a VAD Meeting in the Town Hall, in early June, she had fought to hold back her tears from Fiona but not quite succeeded. Accordingly, in the late afternoon of 10 June, the very first Rolls Royce ever to be seen in Archenford nosed its immaculate way into the Close despite indignant and noisy protests from Gwynne. An equally immaculate chauffeur demanded of the passing archdeacon where Brinsop's house was to be found and a small crowd gathered to gape as the magnificent car parked at his gate. The invaluable Hollingworth marched down the drive to knock at the front door which was opened by none other than Mrs Brinsop herself whose bulging eyes bounced from the tall, uniformed man before her to the car beyond and the bejewelled woman inside. Hollingworth presented Lady Dormington's compliments and requested the appearance of Miss Winifred Price with whom her ladyship wished to speak. Flo sent immediately for Winnie, ashamed at what new mischief the unruly girl was guilty of, and hastened through the growing crowd to beg Lady Dormington to step into the house and take tea – an invitation which Lady Dormington refused so icily that Flo felt her blood run cold. Her husband, arriving from the cathedral and scandalised by the shoving mass at his gate, was soon bowing and scraping alongside his wife, and felt the refusal to set foot inside his house equally sharply. At last, Lady Dormington – Fiona's Aunt Gemma – wound down the window and, in a clear voice that carried clearly to the attentive and delighted throng, addressed the red-faced pair.

'I am removing Miss Price from your employ. If my niece is to be believed, you neither respect nor appreciate this remarkable young woman. I have spoken with her mother and she is to work for the Dormington Estate where her talents will be justly valued. If – in spite of the paltry wages you grudgingly pay her – you feel aggrieved at this action, you are free to pursue the matter in the courts.'

She wound up the window. Flo was scarlet with confusion and Brinsop white with anger. He was angrily starting to stammer his feelings when a cheer broke out at Winnie's appearance. Hollingworth carefully placed her next to her ladyship and stowed away the threadbare bag which contained her few belongings. As the crowd parted to allow the car to reverse and draw away, somebody called for three cheers for Lady Dormington, after which a grinning man in a blue suit, white shirt and red tie demanded three cheers for Winnie. The Rolls Royce sailed towards Main Gate and the admirers began to disperse. Nobody suggested three cheers for the Brinsops who scuttled up their drive to the security of their front door amid giggles and whistling.

The new offensive began in France two weeks later. British guns began a nonstop bombardment of the enemy trenches along a 45 mile front whose daily 150,000 shells could be clearly heard almost eighty miles away. Four of the five days of shelling were misty and damp but on 1 July, at seven-thirty on a warm sunny morning, the guns fell silent and the Big Push forward began the battle of the Somme. It was a disaster. At the end of that first day, the British Forces had suffered 60,000 casualties of whom 20,000 were dead. Among the September reinforcements were Private Carpenter and Private Davies.

PART TWO

The Somme, France:
Autumn 1916

1

The Doullens Road

The three platoons of C Company swung south along the road from the railhead at Doullens glad to stretch their legs and happily involved in an obscene marching song. At their head, mounted on a dappled grey mare which, a year ago, had won a famous victory in the Ludlow Point-to-Point, Major Challenger sang as loudly as his men. The road was not crowded in the early evening as the Company approached the transit camp at the side of the Amiens road. It had been a short march – only an hour. Now everyone was looking forward to a hot meal and a comfortable night. The Major passed back the word to pipe down and smarten up.

When the 12th Salopian Battalion had disembarked at Boulogne, a week before, wide-eyed at the strange sights and seasick from the crossing, there had been three companies in the battalion. It had soon been made embarrassingly clear that they were nothing more than a stop-gap outfit of hastily-trained reserves. At almost every stage of its progress from the coast it had lost troops to other regiments – a section here, a platoon there and once, even, an entire company. The desperate fighting on the battlefields of the Somme – now only one day's hard march ahead – was continuing to cost dearly in terms of human life.

By the time each section had been shown to its tent and visited the barn in a corner of the field to stuff empty mattresses with straw it was almost dark. They ate meat of some sort, potatoes and cheese which they washed down with mugs of strong tea. When they had washed their mess-tins they had at last time to look around them before darkness fell.

Alex and Seb ambled along the banks of the Authie brook which bordered the camp. A few late birds were singing and an occasional fish plopped in the stream. Every now and then a gust of laughter drew their attention back to the camp but the relaxed chatter of several hundred men was generally no more than a hum in the air. Seb looked up. The sky was clouded and a sudden breeze flicked across the water. He sniffed. 'Weather's due for a change.'

Alex dug his heel into the soft earth. 'It's wet enough already.'

They fell silent as three farmworkers trudged silently towards a distant clutch of cottages on the opposite bank of the brook. Seb and Alex were not confident enough to try out their schoolboy French. It seemed strange to pass without greeting.

'They don't seem particularly pleased to have us here,' said Seb glancing back at them.

'Would you want your Broxwood fields taken over by hundreds of foreigners?'

Seb agreed that was a point. The three Frenchmen had surely not asked for a war on their doorstep.

'I wish I knew where Luke is,' Seb said.

A far-off cacophony cut into the night somewhere behind them. A series of rapid rachetlike clackings split the silence and, as they turned, their faces were tinged by dim green light which etched itself along a section of the horizon. There was a mess of noises like spitting, then several deeper, drier, slower sounds. In every part of the camp heads swung towards the disturbance. Instantly concentration tightened.

Thirty kilometres to the east a dusk raid was being countered by rifle fire and grenades. The action was constant for perhaps four minutes and then broke off as suddenly as it had begun. The newcomers found themselves once again in silence – except for the birdsong, crickets chirping and laughter from the sergeants' Mess.

Birds, insects and old soldiers were well used to such outbreaks. The young men were not. Alex and Seb hurried to their tent, needing to be with the rest of the section. As the bugles sounded 'Lights Out' and even the laughter from the Mess died away, a mood of thoughtful apprehension hung over the transit camp and was a trouble to the sleep of the tired men. So was the constant rattle of rain on the canvas and the chuckle of the Authie brook as it slowly rose.

Next morning, C Company paraded before Major Challenger in full marching order at a quarter-past eight. Each platoon commander then inspected his three sections.

Seb and Alex liked Lieutenant Gould, commander of Number Four Platoon. Although he was as young and unsure of himself as any of the men under his command he hid the uncertainty behind the two pips on his shoulder and a friendly, confident smile. When the major had left the parade, Lieutenant Gould told Platoon 4 to stand easy and listen to the plan for today. He told them the company was to march to a village close to the town of Albert – he pronounced the name both ways, French and English. The village itself was called – he grinned – Bouzincourt. A roar of laughter went up as he again pronounced it both ways. There was a scattering of comments from the platoon wits.

'Silence in court.'

'Booze in court.'

'Don't let the major get caught boozing, sir.'

Tony Gould let the laughter run its course. Unlike his men, he had an accurate idea of what awaited them in the deadly triangle enclosed by the towns of Peronne, Bapaume and Albert. He was grateful for the laughter. Finally the platoon sergeant called the men to order and Lieutenant Gould continued. 'We leave at eight forty-five.' He glanced down at his watch. 'That's in ten minutes. It's going to be a longish day's march. Thirty kilometres.' He looked to his platoon sergeant. 'What's that in real distances, Sergeant?' The platoon chuckled appreciatively.

'Eighteen miles, sir.'

'So it is. Very well. Check your boots, check your packs. We don't want Number Four Platoon falling to bits on the way.'

The company halted at noon to eat its rations in the village of Arquèves where the boldest of them bought wine, cider and bread until instructions emerged from the three-table Café-Restaurant (For Officers Only) to stop. This saddened the soldiers, who were enjoying the novelty of shopping with a few foreign coins, and the shopkeeper, who was happily charging them double.

Seb sniffed rain in the air during the first hour's march after the stop at Arquèves and twenty minutes later it was drizzling sufficiently for the company to be halted to put on waterproof capes. There was no singing in the early afternoon. The first two hours after the midday stop were always the worst. Miles behind but miles still to go; muscles stiff after relaxation, feet swollen inside boots and puttees tugging tighter from ankle to knee.

For the final hour of the journey the main Albert road was so packed with traffic that it became impossible to march and the Platoons were forced to break step and thread their way through until they were past the cross-roads at Hédauville and able to make better time. A very long convoy of trucks and ambulances was struggling back towards Doullens and the men in it were silent and sullen. Through masks of mud, red-rimmed eyes watched the new arrivals without emotion. The vital village of Ginchy had been taken the day before in bitter fighting. These were the victors.

It was after four o'clock when C Company paraded on the edge of Bouzincourt. The drizzle had broken up into showers and rain slid down capes into boots and puttees, tightening, chilling and restricting the blood vessels so that legs ached – but feet ached too, and so did shoulders and necks. It was always the same at the end of a long march. Nevertheless, they were all grateful for the training slogs up and down the Shropshire hillroads of the Wrekin. The company had arrived in good order; nobody had dropped out. Everyone was quietly pleased and proud. The hundred and ten men from the borderland of the Welsh Marches shifted weight gently from foot to foot and looked round them.

Bouzincourt seemed less of a French village than yet another British Transit Camp. Incurious infants watched from those houses which were still inhabited but most villagers stayed indoors.

Heavy guns began an evening duel. The exchange was several miles away but several miles closer than the light rifle and machine-gun fire they had heard the night before. The experienced soldiers took no notice, as ever, but the recruits grew suddenly tense. The explosions were flat and dry but there was a new element. Seb and Alex felt the ground vibrating beneath their boots. Others felt it too and looked nervously round to see how their companions were reacting.

'If it's like this, here, at this distance,' murmured Alex to Seb, 'what's it going to be like there – close to?'

Before Seb had time to reply, all eyes were pulled to Major Challenger, stalking into the street from a meeting with the senior British officer. Seeing his set and angry face the platoon commanders stopped their chatter and the Company Sergeant Major, who was having a quiet smoke with the sergeants, inhaled thoughtfully and moved discreetly within easy calling-distance. He knew trouble when he saw it.

There had been a change of plan, the major told his platoon commanders icily. Regrettable, naturally, and a damn nuisance but things move fast in a fighting zone. The company was being split up – yes, yes: he appreciated their concern but orders were orders. He ran through those new orders. Luckily most of the company would stick together. He nodded for the four lieutenants to disperse and beckoned over the CSM to discuss the practical problems.

Tony Gould did his best to stay cheerful as he explained to his platoon that they were breaking off from the rest of the company to march west and bivouac overnight at a place called Warloy. No distance at all really: about five miles. A temporary move. He held on tight to his grin as he told them that the next morning the platoon was to march back to the camp at Doullens.

There was a disbelieving silence and the beginning of a storm of grumbling which the platoon sergeant silenced immediately. At last Lieutenant Gould's smile slipped away. 'I know,' he said. 'I'm as disappointed as anybody.'

The lieutenant paused briefly and the sergeant looked down at the ground. The men waited; they suspected they would not like what was coming.

'It's really about the chaps we saw today – the ones who did so brilliantly at Ginchy. The plan was to get them straight on to the trains at the railhead and back to a rest camp near Boulogne. But you saw the state of them. Their CO thinks they're not up to the journey yet. So they're having a few days to recover at Doullens. Trouble is, another battalion's on its way to Doullens already and it can't be stopped; the men are experienced fighters – needed at the front. So. The camp's going to be full-to-overflowing and we're needed to lend a hand in the running of it. General dogsbodies. That sort of thing.'

Another stunned silence. Then . . .

'We're not Service Corps, sir.'

'That's right, sir.'

'We're a fighting unit.'

The sergeant barked out, That's enough, and the grumbling subsided. Suddenly Tony Gould grinned again.

'It's no good bellyaching. We're in the army and we've got our orders. Let's see what's at this Warloy village. You never know. There's probably a nice little *estaminet* – that's French for a pub – and maybe even a pretty mademoiselle or two. Who knows?'

'I thought we were Infantry,' murmured Alex to Seb. 'Not bloody nursemaids.'

Seb nodded, dispirited, 'If this is the way we run the war, no wonder it's going on for ever.'

2

Captain Dev

The lieutenant's dream of a relaxed night among his platoon in a friendly *estaminet* exploded the moment Number Four Platoon marched into Warloy about half an hour before dusk. It was as heavily militarised as Bouzincourt and top-heavy with officers.

Tony Gould made contact with the billeting officer who offered him a comfortable room in the priest's house in the village square and quite near the field where his men would spend the night. There was a good little restaurant – reserved for officers, of course. There was certainly an estaminet but it was out of bounds to the men; some trouble last week. To the astonishment of the pale-faced major, the young officer declined both room and restaurant; he preferred to stay with his troops.

The major disapproved strongly. 'You'll see more than enough of them when you're in the trenches, Lieutenant, believe me.'

'All the more reason to be with them now, sir.' Tony Gould saluted politely and left.

When the Lieutenant returned to the small sheltered square outside the church he found his platoon had vanished. Night and rain had begun to fall about the same time and he wondered if he could have missed his way. Maybe Warloy had two churches and he'd somehow found the wrong one.

'Lieutenant Gould?' A figure emerged from the shadows beneath the dripping trees. Tony peered into the gloom and made out an officer's cap but since a riding mac covered the figure's shoulders he couldn't see his rank. They were about the same age.

'Yes. What have you done with my platoon?'

The figure held out a hand.

'I'm Devereux.'

Tony shook it cautiously.

'How do you do?' he said. 'I'm afraid I can't see your rank so I don't know if I should be saluting you or not.'

'There's nobody watching so we won't bother with all that nonsense. Let's get out of this rain. I've got a car over there.'

As they walked to the edge of the square Captain Nicholas Devereux of the Army Service Corps explained the disappearance of Tony's men. 'There's a farm about three-quarters of a mile away,' he said. 'The farmer does business with me and owes me a favour or two so I thought I'd put him to the test. I've billeted your men on him.'

The captain's Citroën finally drew up outside a large barn from which the officers could hear the cheerful shouts of men who had expected the worst but found something good instead. Inside was plenty of dry hay for bedding and the roof was watertight; there was more than enough room for the platoon.

Tony looked round. He imagined the muddy bivouacs in the wet open field.

'Lucky for us you came along, Captain Devereux.'

'Friends call me Dev.'

They turned and stood in the doorway looking out at the rain which was heavier now.

'It wasn't only a matter of luck: I'm here under orders.'

'Oh dear.'

Dev grinned. The platoon sergeant came to them.

'I suggested we wait for you, sir, but the captain here told us to move before the rain began bucketing down.'

'Quite right, Sergeant. Everything under control?'

'Highly satisfactory, sir.'

The throaty roar and rattle of a labouring engine could suddenly be heard approaching. Dev glanced at his watch.

'Here's your supper arriving.'

'I'll go and get the men organised, sir.'

The sergeant hurried away as a three-quarter-ton lorry hauled into sight, drowning all other sound. Platoon Number Four pressed forward to see it pull to a halt directly outside. The engine was turned off and talk was possible again.

'This is my first order – to get you fed. I'm afraid you'll have to cope for yourselves at breakfast but at least there'll be something hot tonight.'

A figure came hurrying towards him, pulling on his forage cap.

'Ah, Corporal Massey. Meet Lieutenant Gould and tell him what's on the menu.'

The corporal was not a young man but the spring in his step and his dapper appearance was deceptive. He looked like a man who enjoyed his work as he saluted extravagantly. It was hard to tell if the expression on his face was a grin or a grimace. 'There's a good hot stew, sir. Only bully beef, I'm afraid, but the vegetables are fresh. I have good local cheese and bread just baked. There's tea, of course. Also a tank of fresh water for the platoon's flasks and morning tea.'

Massey saluted eccentrically and hurried away to supervise the lorry's transformation into a well-stocked, well-organised kitchen. Gas lanterns were lit and three Service Corps cooks began to prepare supper. The platoon watched hungrily. Tony Gould turned to Dev in amazement.

'What on earth did we do to deserve this?'

'For a start, you're helping us out at Doullens – that's where I'm based, by the way. Also, Massey happened to have the mobile kitchen overnight and it seemed a pity not to use it. Then again, I have a friend on the staff of the senior officer at Bouzincourt who told me how your nice major stood up to his nasty colonel. And finally there's the orders you haven't heard yet.'

Rain battered down on the tarpaulin that Massey and the Sergeant were rigging as cover between the barn and the truck. Dev and Tony scrambled to sit in the Citroën and take a swig from a bottle of whisky. They discussed the orders.

'Will this be permanent or temporary?' asked Tony Gould.

Dev handed him the bottle again. He knew his instructions could not be popular. 'Out here, Tony, my friend,' he said, 'everything is temporary.'

In the washed-out glow of paraffin lamps, the platoon stood in a half-circle before the two officers and their NCOs. Rain drummed steadily on the roof; from the AEC truck came muted voices and the occasional scrape of a pot being cleaned. The Captain explained that there was a row going on at home over soldiers who had lied about their age when they enlisted. Questions were being asked in Parliament. Civilians were getting jittery over newspaper stories which played up the army's problems without praising its gains. Some parents had

100

lost their nerve and were bombarding the army in Britain with birth certificates, saying please can we have our sons back.

Everybody laughed. Typical of civilians. Dev went on. 'So if there's anybody in this Platoon who is under military age, he should stand forward now.'

Seb heard Alex's sharp intake of breath. Someone coughed but nobody moved. Lieutenant Gould spoke from Dev's side. 'It's no disgrace,' he said. 'In fact it's honourable to want to do your bit for King and Country at any age at all.'

'It's not a case of sending people back home,' Dev added. 'I have no intention of forcing anyone here to leave the army.'

No one moved. Seb, Alex – and others – kept their eyes on the ground. The Platoon Sergeant spoke up.

'Nobody in the Platoon under military age, Sir.'

Captain Devereux and Lieutenant Gould looked at each other. Tony shrugged and half-turned away. The Captain glanced behind him. 'Corporal.'

Corporal Massey came quickly to one end of the half-circle, a heavy torch in his hand. Concentrating, his teeth bared in that strange grin-grimace, he moved sideways like a crab, shining the beam at each face he passed. 'You . . . you and you . . .' Corporal Massey paused before Ted Culpin. 'You.'

He was almost at the opposite end before he found Reuben Yapp. 'And you.'

He snapped off the beam of the torch, gave his wild salute and stalked back to his place behind his officer. Tony Gould stepped forward. 'Fall out Brown, Carpenter, Davies, Culpin and Yapp,' he said softly.

The two officers retreated, leaving the Sergeant to settle the men down for the night and Massey to gather together the five sullen boys who, huddled together, truly looked little more than a clutch of anxious children.

They jammed as closely together in the back of the truck as their equipment and other occupants would allow. The Citroën had already left and the barn was in silence. Corporal Massey shone his torch beam over them before preparing to lock the doors.

'Where are we going?' asked Roy Brown miserably.

'Pavé.'

'How long's it going to take?'

'Depends.'

Alex spoke up. 'Depends on what?'

Massey was irritated. 'Sentries, the state of the roads, Jerry gunners, moonlight, luck. Don't ask silly questions.' He slammed the bolts home from the first door. Seb shut his eyes and laid his head against his pack. 'Don't ask silly questions, Private Davies,' he echoed.

'What other sort are there in the army?' Alex replied. But nobody laughed.

3

Cocky's Kingdom

The River Ancre was a tributary of the much larger Somme which it joined south of Albert. Among the network of minor roads, lanes and tracks on its banks stood the small group of buildings called Pavé. It had been a farming community. Two houses shared a wall and a high barn leaned against the smaller of the pair; there were a few outbuildings. A good, metalled road ran past which presumably gave the place its name.

Now Pavé was a ruin. In the early days of the war it had been shelled by the German guns as a matter of course, to deprive the enemy of its shelter. The central buildings leaned inwards at a number of crazy angles and an isolated chimney survived. Pavé looked as if the first strong gale of winter, or a single howitzer shell, would flatten it once and for all. It looked finished. Useless. Appearances were deceptive. Below this unpromising wreck Regimental Sergeant-Major Allcock had established his small and effective kingdom.

It was Corporal Massey who had discovered the cellars of Pavé. Lost in the network of paths he had come across the farmstead and, since he was not due to report back to Bouzincourt until the evening, he had idly explored the ruins, hoping to find something useful or valuable. Instead he had almost fallen through a smashed trapdoor into a cellar beneath the largest of the buildings. He could see very little from its stone steps but it felt dry and clean. He hauled the trapdoor back in place, covered it with rubble and had a private word with his RSM.

The RSM devised a plan. He handpicked a section of his men for cleaning, clearing and repair work. He saw that they were well supplied with food, transport and equipment and placed Corporal Massey in charge. Instead of being taken to some deserted system of collapsed dugouts, they were driven to Pavé where they worked throughout early August. After two weeks they had created Cocky's Kingdom.

The masterstroke of the plan was to convince officers at Bouzincourt that it would be useful to establish a service post closer to the forward trenches, somewhere perhaps among minor roads near the Ancre, north of Albert. They were only too pleased to agree. A new officer was at Doullens – Captain Devereux, fresh from England, knowing nothing of Allcock. He was the ideal officer to be put in charge of the experiment. Allcock was pleased; they were delighted. The truth was the officers at Bouzincourt were only too glad to get rid of the RSM.

RSM Allcock – 'Cocky' to his friends – had joined the army as a boy soldier like his father before him. He was now almost forty, a difficult, solitary man with a sensible wife, Doris, and a house near the Regimental Barracks at Warrington. He also had a Golden Retriever called Barney. Officially he was no longer a regimental sergeant-major but nobody who knew his story begrudged him the title.

His regiment had crossed to France in summer 1914 as part of the British Expeditionary Force and fought well to block the German advance at the River Marne in September. It had then been transferred north to Flanders on the Belgium border where, again, it had held out against heavy enemy attacks and seen the war solidify into the pattern of opposing trenches. Cocky had fought on the Marne as a corporal and at Ypres as a sergeant-major – heavy losses meant quick promotion. Winter arrived and Cocky went home on leave to Doris and Barney. He refused to speak one word about the war, but when he left to return to Flanders, he told Doris bluntly that she must not expect to see him again; her army widow's pension would keep her life comfortable.

At Ypres he found that the survivors of his regiment had been amalgamated with the remnants of three others and that he had been promoted Regimental Sergeant-Major. He became a good leader of men, an example in courage and in attitude towards authority. His best skills were in sorting out unforeseen problems, or finding swift, unusual solutions.

All this changed in April 1915 when a shell scored a direct hit on the regimental forward HQ. RSM Allcock was the sole survivor of the dozen in the dugout and spent a terrifying six hours buried beneath ten feet of clogging soil among the shreds of his companions. A sheet of corrugated iron was sliced deep into his side. He owed his life to finding a pocket of air and he was conscious as they dug him out. He continually begged them to take care of his runner who was in a bad way; he told how they had kept each other talking and joking their hands clasped, throughout the ordeal. The RSM was gripping a hand – but above its elbow there was nothing.

That was when Cocky began screaming.

He spent a month in hospital at Rouen where the gash in his side healed better than his memories. He returned to the regiment but his nerve was gone and he began drinking heavily to deaden his fears. His nightly screaming disturbed everyone, though in the morning Cocky could never remember it. Worst, from the military point of view, he began to question orders and refuse those he felt would put men in unnecessary danger. He took refuge in cynicism which could not be allowed in a man of his rank. He was transferred to the Regimental Transport Depot where his influence was just as upsetting. The only man who took to him was a Lance-Corporal Massey – a bit of a rebel himself.

In Britain the Reservists and territorials were called up which allowed greater reorganisation and in July 1915 RSM Allcock was loaned to the Army Service Corps at Doullens, on the Somme; newly-promoted Corporal Massey went with him. In a new outfit among new surroundings, he was better able to cope and at the end of the year the posting was made permanent. But the drinking, the cynicism and the nightmares returned and began a sad spiral – the more he drank, the more depressed and cynical he would be – and the more frequently bad dreams woke him, the more he needed a drink to get him back to sleep.

There was talk of invaliding him from the army altogether but Cocky confided to Massey that this would be impossible. How could he inflict himself upon his wife in his present state? And what could he do at home? All he knew was the army. He would be forced home useless, without even the disability pension which was reserved for soldiers wounded in action not for drunks with bad dreams. Massey sensed the despair in his friend; it was one problem the RSM was unable to solve. But then Corporal Massey lost his way near Bouzincourt and stumbled upon Pavé. RSM Allcock and the selected few moved in and worked well together. Nightmares ceased; drinking steadied. The critical view of his masters remained, however, and the cynicism, if anything, increased.

The arrival of five teenage boys on a wet September night two days before a major battle did nothing to alter this.

'Dear God,' he groaned as Corporal Massey paraded them at the foot of the steps beneath Pavé. 'What does Dev think I'm running here? Doctor Barnardo's?'

'What have I done to deserve you?'

No reply was expected. As far as Seb was concerned, none was possible. The boys were wet and miserable; they looked down at the packed earth floor.

'Have you got blankets?' The boys nodded.

'Dry blankets? Clean blankets?' The boys shook their heads.

RSM Allcock gazed reproachfully at Corporal Massey who despairingly shrugged. It got worse. Yes – they had wet blankets; no – they didn't have food. Yes, they knew why they had been picked out from the rest; no, they didn't know for what purpose. They knew where they were: Pavé – but they didn't know where Pavé was. Silence hung gloomily round the bedraggled group in the dim light of the Corporal's lamp. Alex noticed with surprise that the RSM was wearing carpet slippers and cheered up slightly.

The senior NCO looked at each of the dispirited boys in turn. He gazed down upon Ted and his nose twitched. Ted squirmed in shame, expecting the usual mockery.

106

'Anybody still in the kitchen, Corporal?'

'Expect so.'

'Hot water. Get them scrubbed and polished. They may look more useful then.' RSM Allcock turned to a door in the wall of corrugated iron and wood. 'Then sleep. As soon as you can. And don't disturb the others. Nobody's going to get much sleep after tomorrow so get some now.'

Before Ted could realise he was not to be made fun of, the RSM nodded, opened the door and left them with Corporal Massey in the narrow corridor. The Corporal lifted his lantern.

'Come on.'

He led them through a rough archway into a second cellar. There was a door almost at their side. The Corporal tapped on it and looked in. 'Chef?' he asked. 'Hot water? Cocoa?'

The boys heard a sleepy voice grumble from the kitchen.

'Who says?'

'Himself says.'

At the end of the corridor was a small, elegant wooden staircase leading back up to ground level. Corporal Massey ran a loving hand along its fine woodwork. It was splendidly out of place in the tin and plank cellars. The man turned proudly to the bemused boys. 'I liberated this personally from a burned-out house in Albert.' He raised the lantern and led the way up.

'What does he mean "liberated"?' whispered Reuben Yapp.

'He means he stole it,' explained Roy Brown.

The room at the top of the stairs was large. There was a strong smell of corn and old apples.

'Dump your kit here for now.'

The boys gladly dropped their packs and rifles. They were very tired – it was almost fifteen hours since the buglers had sounded reveille at Doullens. The corporal lit another lamp and the room took shape round them. They were in some sort of barn stacked with crates and other equipment. Seb spoke.

'What did the RSM mean, Corporal? About nobody getting much sleep after tomorrow?'

Corporal Massey shook his head sadly at the ignorance of the world in general and this young man in particular. 'The bombardment,' he explained patiently. 'We'll have heavy guns shelling overhead from tomorrow until the Big Push begins in four days' time. Night and day.'

The boys were awed into silence. Information of this importance usually came down the chain of command very late in the day to those right at the bottom.

'Clean blankets.'

Massey pointed to an open crate in the corner. 'Leave your wet blankets out in the wash-house. We'll dry them tomorrow.'

'We could leave them to dry in here, Corporal,' said Reuben helpfully.

'Have you ever smelt the smell of wet blankets drying?' He pointed to a cubicle which had been built in the corner. 'Moreover, that is my room, there.'

'What's up the steps?' Seb could just make out a broad ladder which rose directly through a hatch in the ceiling.

'We keep the pigeons up there. And the telescope.' He saw their flicker of interest and grinned. 'Never a dull moment in Cocky's Kingdom, my lads,' he said.

He took up the lamp and moved to the top of the liberated staircase. 'After cocoa, it's over to the wash-house and a good all-over scrub. Himself gave the command; you heard him.'

As he led them back underground he noticed Ted's tight, unhappy face. Chef heard them coming and opened the kitchen door; warmth and good cooking smells drew them in. Corporal Massey held the lamp high to light their way. He put a hand on Seb's arm as the others hurried gratefully through Chef's door. 'What's up with your chum at the front?'

Seb had seen Ted humiliated many times before. Ted was one of a number of recruits brought up strictly on lonely farms to a degree of shyness that was almost crippling.

'Well, come on.' Massey was impatient.

Seb decided to trust him. 'Ted's shy. He's not used to stripping off in public. He gets upset,' Seb explained, keeping his voice low.

'Nothing wrong with a bit of modesty,' declared Massey. 'So let him have the place to himself.' He waved Seb past into the warm kitchen. 'Good God Almighty,' he said wonderingly as he moved up to the barn, 'what does he think we are here? Barbarians?'

After they had drunk the cocoa and rinsed the mugs, Private Bishop – known as 'Chef' – helped them fill buckets of hot water to take to one of the small out-houses, but as they were about to move outside, Corporal Massey suddenly appeared and demanded certain detail of the Doullens camp. He put a hand on Ted's shoulder.

'You – you can tell me. You can go out to the wash-house later.'

It was almost midnight when Ted handed back to Corporal Massey the bar of expensive and highly-scented soap he had liberated from the unlucky Albert house. He climbed quietly down its antique staircase to the kitchen where Roy was smoking a last cigarette and discussing the finer points of pastry-making with Chef. Roy led him to where they were to sleep.

Ted Culpin found that Alex and Reuben had already made up a bed for him and stowed his pack underneath. By the glow of a candle he could make out several sets of bunks. Roy whispered goodnight and hauled himself up and out of sight on to the bed above. Ted undressed in the shadows and listened to the regular breathing of his sleeping comrades – old and new. It had been a strange day. He blew out the candle and slipped between dry, clean blankets. He was just working out if he was pleased to be part of Cocky's Underground Kingdom when sleep suddenly ambushed him; he had been about to decide that he was.

It was the strangeness of the kingdom that attracted Alex and Seb. Yet it was slightly familiar – a kinder, more useful, more real School House. All the newcomers were dazzled except Reuben, who had come to France to fight; not to play games in some backwater, no matter how close to the front lines.

Roy was appointed assistant to Chef – the conversation about pastry had decided that – and Roy was pleased. Cooking and baking had always been among his interests but he had never been encouraged to follow them; there was no place for hobbies like that in the small-town foundry where he had worked and the kitchen was considered strictly for women only. Cocky's Kingdom took its food seriously (another reason why Reuben mistrusted it) and the moment he realised that there would be no jeering, no jokes, Roy knew he would be happy. Chef Bishop was pleased, too.

Ted Culpin's responsibilities at Pavé were mostly decided when Corporal Massey heard that he and his father kept racing pigeons back home in Clun and clinched when the corporal saw the firm gentleness with which the young man handled the creatures. One of the clerks had looked after the birds until then and offered to share the work but Ted shook his head. He had found something he was confident in; he wanted the pigeons all to himself.

Seb and Alex had no choice – but they were used to that. They were the only youngsters who had joined up from school; the others had left school at eleven or twelve and Reuben, who had left at ten, could barely read or

110

write. They joined the office clerks and although they knew theirs was a vital job, they felt it was almost the least exciting.

At least they had a definite place at Pavé. Reuben did not, which strengthened his resentment. The pity of it was that he would have been very useful in the yard behind Pavé where surly Corporal Sullivan cared for the post's vehicles and undertook essential repairs to other army transport. Reuben had worked in a garage near Ludlow and was a clever mechanic. Sadly, Sullivan was possessive about his yard and workshop; he had no time to keep an eye on children keen at playing with cars. (It was only under protest that he accepted a hand now and then from the post's two drivers.) So Reuben was left with the unlikeable job of filling in whenever he was told. A dogsbody. He hated it.

Pavé was unique. It functioned with great efficiency because, unlike other depots, it had no rigid limits. It tried to do whatever was needed for whoever asked. At ten o'clock on that first morning, for instance, Dev hurried down to the office where the clerks were explaining the information and filing systems to Alex and Seb with two large satchels of mail for soldiers in the front or reserve lines. The army's postal services had been unable to keep up with the splitting and rejoining of units in the chaos a couple of miles up the road. The letters were already very late and Dev wanted them sorted and delivered as soon as possible. Could Cocky help? (It took Alex and Seb two hours to break down the jumble of envelopes into specific piles. With the help of the clerks, up-to-the-minute maps and the office's cross-filing index, they enabled a driver to set out before nightfall with 136 re-addressed letters in ten bundles to hand over to identified companies. RSM Allcock was determined as many men as possible should have news from home to read and re-read during the massive bombardment and before they went over the top in attack. Sixty-seven letters remained at Pavé – mostly with wrong names and inaccurate units; Alex and Seb were told to go through the process again, the next day, to see if more might be delivered.)

An hour later a runner came in from the headquarters of a battalion in the support line directly ahead of Pavé with a message from his major. The men were bogged down in a quagmire of trenches as they struggled to carry ammunition to the forward troops. Could Cocky do anything? (Corporal Massey found two water pumps in the barn and sent word out to Sullivan to prepare the Austin to take them as far forward as possible. He also sent back with the runner the map reference of a dugout, deserted since July, where corrugated metal sheets and wooden shoring were to be found.)

And so the day continued. Just before noon Chef supplied a Mess-sergeant with a couple of bottles of wine for an ill-tempered brigadier who had called un-expectedly at company headquarters for lunch. (Chef took Roy to the wine-rack and showed him where the good and the not-so-good wines were kept. They gave the sergeant two bottles from the not-so-good rack since the brigadier's bad manners in turning up at a busy time should not be encouraged.)

A subaltern whose platoon was to be in the first wave of the attack in three days' time brought an ammunition-box containing anything of value his men possessed as well as letters home which were to be posted if the worst came to the worst. (The RSM himself sealed the box and showed the officer where it would be buried secretly, ready for collection, hopefully, when the platoon came out of the line again.)

That was the sort of work Pavé did. Senior officers usually hated the place for its lack of spit-and-polish. The men that mattered – the fighters – were only too glad to have such a post close at hand. Like the other boy-soldiers, except Reuben, Seb and Alex felt their lives running faster with more excitement. They began to bless their luck and feel they were needed.

4

The Madness

As if to prepare the troops for the massive British bombardment there was a thunderstorm that night. The sudden downpour did not hamper the feverish antlike activity that was crammed into a narrow band of about a mile either side of the front line snaking across the Albert-Bapaume-Peronne triangle. Orders had been given hours, sometimes days before. Under cover of darkness the final preparations for the Big Push continued and would proceed beneath the massive two-day shelling.

The fighting companies struggled through the mud and rain up to the front line. The final part of their journey along the trench system, hampered by heavy and bulky equipment, was always the worst. They carried with them all the ammunition and supplies they could – once they had scrambled over the top in the first attack nothing could be relied on, certainly not deliveries of food or bullets.

The holding companies who had been guarding the front trenches pushed gratefully back down the same system, leaving their rubbish, filth and dead behind. The pressure in the gulleys was immense as they headed away from the front, squeezing, pushing, shoving past companies moving up in reserve and support to form the second wave of attack and hold any captured trenches against counter-attack.

It seemed impossible that the narrow ribbon which sloped across the triangle could contain all these men and all their equipment: the Infantry with its rifles and light machine-guns, the heavy machine-gunners, the Signallers, the Light Artillery. Behind these – with lower priority – came the Medical Corps, to set up first-aid posts near the front and casualty clearing stations close to the roads where ambulances could take them to base hospitals and railheads.

Every approach road to the front was blocked as breakdowns, repairs to the surface – for crossroads were regularly shelled – or the sheer chaos of numbers added to the mad pressure. A traffic control post at Fricourt – seven kilometres from Pavé – had tried to make a full count of traffic on one road, three weeks earlier. It had been hampered by a gas-attack but had counted, during a twenty-four hour period, 2,423 motor vehicles (lorries, cars, buses, motorbikes and ambulances), 4,000 horse-drawn waggons, 5,404 officers on horseback and 1,043 men riding bicycles. The Infantry, slogging forward to the line or stumbling back, numbered 26,536.

'Madness,' murmured Cocky as he reached for the bottle. It was sheer bloody madness.

The storms had passed over and the sky was clearing fast. From the look-out post, high on the barn, he leaned back and breathed cool air. Lights flickered eerily here and there over the dark landscape. Raids were in progress. Both sides were checking what troops would be opposite them at dawn. Cocky heard the clockwork winding down as the needle scratched to the middle of the record. He took a slug of whisky and stood, stretching, before winding up the gramophone again and putting the needle back to the beginning.

Elgar's 'Serenade For Strings' hissed softly into the air. Cocky sighed and settled himself in the carved chair (liberated from a deserted abbey near Saint Omer) to

114

listen to the music of old, peacetime England. Corporal Massey had liberated the records from the officer's club at Rouen and the RSM, recognising the composer of 'Land Of Hope and Glory', which always made him wince, had not been impressed. But then he had heard the 'Serenade' and, the next day, had persuaded the Corporal to liberate what other records by Elgar the club possessed. Massey had eventually found the 'Introduction and Allegro', and with these two works Cocky's musical needs were satisfied. The 'Serenade' soothed him; the 'Introduction and Allegro' steeled him.

'Madness,' he muttered again, hearing the stutter of guns. Tonight he needed the nostalgia of the pre-war never-never-land Elgar was suggesting. It must be well after eleven o'clock. Most of his men were sleeping, he supposed; he longed to be able to drift off fast, as they did. Probably Chef and his assistant were still talking food and drink in the kitchen: he hoped so.

Another burst of machine-gun fire to the east drew his attention. There was a crackling of rifle fire and the thump of a Mills bomb. A flare arched into the sky about three-quarters of a mile away; it lit an empty expanse, flickered, dimmed, died. It's the sheer bloody ingenuity of it all that's so horrible, he thought. The ways we coldly choose to kill each other. Guns, grenades, phosphorous flares. What next? As if in reply a donkey brayed not far away, down by the river. Yes, yes, Cocky thought. We use you as well. We use mules, horses, anything.

Behind him, the pigeons shifted and chuckled on their perches. 'And even you,' said the RSM aloud, 'the doves of peace.' He turned to the coop and froze, startled at the figure suddenly there. 'Who is it?'

'Sorry, Sir.' Alex was uncertain, too. 'I heard the music.'

Cocky screwed up his eyes against the darkness.

'I said, "Who is it?"'

115

'Davies, sir. I didn't realise it was you. Sorry. I'll go.'

'Wind the box, Davies. It's running down.'

Alex moved to the gramophone and wound it tight. The first side was almost finished. 'We do a lot of Elgar,' Alex said quietly. 'He lives in the next county and we met him once at a concert.'

Cocky had a feeling he was about to be impressed. 'How do you mean?'

Alex explained briefly about Archenford Choir. The RSM was right: he was impressed. 'Do you still sing?'

Alex laughed softly. 'Not what our Choirmaster would call "singing". But we still sing a bit.'

As the needle hit the final groove, Alex lifted it and turned the record over. RSM Allcock sat in silence, trying to put a value on a pair of choirboy soldiers hired out to concert parties and church parades. He cheered up.

Alex stood by the gramophone looking out over the battlefield, listening. He felt a strong pang of sadness for the past – the first time it had ever hit him.

'You should be asleep, Davies.'

'I get trouble with sleeping, sir.'

The RSM grunted in what might have been sympathy or scorn. He asked Alex his Christian name and told him he preferred not to be called sir once the working day was over. Alex moved to sit on the floor beside the telescope.

'Watch out for that bottle.'

'Sorry.' Alex had almost kicked it over. He picked it up and handed it to Cocky who took a swig. He felt Alex's disapproval and misunderstood, not having known Tarrington.

'You disapprove? Hasn't Corporal Massey related my sad, sad story?' The tone was half-mocking, half-defensive and Alex was embarrassed, for Massey had indeed told them about Allcock's past. He shrugged. Cocky raised a vague hand to point out a rash of bright pinpoints; the sound of rifle fire drifted up distantly, seconds later. Cocky lowered his hand. 'Don't despise anybody who has some special need, young man.'

Alex stared into the night, seeing an almsbox on a stone column.

'It can happen to anyone. It might happen to you one day.'

Alex laughed quietly. 'I know.'

The bitter certainty in Alex's reply silenced the RSM. He was a sensitive man and guessed at dangerous depths beneath the boy's words. The needle scratched rhythmically at the label and Alex got up to find the second disc. He wound the machine and was about to lower the needle when there was a creaking from the ladder rungs and Ted's startled eyes rose through the floor, took in the scene and immediately descended again. The RSM said, 'Who in the world is that?' And Alex called, 'Ted – it's all right.' Ted's eyes appeared again, followed by the rest of him. Alex put the needle in the groove and returned to his place alongside the telescope tripod. Ted turned to his sleeping pigeons.

'Come to check up on them, lad?'

Ted nodded and knelt to unfasten the door. The man watched him reach gently inside for one of the birds. He turned to watch Alex gazing into space as the 'Serenade' played. He and Doris had no children. The two soldiers looked very young.

'Do you know what a war is?' he suddenly found himself asking. It was one of his questions that expected no answer. He slotted careful thoughts into place. He needed to tell them something important. A flare soared over the British lines, close by; the barn roof and the three of them were tinged briefly with pale blue-white. 'Old Men killing Young Men. That's what war is.'

Another flare hovered above the lines. 'And all that down there – that's the way they've decided to do it.'

Total silence followed. Neither of the young men knew what to say; neither fully understood. The RSM felt

117

he had said too much. He coughed. 'At least I can keep you lot clear of it,' he muttered, reaching for the bottle. 'And that's something.'

Ted stroked the pigeon fearfully and Alex felt the man's gaze rest on him, needing response. He nodded slowly: it was more than something. Cocky raised the bottle – then set it down; he had had enough. He didn't want to scare the boys any more than he already had. 'Dogs,' he said. 'Ted? You like dogs?'

Ted looked over at Cocky, uncertain, still scared. He nodded as the bird stirred in his hands. 'I like dogs,' he said seriously.

'Retrievers?'

There was a brief pause. Ted nodded solemnly again. 'I like Retrievers.'

'Golden Retrievers?'

Ted realised, far off, that this was some sort of game, a joke. The beginnings of something very near a smile started to approach his lips. He nodded. 'Yes,' he said tentatively.

'Golden Retrievers called Barney?'

Alex smiled in the darkness but Ted laughed out loud – the first time it had been known. Further south, on the river bank, the donkey began braying. It sounded as if the animal was enjoying the joke, too. All three on the roof laughed and the donkey brayed again. They laughed even more. (Dear God, thought Cocky, behind his laughter, I'm going soft. This is ridiculous. It's worse than Doctor Barnardo's. It's Happy Bloody Families.) A voice rose petulantly from the foot of the ladder.

'If you don't mind, there happens to be at least one member of this post who is tired and trying to get some sleep.'

A door clanked, rattled and slammed shut tinnily. There was silence. Ted's mouth gaped in delighted dread at having been caught in the act with the RSM disturbing Corporal Massey.

5

The Big Push

Bombardment began.

It was concentrated on Bapaume to the north and a handful of German strongholds which had chopped down all attacks since July. Enemy trenches were deep and well-made; the occupants steeled themselves to sit out the shelling half-deafened but safe.

Work at Pavé grew at a chaotic rate as the build-up to the Big Push intensified. There was a time when heavy enemy guns duelled with the British artillery and Corporal Massey found time to teach Roy and Reuben actually to see shells flit like insects across the sky by fixing a relaxed gaze on the highest point available. Dev took Sullivan to see a tank squadron waiting to move up and the man returned enthusiastic – the power of it; the size; tank warfare would revolutionise battle and, yes, this might be – as politicians were fond of saying – 'The War To End All Wars'. Surely after such weapons as the tank there could never be another.

'Never be another?' Cocky was scornful. 'If we're daft enough to fight this one to the bitter end, we're too daft to change.'

(Nevertheless, in the interests of science, he persuaded Dev to pack the five young Salopians into the Citroën and give them a sight of the 'Secret Weapon', too. They returned as excited as the corporal had been and Reuben pestered Massey for information on how to join the Tanks Corps.)

Shelling continued all day and, as the RSM had forecast, there was no sleep during that night, even underground. A bright moon slid through the sky and made night raiding hazardous but helped troops struggling up to their positions of attack. It was essential to the tank commanders for their lumbering weapons lacked headlights.

The next day – forty-eight hours before the Push – the British General Staff issued a directive to its forces from headquarters at Montreuil (a convenient 13 kilometres from the hotels and casinos of Le Touquet and a healthy sixty miles from the Peronne-Albert-Bapaume triangle.) The enemy – it told the troops – was heavily outnumbered, his defences enfeebled and reserve troops demoralised. It demanded risks of bold, vigorous action to the limits of endurance.

Even deep in the cushioning ground those limits were felt to be fast approaching. Seb, Alex and the other clerks tried to concentrate on their work as their heads ached and the ground reverberated round them. The air was thick with dust from falling rubble and when, during the course of the day, the bombardment redoubled, by common consent, all but the most essential work was abandoned. Shortly after nightfall Seb and Alex crept out into the protection of darkness for fresh air but the sharper explosions and the concussion of shells pounding through the sky had their heads ringing at once and just before they retreated underground it began to rain heavily. Neither friend could find much to say to the other. If their discomfort was bad in the cellars of Pavé, the misery of the thousands bivouacking in the open was too terrible to consider. They would be glad to see the dawn when perhaps the rain might stop and there would be only one last day of waiting.

Zero hour was 06.20. Along the six-mile front whistles blew; curses and encouragement pushed the British and Empire troops over the top into No-Man's-Land. The barrage of shells maintained a momentum, pouring explosive ahead of the advancing men, raising sights in a lifting barrage. It was expected – as it was always expected – that the thick entanglements of barbed wire would have been blown apart by the two-day bombardment. But it turned out – as it always turned out – that there was more than enough of it still intact to slow progress and offer targets to machine-gun posts brave enough to take the chance.

In spite of the GHQ directive, enemy resistance was as strong and stubborn as ever. The tanks were to have made all the difference. They were to have ripped away every obstacle that had created the deadly stalemate of trench warfare. Supported by infantry, they were to have punched great gaps in the German defences through which the Cavalry stood poised to pour, eager to gallop spectacularly into that untrenched and undefended countryside beyond the front lines and capture headquarters, railheads, ammunition depots. By the end of the day, British GHQ expected to draw a new front line across Picardy. That was the plan.

'Plan,' said RSM Allcock scornfully. 'They sit on their aged arses and think they're playing chess.'

He was in the office at Pavé with Seb, Alex, Reuben and Captain Devereux, waiting for the first news.

'Plan,' he sneered again.

Seb looked up.

'There's got to be a plan.'

'How else can they do it?' asked Alex.

Dev turned towards the RSM.

'Well?' he said. 'And isn't it like chess when all's said and done?'

Cocky treated Dev to a pitying expression which seemed to say all he had ever thought about officers.

'First,' he said, 'there isn't any chess board. The generals think there is, because the maps at headquarters show woods, farms, and even the occasional hedgerow but that's all gone. The bombardments that continually fail to wipe out enemy resistance succeed all too well in destroying landmarks and slowing advances to slightly better than snail's pace.'

Reuben stirred uneasily; he hated talk like this. 'There's territory that's ours and territory that's theirs,' he murmured. 'Isn't that like a chessboard?'

Cocky shut his eyes in frustration. He opened them again and looked full on Reuben. 'In chess a player makes one move, then his opponent makes another, then the other responds, and so it goes on.' Cocky slammed a hand flat against the wall. 'Out here there's a thousand different games going on at once, starting and finishing. Every result affects the games all round it, so it's chaos. And chaos is the opposite to chess.'

Cocky leaned back against the cool wall of the cellar. The guns were very apparent, even below ground. Nobody spoke for fully three minutes.

'They'll need to push the cavalry through the gaps pretty soon if they're going to be any use,' said Dev quietly.

'I'd like to see the cavalry in a charge,' said Seb.

'Me too.'

'Spectacular.'

'Horses and chess.' Cocky smiled infuriatingly. 'What wonderful pastimes for an autumn afternoon. A weekend with the gentry; it shows how our betters at General HQ think, my lads, eh?'

Reuben swung his feet to the floor and left without a word.

Seb glanced at Cocky. 'When you're in this mood, Reuben passes everything you say to Corporal Sullivan. You want to be careful.'

Cocky laughed. 'A shell came through my dug-out roof, Seb. It must have exploded nearer to me than you are. I should have been blown to bits but I wasn't and I should have suffocated but didn't. So don't tell me to be careful.'

'It's a different sort of war,' admitted Dev. 'Tanks, horses, lorries, planes – all built for speed yet the war's stuck fast in lines of trenches half a mile apart.'

'Another difference,' added Cocky. 'All battles up till 1914 were over in a few hours, a few days at most. From now on it's inch by inch and if you're seen you're dead; so dig down and keep quiet. Battles out here go on for bloody months.'

'Not even time to clear up the dead.'

Cocky laughed again. 'Horses and tanks,' he hooted. 'I ask you: horses and tanks. How can you have horses, tanks and planes all in the same war?'

There was no talking for a while. Seb worked at lists for Corporal Massey and Alex filled in the latest information on the maps. Dev looked at his watch and stretched; he began to get to his feet.

'I've got a plan,' said RSM Allcock suddenly. He looked at the young officer. 'Shoot one general at GHQ for every five hundred men that his plan kills. On both sides. For every ten generals shot, hang a politician. We'd have peace within a fortnight. What do you think, Dev?'

Dev got to his feet and reached for his coat and cap. 'I think Seb's right, Cocky. You should watch what you say.' He turned at the doorway and grinned. 'There are people who don't think you're as lovable as we do.' He waved and was gone. The boys worked. Cocky put his head against the wall and dozed off.

The tanks made a difference where they arrived at the right place at the right time. Two hours after Zero Hour, for instance, a tank was in the street of Flers, two miles behind the enemy line, followed up by delighted infantry as three other tanks crushed the last resistance on the village outskirts. The General Staff was jubilant. It was, for many, the best news of the war. Demoralised Germans surrendered in crowds.

It had been the best of the tanks, for the extensive and exhaustive trials had not only run the engines in, but gone some way to wearing them out. Forty-two tanks had been able to muster at their starting-points ready to spearhead the Big Push. Just over half of them had been able to move when required and of the twenty-five that began the attack, only eight saw the action through. Dotted around the battlefield, seventeen tanks lay ditched, destroyed or broken-down.

6

Comrades and Enemies

After supper Seb and Alex sang.

15 September had been a good day. The enemy were driven back a few kilometres and now it was dark and raining which reduced the chance of counter-attack. The day had even been historic – the first use of tanks in battle. More important to Cocky was the fact that all the members of his kingdom had come safely through the first day of a major battle.

Chef and Roy had given them a wonderful meal of duck paté and red cabbage. Roy had baked his first batch of bread and there had been sharp white local cheese. Dev had turned up with another local delicacy – macaroons from Amiens – and there was cider for the young men and a couple of bottles from the special rack for the others. Seb and Alex were beginning to realise that alcohol was almost as important to a fighting man as petrol was to his vehicles. Anything that dulled reality was highly valued.

The two young men sang in simple harmony. Seb's voice had begun to change almost as soon as he left

Archenford but he managed an accurate and pleasing light baritone voice. Alex, amazingly, could still sing treble so long as he avoided the higher notes. They stood together in the corner near the door:

> Roses are shining in Picardy,
> In the hush of the silvery dew.
> Roses are flowering in Picardy
> But there's never a rose like you . . .

It was a sentimental song and highly popular even in Picardy where a shining rose was a rare event, especially in the killing grounds. The voices flowed skilfully on. All eyes were down as the men remembered wives, girl-friends, mothers.

Cocky thoughtfully sipped his burgundy, thinking partly of Doris and Barney but mostly of tomorrow. It would be a hard day. There would be repairs, re-supplying, bringing records up to date. There had been many German prisoners for whom the Service Corps would be called on to provide blankets, clothing, food, clean water, cutlery and mess-tins. It would not be popular work: there was little enough food and equipment to go round anyway – and many Britons, officers and men, strongly believed no prisoner should be taken alive. Tomorrow would be difficult; that was why tonight was important.

The song came quietly to an end and after a second or two of silence there was cheering and clapping. Seb and Alex grinned – Seb even bowed – then they took their places back at the table and the RSM looked proudly at Dev. 'You might pass the word to the appropriate people,' he said, 'that Pavé can supply trained singers for Church parades and concert parties.'

Alex and Seb protested. Corporal Massey waved them to silence.

'At a suitable fee,' he added.

Cocky agreed. 'At a highly suitable fee.'

One of the Pavé drivers, Sam Tranter, asked for tea and Roy hurried out to see to it. Cocky took yet another swig of his wine; he found that heavy red wine made him argumentative which he rather enjoyed. He looked round for a good target and found Corporal Sullivan sullen at a corner of the table. Sullivan disliked French food and was looking forward to making an early escape to his garage where he had some corned beef hidden away.

'So,' Cocky said, 'your tin boxes turned out to be a mixed blessing, Corporal.'

Dev had come to Pavé from a tour of Battalion HQs and observation posts and had reported that there had been a few notable successes but a high failure rate, too: a couple of the tanks had lost their way completely and fired upon their own troops.

'Tin boxes,' repeated Cocky firmly. 'Ugly, unhygienic, unreliable and noisy.'

Cocky and Massey waited expectantly for Sullivan to react. He scowled, murmured goodnight, left the table and was gone. The RSM and Corporal Massey exchanged satisfied looks but Sullivan's exit left an awkward silence.

'Sir? Captain Dev, Sir?'

All eyes swivelled to Ted. It was a rarity for Ted to enter a conversation. For Ted to address an officer was unknown. For Ted to call an officer by his nickname (though Ted probably didn't realise he was doing this) was impossible. Everyone in the smoky, warm room tried hard not to gape. Dev turned, as surprised as the rest. 'Private Culpin?'

'The pigeons come back.'

Dev didn't understand. He had been fixing up a supply column at Doullens when, during the first hour of the battle, a signaller had come to take two of Ted's

126

messenger pigeons to replace his own which had been lost. Everyone else in the room knew what Ted was talking about and as they saw his nerve begin to falter they all jumped in to help him.

'The company in the line just over near Pozières.'

'Needed pigeons.'

'Ted gave him two.'

'His best two.'

Corporal Massey banged on the table with his spoon for silence. 'This is not a kindergarten,' he said. 'We are not Barbarians. As I recall it, Captain Devereux was in conversation with Private Culpin.'

Dev said smoothly, 'And they came back?'

Ted nodded.

'Were they hurt?'

And suddenly Ted was pouring out the whole story: why he'd picked that particular pair, how he'd felt as he waited, his excitement when he saw the first one circle round, how he'd coaxed it down and removed the message which had continued to Bouzincourt with Sam Tranter. Ted was happy; he had found his place. He suddenly realised that he not only loved his pigeons but he loved Pavé too and his friends there. As he concluded his story, seeing Dev's approval and the pleasure of the others, he swore to himself that he would never let them down – not even Sullivan who frightened him or Reuben who was rolling a cigarette as if nothing unusual had happened. Ted had discovered comradeship.

Much to RSM Allcock's surprise, the Allies' initial advances were continued during the week, though he was quick to point out that struggling forward over a few kilometres of mud, flesh and blood was a strange definition of success. There was, however, optimism in the air, particularly among senior officers. Two cheery colonels called at Pavé for repairs to their car and invited themselves to lunch. When they had gone, Alex remarked that they reminded him of a school team celebrating a good win.

'Exactly,' agreed Corporal Massey. 'Never grown up, you see. That's what happens to the upper classes. They all go to the same schools and they never grow out of them. I mean to say – "Old Boys". What a thing to be called for the rest of your lives.'

Seb grinned. 'Our Headmaster used to call us "Little Men".'

Cocky and Massey hooted with laughter. 'Old Boys and Little Men.'

'It's all wonderful nonsense,' gasped the RSM, wiping his eyes. 'Our Good King George the Fifth is first cousin to their Bad Kaiser William. And look at the name of the British First Sea Lord – Louis of Battenberg.'

'It's a trifling family disagreement,' giggled Massey, 'in which we have been invited to partake.'

That set them off again. The door slammed as Reuben and Sullivan left.

'How nice that Corporal Sullivan has found himself a friend,' purred Corporal Massey. 'And there was I thinking nobody could be as boneheaded as him.'

By October the First, British forces were within six kilometres of Bapaume in the north and Peronne in the east. With most of the triangle clear of Germans, the General Staff shifted its attentions to the few villages along the River Ancre where the enemy still held strong positions. Fighting came close to Pavé.

There were long debates about the Service Corps advanced post. The enemy had never shown an interest in the place but now the focus was moving and Captain Devereux was concerned for the safety of RSM Allcock's staff. Finally a compromise was struck: Pavé was to continue its useful work but an extra keen watch was to be kept on enemy activity and evacuation plans were to be drawn up if Cocky's Kingdom ever looked in danger. There was talk of sending the youngsters back to a safe post near Amiens, though none wanted to leave the team. Only Corporal Sullivan and Reuben occasionally felt outsiders but at last the boy was allowed to help Sullivan in his workshop where they spent many happy hours grumbling about the war in general and Pavé in particular.

As the months changed, so did the weather. October brought heavy rain which in turn brought clinging, clogging mud. Conditions deteriorated rapidly and equipment was under a heavy strain. Loads of water-pumps, waterproof tarpaulins and capes moved up to Pavé which was soon crammed to overflowing.

Fighting along the whole of the front line gave way to vicious skirmishes for key positions as both sides struggled to gain as much as possible before surrendering to winter whose harsh advance continued. When the rain held off, frost attacked; if frozen mud thawed, there were violent thunderstorms. Transport became even more unreliable as road surfaces broke up. The River Ancre began to flood.

The Cavalry was reluctantly sent to its winter quarters, much to the RSM's malicious glee. Cocky ordered a small celebration, for the move signalled clearly that no further offensives were planned for the year. More good news came with the recapture of Verdun by the French and he held a party for that, too.

Life at Pavé settled into a long, hard routine of lists, loading and unloading, checking, repairing and keeping half a dozen key maps exactly up-to-date. The occasional celebrations helped bind the team together, though it would have been shocked to learn that Corporal Sullivan and Private Yapp had taken such offence at their sergeant-major's barbed and satirical toast to the departure of the old cavalry and the uselessness of the new (he meant the tanks) that they had written to the commanding officer of the Service Corps at Doullens outlining the many occasions on which RSM Allcock had insulted and mocked the gallant effort and sacrifice of King George's best men.

Official complaints like this were not lightly made. The results could be serious. Sullivan knew this very well. He also knew the low opinion of RSM Allcock at Headquarters. He thought there was a good chance of a change of leadership at Pavé when his letter was read.

7

Massey's Maestros

The two ex-choristers began to be known outside Pavé. The first Church parade had been a novelty but after the third the novelty wore off. It felt wrong. First there was a practice with some out-of-tune harmonium, usually played by a junior officer who had probably boasted that he was something of a musician and would very soon wish that he hadn't (because he wasn't). Then came the arrival of the troops to form three sides of a great square. The men were cheery enough, singing popular hymns with gusto, but Seb and Alex knew that most of them resented rest-time spent on spit-and-polish just to say prayers, sing hymns and listen to a sermon. There was the familiar sense of a big Church parade being obscurely to the greater glory of the senior padre and officers. The sermons were familiar, too. There were fewer references to blood, sacrifice and honour than the ones they had heard at Archenford but there was still enough to show how out-of-touch the Men of God were with the men at the front.

According to the preachers, lives were still 'laid down' as if they were loads too heavy for the owners to carry.

But most of the men knew how desperately most men clung to life, no matter how dreadful their injuries. The only soldiers who had made a willing choice to lay down their burdens of life were the suicides – and they were a strictly taboo subject.

Their performances at officers' mess nights felt wrong, too. It was interesting to report to the chateau which some regiment had made its headquarters for they were usually given a quick tour. The singing, however, was another waste of time since they soon realised that the officers present at such formal dinners had no interest at all in music and would have been just as happy – probably happier – with performing dogs. Mess nights were unreal, oozing false pride, and snobbery.

They loved the concert parties. Crammed into smoke-filled halls the men were riotous with good humour, desperate to have a good time and forget the war for a couple of hours. Unlike the Church parades or Mess nights, the noisy appreciation from the ordinary soldiers was genuine. The boys were called various titles on the programme-usually chalked on a board. They had been Cocky's Canaries, The Two Tonsil-Ticklers and Massey's Maestros; many late-night sessions at Pavé had been devoted to finding the right name but all had ended in hysterical laughter. At first they had sung decent patriotic songs but Corporal Massey, who loved Music Hall, taught them indecent and unpatriotic songs instead, and these always made the rickety roofs ring with applause. They were much in demand.

The rain drummed on the truck cab's roof as Alex and Seb tried out several elaborate ways of sliding from the end of 'Land of Hope And Glory' into 'For He's a Jolly Good Fellow' without a pause. They were thankful that they would be singing without accompaniment, which meant they could slither through as many shocking key-changes as they liked. Eventually they were happy with the solution and settled back to make the most of the journey. This was to be their grandest performance so far. They were on the way to a château near Amiens where a brigadier was celebrating his promotion and birthday. Corporal Massey himself was driving. It was his intention to liberate a piano, a case of fine wines, a second gramophone and a new recording of Elgar's 'Serenade' as a surprise for Cocky.

'Thou Shalt Not Steal,' intoned Seb in the comically righteous manner of many clergymen he had heard. He was annoyed with himself as soon as he had spoken – though at his side Alex said nothing.

Massey turned an offended face to Seb. 'I do not steal. Nothing so vulgar. I am simply intending to rent the piano for a year or so. Your singing tonight is the first payment.'

'But you know you'll never give the piano back.'

'I shall willingly send it back. On the last day of the war.'

Seb smiled. Massey increased speed. It was a good stretch of road; they wouldn't meet much traffic for another five miles. Alex suddenly spoke. 'So stealing is only stealing if that's the way you think of it.'

'Precisely,' beamed the corporal. 'I personally prefer to borrow, hire, rent, lease or even charter. There is no need at all to steal.'

Seb grinned. 'So the piano's just a trophy of war.'

'Exactly.'

'None of this means anything. Just words. Stealing's still stealing.'

The man who had been clever enough to recognise Ted's sensitivity glanced at Alex. 'Go on, Alexander.'

There was a slight pause. Seb was sure Alex would change the subject or rely on him to do so. He was astonished when Alex spoke up quietly but determined. 'I used to steal. That's the reason I'm here now. That's why Seb's here with me.' He told the story. Massey listened attentively and Seb's surprise continued. He had never heard Alex talk about the stealing in this detail or with this honesty. It was even embarrassing. When Alex had finished, both boys waited for the Corporal's reaction.

Massey laughed. He laughed so much that the truck swerved – then swerved again. He had to brake and halt at the roadside until he recovered. The boys sat bemused. 'Oh you sweet simple thing,' he said at last, wiping his eyes with the back of his hand. He giggled a little and then, seeing Alex's puzzled face, made himself serious. 'Listen,' he said. 'You lost your dad; you were having a bad time. Somebody had to pay. You chose the Dean and Chapter at Archenford. You're no thief – you even put the money back. With interest.'

'And then you were blackmailed by Tarrington,' put in Seb, anxious to help now he could see which way the discussion was heading.

'But the time I was caught . . .'

'Totally different, Alexander. On that final occasion you were indulging in a little thrill. I hope you enjoyed it. Four months in the army seems to me rather a high price to pay for it, but you know best.'

The Corporal rammed the lever into first gear and the truck moved out into the road again. The rain seemed to be easing a little. They passed four sets of lights in convoy.

'Different times mean different habits,' the man said in a low voice. 'We're in a war and it will be a miracle if the three of us survive it. Think of tomorrow – but live for today.' He turned sternly to Alex. 'Now,' he said, 'tonight I must put the powers of my considerable mind into removing from a guarded château a piano; I shall need assistance from many sentries whose job is to stop me doing any such thing. So don't waste my brain on trivial matters like liberating a few pounds from the Dean and Chapter. Forget it. Let it go.'

133

Seb almost applauded. The argument made him light-headed. He grabbed Alex's shoulder urgently.

'What do you say?' he demanded.

Alex said nothing. He pulled his shoulder free and continued staring out into the wild night as the truck bumped and swayed towards Amiens. Seb regretted his excitement. It wasn't until they were turning into the long drive that led to the Château Vallenz that Alex suddenly turned to him. 'Seb?'

'Let it go,' called Corporal Massey who had clearly not been thinking only of the liberation of the piano all this time. 'Let it vanish, disappear, go up in smoke, swirl down the plug-hole.' He grinned at Alex. Alex grinned too.

'It's gone,' he laughed. It was something to do with the comic way the man pronounced 'plug-hole' – like a Music Hall comedian. Massey hooted. Seb began to giggle. Alex couldn't stop laughing. They had to slow down and compose themselves before they approached the sentries of the château gates. But Seb believed it. It had gone.

The walls of the office were thin so Dev and Cocky kept their voices low. Each man sipped at wine from the special rack and Dev wished Massey were here, knowing that the RSM always took notice of what he said. Cocky handed back the sheet of paper on which a friend in the adjutant's office had copied out Sullivan's letter to the Officer Commanding the Service Corps at Doullens. Cocky grinned. 'The letter's almost as boring as the man who wrote it. It's a joke.'

'The adjutant doesn't think it's funny.' Dev leaned forward anxiously. 'Cocky, you've got enemies – a lot of them.'

'You worry too much, Captain Devereux. I do my job. I do it well. They know it.'

'Others would do it just as well,' said Dev bluntly.

134

There was a knock at the flimsy door and Ted came straight in.

'Sam says can you come?'

Cocky groaned and stood.

'Say hello to Captain Dev,' he said, reaching for his cap.

'Hello, Captain Dev.'

Ted wondered whether to throw a salute but decided against it when his hand was already halfway up; he changed it to a serious wave. Dev waved back seriously.

'All right, Ted,' said Cocky. 'Tell Mister Tranter I'm on my way.'

Ted ran off. Dev grinned. Then he looked up curiously.

'Trouble?'

'It's ever since things began happening over towards Beaumont Hamel,' the RSM explained. 'There's patrols from both sides creeping around as thick as flies. Sam's up at the telescope. I've got a twenty-four hour watch up there.'

Dev joined him as he left and they hurried through the arch between the cellars. Cocky tapped on the kitchen door and put his head in. 'Sorry, Chef. Better hold supper. We'll eat late. Ten?'

He withdrew before Chef could protest. As they reached the gilded staircase to the barn they could hear him complaining loudly to Roy. There was a fusillade of clankings and even louder complaints.

Reuben was relieved from watch by Corporal Sullivan at midnight. They shared a carefully-shielded cigarette before the young soldier climbed wearily down the ladders from the concealed look-out point. He had seen nothing during his hour's duty and neither had the clerk before him. There was some feeling that Sam Tranter had been dozing and dreamed it all in the first place. All the action was well away to the north around Le Sar and the

135

nearest Germans to Pavé were defending the village of Beaumont-Hamel, six kilometres away.

Reuben descended to the cellars and moved towards the office where the look-out log book was kept; the RSM insisted each duty was reported. It was quiet below the ruins, away from the driving rain at the top of the barn. The oil-lamps were low; there was nobody about. He reached for the handle of the office door and heard his name.

'I'm saying that you may be able to get Reuben and Sullivan to withdraw their letter, that's all.'

Reuben froze, then crept silently closer. He could hear every word from inside where Dev and Cocky had come round again to the Doullens letter.

RSM Allcock was tired. He leaned back in his chair wishing Dev would go.

'You're not listening,' Dev said.

'No. I'm sorry, Dev.'

'There's a strict procedure laid down for making complaints to Commanding Officers and they haven't followed it. They're supposed to get my permission, first.'

Reuben tightened his fists in frustration. It was typical. Allcock was going to wriggle clear. But how did Devereux know about the letter? He listened intently.

'All right. Give me the letter. Let's have another look at what they say.'

Reuben felt a surge of anger and guilt. They had the letter, there in the office – Devereux and Allcock. It hadn't even got as far as Service Corps Headquarters. Reuben was suddenly worried. He knew that Allcock was popular with everyone except Corporal Sullivan and himself. If it got out that they were trying to get rid of the man . . .

He moved silently and very fast back to the staircase and into the barn.

When Sullivan heard what Reuben had to say, he was as scandalised as the boy. He wondered if Reuben had overheard correctly, but he wasn't the sort to invent things. Sullivan took a quick scan of the countryside where nothing had moved since he came on watch. He told Reuben to get down the ladders and followed him. He needed to hear for himself and maybe confront his enemies. In truth he didn't know exactly what he was going to do; he only knew he was not going to put up with treatment like this. For the only time in eighteen hours, nobody was keeping watch at the telescope.

8

Night Raid

The German *Leutnant* on the river bank two hundred yards away lowered his night field-glasses and waved his men forward. He made sure that the corporal who was to stay knew the signals. Pavé had been under observation for a week. There was too much activity for a ruined farmyard. The rain lashed down and the *Leutnant* was pleased – he had waited three days for a night like this, when raids would be unexpected. This was a dangerous mission – deep into enemy territory – but it would be something to set against the losses of the recent weeks and the disaster at Verdun. He took one last look. He had not expected such luck with the sentry at the concealed telescope. He knew his stormtroops would not be so careless. He gave his field-glasses to the corporal and followed his men, their grey uniforms already merging with the night.

Seb was half-asleep and Alex was snoring, his head on Seb's shoulder. Corporal Massey was fed up with the snoring and would have nudged the boy awake if they had not been so close to base. He came to the bend where main beams must be extinguished and slowed down as he waited for his vision to adjust to the paraffin side-lamps. He cautiously began to increase speed. The piano in the back jangled and clinked against the crates of wine. It had been a highly successful evening. He had managed to locate the gramophone, too, and had actually been presented with the Elgar records in grudging admiration. Massey smiled.

'Stop.'

Massey braked at once. Seb's shout was positive. There was more discordant music from the back. The jerk woke Alex.

'What is it?'

Seb was staring intently into the darkness. Massey was worried. He could see the boy was alarmed. He wished his own eyes were sharper.

'Don't frighten a poor old man. What is it?' he repeated.

Seb turned to Alex. 'Can you see it, too?'

'Yes. And another.'

Massey turned sternly to them. 'What is it?' he rapped out.

It was Ted's pigeons. A dim glow – hardly visible – was lighting the look-out post from below. Pigeons or other birds fluttered in and out of it. 'The trapdoor to the telescope's open,' said Seb. 'The pigeons are loose.'

All three knew Ted kept his pigeons firmly cooped. They knew a continual watch was supposed to be kept. They knew a curtain was pulled to shut out the light rising from Pavé whenever the hatch was opened.

'Out,' Massey shouted. 'I want our lamps out. Now.'

The boys jumped down to extinguish the sidelights and Corporal Massey opened a panel below the bench seat. When Seb and Alex, breathless with fear, climbed back in the cab, he handed each of them a Webley pistol and clips of .38 bullets. In silence he loaded his weapon

138

and watched as the boys did the same. They jammed spare clips into their pockets. Massey turned to the young soldiers.

'This may be something or it may be nothing. We could turn and drive back to Bouzincourt for assistance but it would take an hour and we have friends over there.' He nodded towards Pavé, 'I can't believe we're going to find any problems – we're miles from the front – but better to be prepared.' He looked levelly at them. 'All right?' he asked without fear or excitement.

They nodded, too scared to speak. Massey suddenly grinned. 'Don't expect any orders from me. I've never done this sort of thing before. Let's see what happens.'

He moved into first gear and the lorry rolled smoothly forward. There was less rain and he could see better. He pressed gently on to Pavé trying to guess when the engine would be heard and there would be no more need for stealth. Alex shouted. 'Men. Down by the river. Running.'

Massey snapped on the headlamps and jammed his foot on the accelerator. They surged forward. There was a loud jangling from the back and bottles smashed as the truck pounded noisily the last two hundred yards home.

They looked down into Pavé but could see no sign of life. The first cellar was chaotic. Grenades had been thrown from outside and thick, sickly dust still clogged the air. The blasts had ripped out the interior walls and splintered the furniture. Scraps of paper littered the floor like grotesque confetti. One lamp had survived to cast cold light on a shapeless parcel of flesh wrapped in blood-soaked shreds of khaki; not far away from a boot and a leg. Seb screamed. Among the debris against a wall Corporal Sullivan's head looked up in calm surprise. Behind the heavy upturned table, Captain Devereux lay on his back, arms and legs stretched out and Cocky knelt behind, supporting the young officer's head. The

RSM's hair was matted with blood and there was a gaping wound in his shoulder but he was alive. Dev had been caught in the grenade blast and shot several times in the chest and stomach. Cocky bent over him like a crimson statue. Corporal Massey spoke to the RSM but he only twisted his head painfully to stare at the newcomers in surprise, his eyes congested with blood. The Corporal called his name but Cocky's head lowered, dazed and grieving, to the dead man on the floor.

Cocky was obviously in massive shock and perhaps not even feeling his serious wounds so Massey moved towards the second cellar and the boys followed, sickened and very scared.

It looked as if the raiding party had charged straight through the dust of the explosion and caught everyone in the second cellar by surprise. The sleeping quarters were a tangled mess of bloodied blankets and bodies; the sleepers had barely found time to wake – three were killed in their beds, shot or stabbed. Sam Tranter looked peaceful but his hands were chopped and sliced from his desperate attempts to hold off a bayonet or knife. Chef was clutching a pan; it must have been the only weapon he had time to grab. There were bullet wounds in his side but his neck was angled and twisted back; it looked as if it had been broken. There was no sign of Roy.

They hurried up the staircase into the barn. The outside door was wide open and much of the equipment was thrown about as if a burglar had been carrying out a frantic search for valuables. Corporal Massey's bedroom door was open; there was nobody inside.

'Where's Reuben? Where's Ted and Roy?' Alex stared out into the night, his pistol before him. Seb was peering up the ladders to the open hatch. Pigeons were perched on its edge. One was looking down at him. It was bewildering. Now that the first shock was beginning to wear off, other feelings and thoughts began to stir. Massey was worried about the missing boys. He moved to the door and called, but Alex slipped swiftly past him, shaking off his restraining hand, running into the night. The Corporal heard Seb begin climbing the ladders and decided to see what could be done for his friend in the ruins of the office.

Seb found Ted at the telescope. He was naked and had been brutally bayoneted. His gashed and stabbed body was smeared with blood and a crimson rivulet ran from his mouth as he lay angled round two sides of the hatch. He was alive. He held a towel tight in one hand.

'Pigeons,' he whispered.

Seb dropped the hatch down and knelt in helpless distress as near to the thin body as he could. Ted could barely speak but his eyes swung up to Seb's face. The pigeons were fluttering and settling on top of their coop.

'They're all here,' Seb said. Ted's eyes clouded in concern; his brow furrowed delicately.

'No,' he said. 'Germans. Messages.'

Seb hoped he understood. He glanced at the birds and could see a pigeon carrying a message cannister. 'Yes,' he said. 'There's one missing.'

Ted frowned again; the eyes gazed up at Seb. 'Two,' he said quietly.

'Two,' Seb lied as Ted's cloudy eyes scanned his face. Seb wiped blood from Ted's mouth and the lips twitched into a smile. But then he tried to move and gasped as a wound somewhere opened and blood dripped to the floor. Ted saw Seb's horrified eyes on his body and made an effort to pull the saturated towel over him.

'Shy,' he whispered, worried and embarrassed. Seb eased the towel from Ted's fingers and laid it across him. Ted seemed about to sleep. Seb whispered urgently in his ear, hating to ask but needing to know.

'Reuben – where's Reuben? Or Roy? Reuben and Roy, Ted.'

Ted's eyelids flicked open and he seemed more alert. He was in great pain and sometimes his words were

141

covered by quiet moaning but as far as Seb could make out the raid had begun while Ted was, as usual, late and alone outside in the wash-house. The first he knew of the attack was an explosion and he peeped from the window to see soldiers rushing down into the end cellar. He met Reuben at the barn door but the boy ran into the night without a word. Ted sprinted for the ladders. He knew it would take time for the men to work their way through the cellars to the look-out point. There were emergency SOS messages ready near the telescope and he had managed to get two pigeons on their way and free the others before somebody down the river had blown a series of whistle-blasts and men were climbing the ladders to him. He had closed the hatch but was too slight to hold it against the stormtroops. They had been angry about the pigeons. Seb was overwhelmed. He shook his head. He didn't know what to do. Ted's sticky hand closed on his own. The boy spoke so softly it was like sighing.

'Cocky's Kingdom,' he breathed. 'Love Cocky's Kingdom.' His eyes slowly moved to meet Seb's. Ted grinned. 'Cocky's Kingdom,' he repeated proudly. Then he gasped, choked, bled. Coughing began to shake him as his blood filled his lungs and he started to drown. His eyes were wide with terror as he fought violently for breath. Seb raised him from the planking and held him tight as his struggles eased and Ted began to relax in his arms, tired of fighting, glad to go. He half-opened his eyes, looked calmly at Seb. Then sagged.

Seb threw back his head and howled like a wild animal. The rain washed clear channels through Ted's blood and his pigeons fluttered, grieved and flew tight frightened circles.

The air was still thick in the first cellar where Corporal Massey had done what he could for his old friend. Grey with dust and sickness, Cocky sat propped in a corner. Massey was cleaning up his face as best he could when Seb came slowly towards them in his bloodsmeared uniform and told them he'd found Ted. There was a profound silence. Seb wondered where Alex was but had no emotion to spare. Cocky was suddenly sick. Corporal Massey held his head and wiped his mouth as the RSM gazed round. He took notice of the corporal and Seb as if for the first time.

'Time to go,' he said, distinctly. 'Closed for repairs.'

Footsteps were heard. Massey and Seb reached for their hand guns but it was Alex. He had found Reuben hiding in the field behind Pavé. The boy was in shock and kept shouting that it was all his fault. He suddenly paused and asked where Sullivan was. Seb was glad Massey had thrown a torn greatcoat over the head. Reuben could partly remember what happened. He remembered standing outside the office behind Sullivan. He remembered two stick-grenades in mid-air. He remembered diving for the shelter of the second cellar and the explosions blowing him to the foot of the staircase. That was all. Reuben looked round. He could take in none of this. He gazed with horror at Cocky.

'Time to go,' the RSM repeated. 'Corporal, get these men out of here.'

Massey thought he was delirious and murmured comforting words about rest and being quiet until help arrived but Cocky shook his head. He shouted, 'Get them out. Before it starts.'

And Corporal Massey understood. 'Out to the truck. Quick. Help me here.'

But Cocky refused to be moved. He was growing feebler. The shoulder wound was very deep. He kept murmuring that they must go. 'Closed for repairs, Doris,' he said.

Massey herded them outside with urgency. As the man swung the starting handle, Alex shouted into the night for Roy but there was no answer. Reuben thought he remembered seeing them carry Roy struggling away. 'It's my fault,' he shouted. 'My fault.'

'Into the truck. Now,' the man called. The truck was not starting easily. He swung the handle again and cursed. Seb took over. 'I don't understand,' he said. The engine spluttered and caught.

'They came to see what was here and found Aladdin's Cave. They can't have Pavé, so they'll make damn sure nobody else can. If they've got the co-ordinates, they'll shell the place flat before there's time to shift the goods.'

'But we can't leave Cocky.'

'Do as he wants, lad. Do you think I like the idea any more than you do?'

Alex was rummaging in the back of the truck.

'Will you get in the cab, boy?' Massey shouted.

Alex clambered down with the gramophone in his arms and hurried back into Pavé. Seb shouted at him and turned to follow but Massey held his arm. 'No you don't.'

'I'm not leaving Alex.'

'Nobody's asking you to. So long as he's quick.'

They were ready and waiting when Alex ran back. It was a crush with all four of them on the bench seat but Massey hit first gear and the truck bucked and bounced from the yard. As it took the Bouzincourt road at its best speed the snarling engine grew more distant and Elgar's 'Serenade For Strings' took its place.

They were in Bouzincourt by 2.15 and an hour and a half later the shells began landing round Pavé – it had taken the raiding party a long time to get back behind the nearest German line and arrange matters with the artillery. When the survivors of Cocky's Kingdom saw Pavé again, six hours later, it had been obliterated. Another name on a map with nothing to mark it except memories.

9

New Lives; Old Friends

Four days after the destruction of Pavé, Seb, Alex and Reuben waited to begin the journey forward to their battalion. The experience had affected each in a different way. Seb seemed the least upset but it was his nature to keep his problems to himself. The end of Pavé was a deep grief to him. He was sentimental and the sound of Elgar's music drifting up from the doomed cellar would haunt him the rest of his life, though not as much as Ted's terrible death, clutching his pathetic towel among the pigeons. Seb was strict with himself. He knew that if he once allowed himself to open the door and release these feelings, he would be destroyed as surely as Pavé. So he kept the door of self-control locked and barred. There would be time to mourn for Pavé and his friends, but it was not now.

Part of Alex had frozen. He became more aloof and talked less. He spent more time on his own. The change had come over him, suddenly, like an ice-cold wave and it had happened the moment he had jerked awake to see pigeons circling in a dim, distant light. Earlier, Seb and Corporal Massey had almost convinced him he was nothing special, not even a thief, but then had come the icicle thrill of those pigeons, the race to the cellars, the joy of striding alone into the dangerous darkness to find Reuben. He was a tightrope walker. That was the truth. He needed and craved danger – the feeling of that sharp, thin line as his only security against the deep space under his heels. Everything made sense. The danger of singing solo, the danger of choosing to serve Tarrington, the unstable terror of the journeys to the almsbox. The truth was he was a little mad; he knew now that he lacked feelings that made others human. He had seen Dev, Cocky and other friends torn into death or dying but felt only excitement. He was made for this war and felt superbly in control of himself. No wonder his mother had left, then his father; no wonder Aunt hated him, and Tarrington, Collett, Brinsop and all the rest. They had all feared him. All his senses hummed like the invisible wire taut below his heels. He had to be careful. He must not let that wire snap and fall wheeling through space into total lunacy.

He would revenge Pavé – not because revenge was important but because each event demanded a larger event; each new thrill must be greater than the last. Alex was an addict to danger, needing bigger and bigger doses. He hugged this mad knowledge to himself and pushed everybody else out to arm's length. Even Seb. Particularly Seb, who must not be allowed to guess his friend was mad. If he had a question, it was why Seb loved him and stayed loyal. It made no sense.

Reuben wore his feelings openly; in that way he was more honest than the others. He took full responsibility for every terrible thing that had happened. It was Reuben who had called Sullivan down from his watch and left Pavé blind and open to attack. Others had told him it would have happened anyway but Reuben knew better. In any case, it was his letter – his and Corporal Sullivan's – which had kept the captain and the RSM in the office and had brought the two of them to the door. Reuben blamed himself for everything. For having eyes sharp enough to glimpse those stick-grenades spinning in mid-air and instinct quick enough to dive for shelter. He blamed himself for being the only survivor. He almost wept with shame every time he thought of himself staggering out through the barn door into the safety of the night past the simple Culpin heading for the

146

look-out post to save his stupid pigeons and send the SOS.

Reuben knew Alex hated him; Alex refused to speak to him. He knew Seb was trying hard to hide his contempt – but then, he would; that was Seb's character. Reuben also knew he should have accepted the major's offer to stay at Doullens as part of the Service Corps but he needed to be with Alex and Seb. He didn't know why. It made no sense. When the other two had chosen to return to the 12th Salopians in the Support Line, he had nodded dumbly in agreement.

All three would have liked to talk it all over with Corporal Massey but Massey had disappeared – had walked out of their lives. After the silent journey from the ruins of Pavé, he had parked the truck on the transport yard at Doullens, climbed from the cab and simply walked away as if he had never known them. They had watched and waited for a sign but he gave none. Corporal Massey never looked back and they never heard of him again.

A heavy van laboured to a halt near the sentry post and the youngsters picked up their packs and rifles as the driver wound down his window and shouted above the noise of his engine. 'You the lads I'm taking up the line?'

The entry to Major Challenger's dug-out in the Reserve trenches was a narrow, low opening in the angle of two systems. Three steps of chalky mud led down into the room where the major and his second-in-command slept; there was barely room for two bunks and the upturned boxes which served as seats and table. Another doorway led four steps deeper to a larger space where all the officers ate and three of the Platoon Commanders slept. A cubbyhole, no bigger than a wardrobe, was carved near the doorway where the remaining commander had a bed of sorts – usually the smallest of them for

147

obvious reasons. The dug-out was dark and damp. In the early evening it felt clammy and in the hours before dawn it was bitterly cold. Since each set of officers stayed there only one week before moving up into the support trench, there was little attempt at clearing the place out as they left. Major Challenger had been disgusted at the state of the trenches in general and had complained to the commanding officer of the company they were replacing. The man had smiled. He recognised the attitude of a man new to the front.

The major was very keen that his Company should do well if called upon to fight. It had been four days in the reserve trenches and would move up to the support line at the end of the week. Three days later it would take its place at the cutting edge of the entire British Army – in the firing line, the most forward trench of all.

Major Challenger's teatime briefing lasted ten minutes; there was little new to discuss with his officers. They discussed sanitation, the problem of storing clean water and swapped ideas on how to keep the men alert and occupied when there was little to do and nowhere to go.

The major drained his mug and gave it to one of the Mess servants. It was the accepted signal that the daily briefing was at an end and the officers drank up and began to move towards the entrance.

'A word with you two, please.'

The last two officers turned back to Captain Rivett, the company's second-in-command.

'There are three men rejoining the company tonight or tomorrow. They've been involved in the nasty business over at Pavé. I don't mind which of you has them but I want them kept together.' He glanced down at the scrap of paper in his hand. 'Yapp, Carpenter and Davies.'

Tony Gould smiled. 'They were originally with Number Four, sir. I'll be glad to take them back.'

Platoon Three's Commander interrupted. He was

almost new out from England. He'd been transferred to the Salopians from the Borderers and was desperate to prove himself. A little too desperate, Tony Gould secretly thought.

The new man turned to Tony. 'Sebastian Carpenter? Alexander Davies?'

Lieutenant Gould nodded.

'I'll take them,' said the second-lieutenant. 'We were at school together.'

'Good. That's settled then,' said Captain Rivett handing Lionel Tarrington the names.

Seb, Reuben and Alex all felt the strangeness of leaving the road and heading across country in the direction that the Pioneer corporal had pointed out. Much of that feeling came from knowing that they were now part of the landscape that each one of them had studied so intently through the Pavé telescope. In spite of this, none could work out where they were.

A row of heavy guns suddenly started firing from a field close by, to their left, and the noise briefly deafened them while cordite irritated eyes and noses. It was a shock on all five senses, for the flash of the guns dazzled the eyes and the concussion in the air could definitely be felt. The young men moved off as fast as they could. Soon they were part of a line of men and loaded horses trudging through ankle-deep mud, pushing forward against a line of men pushing back towards the Thiepval road. Even when the brief bombardment stopped – though the ringing in the ears stayed for some time – nobody spoke; there was none of the chirpy conversation and good humour they remembered from other marches. This was a grim and determined procession of tired men. The three took it in turns to call out to those who were passing.

'Salopians Support Line?'

Mostly they would get no reaction at all. Occasionally

149

a sullen shake of the head told them at least their question had been heard. Once or twice somebody bothered to reply. 'Keep going, mate.' 'Straight on.' In the end it was the man directly before them in the long weary line who turned and spoke.

'See that tree? There? By the stones? Your lot's down there.'

The Salopian sentry had no orders to allow anybody into the Support Line but the corporal of the Guard gave the boys a long look over and decided they were harmless. He was about to give directions to the nearest dug-out where they would at least get some sleep when the guard was called to attention behind him and footsteps could be heard, splashing through the mud. The corporal came to attention; the boys followed suit.

'What do we have here?'

The corporal explained. The newcomer stood close to Reuben and stared at him in the pale light of the night sky. 'Who are you?'

'Private Yapp, sir. Looking for Four Platoon, sir.'

'You've found Three Platoon, Yapp. Welcome.'

'Sir?' asked Reuben, puzzled.

Seb and Alex were not puzzled. They knew exactly who this officer was. The knowledge struck like a blow. Tarrington smiled at them.

'You look like you've seen a ghost. You haven't. Only your Platoon Commander.'

Seb spoke, trying to keep his voice level. 'No, sir. We have to report to Four Platoon. Lieutenant Gould, sir.'

Tarrington's voice was sharp and precise, like a whip. 'No, Private. You don't listen. I said now you're mine.'

The three kept stiffly at attention while Tarrington took his corporal of the guard to one side and gave instructions where the young Salopians should be taken. And in the darkness Alex began to smile. There was no joy – only the sense of recognising cold waves of danger suddenly flicking at him. Of course. Of course it had to be Tarrington. He should never have expected anything else.

10

In Support

The three newcomers stumbled out into the darkness to take part in the dawn stand-to, ready to throw back any attack at first light. Section Four's dug-out reeked of wet uniforms, unwashed bodies and fat food and the air was thick with smoke from oil-lamps and cigarettes. They were glad to be outside. Seb had a sharp headache, Reuben felt he had not slept at all and Alex believed he no longer needed rest and, like a cat, trained himself never to fall more than half asleep. It was raining, of course. Dry-mouthed and gummy-eyes the section stood in its position draped in waterproof capes with rifles at the ready. Intelligence had forecast no enemy action but a surprise attack was always possible as Seb, Alex and Reuben knew only too well.

Breakfast was a miserable matter of stale bread, tinned cheese and strawberry jam. There was, naturally, tea – hot, strong and very sweet. The section's way was to soften the bread by dipping it into the tea and then to eat the cheese piled high with jam. Meals were a high point of the day when men could relax, joke and be noisy. The awfulness of the food united the entire company.

After breakfast, the dug-out was made as clean as possible for the morning inspection. Tarrington saw no sport in this and his platoon sergeant made the rounds in his place.

Like time in hospital, the morning seemed to pass

quickly enough, in spite of the early start. Most of the section's work was to make their trench stronger, cleaner and dryer. The men spent time shoring up crumbling walls and pumping out water. The duckboards were scraped to give better footing and raised above the liquid layer of mud where possible. At midday the sentries were changed again and a simple, indigestible lunch was eaten – usually dry biscuit and corned beef. Corporal Ross' huge tin of strawberry jam was available to help the army biscuit down.

Like a hospital, too, time dragged during the afternoon. The repair work was supposed to continue and the men were expected to make sure their clothing and personal equipment was in good shape but that was soon done. Unless Corporal Ross kept his keen eyes on his men, often it was not done at all. And, in fact, Corporal Ross' eyes were otherwise engaged, staring intently into the wet expanses of mud where once there had been grass and trees. He was at a point where the zig-zag trench had collapsed and it was possible to leave the network under cover. The corporal was satisfied – there was nothing moving. He beckoned the youngsters to follow him. They crawled through the muck and debris until they were able to haul themselves upright behind the shattered stones of a house and look around.

A pitted black porridge lay desolately around them in the grey November afternoon. They could make out where they had entered the support line, the night before, and Ross pointed out the position of both the front and reserve lines. Nothing could be seen of the German trench system three hundred yards away but the corporal was able to give them an idea of where it ran. 'They fight different from us in an attack,' he told them. 'Fritz is clever; Fritz is cunning. He doesn't hang on to his front line at all costs like we do. He gives it up as soon as he can and falls back to his second line; that's always the strong line and the one he fights from. And our lads are left in his weak trench and facing the wrong way.'

On the way back into the trench system he gave other examples of the differences between the two sides. He'd heard several times of the enemy concealing flasks of poison gas along the edge of their own trenches. 'Then when they've pulled back and given that trench away, a sniper will smash those gas-bottles and down it'll fall on to our lads.'

They came at last to the crumbled section of trench and slithered back in. Corporal Ross and Reuben smoked a cigarette as all four stretched arms and legs, cramped from crawling.

Seb closed his eyes and let himself doze. It would soon be tea – a meal, he was told, identical to breakfast. Then there would be the dusk stand-to. Then another night in the crowded dug-out.

Everybody knew about the stormtroopers at Pavvy (as it was called). Seb, Alex and Reuben found themselves famous – particularly Reuben who was the only one to have survived the ferocious attack. The two Archenford men refused to talk of Pavé but Reuben found he could hardly stop. He never spoke in the presence of Alex or Seb but the more he told of that terrible night, the better he felt about it. He began to embroider his own part until he began to believe his own account rather than the truth. It was not only the soldiers of Section Four who were keen for details but men from other sections would seek him out at slack times, too.

Reuben began to be a hero. In his version, he had seen the entry of the Germans and dived for shelter one split second before the grenades exploded. Dazed but determined, he had raced for the out-house where flares were stored but had been forced to go to ground by prowling stormtroops. When the enemy had withdrawn at the approach of the truck and release of messenger pigeons, he had wisely waited until he could identify the arrivals.

'But what was Pavvy about? Who were your officers?' Reuben soon learned that he could make himself feel even better by talking Captain Dev and Cocky down, even though it meant talking Corporal Sullivan and himself up. This should have made him even more ashamed but it didn't.

Seb and Alex also had a claim to fame: some of Company C had heard of the performance at Concert Parties and one man from Two Platoon had actually seen them. There were many requests for songs but Massey's Maestros and Cocky's Canaries were part of time they did not want to be reminded about. They made themselves unpopular by always refusing.

The first clash with Tarrington came that night.

After a hot supper – the best meal of the day – with the dug-out full of smoke and chatter, the platoon commander's servant pulled open the sacking at the door and told Corporal Ross that he was wanted at once. So were Privates Davies, Carpenter and Yapp. The corporal tugged his tunic on. 'What the hell does he want us for at this hour?' he grumbled.

Seb and Alex passed a glance between them which said 'Be careful'.

'I am told you deliberately left the support trench this afternoon. Is this true?' Tarrington watched the four men at attention before him. Ross felt angry and embarrassed. This wasn't the way to do it; he didn't expect to be reprimanded in front of his men.

Outside in the drizzle, the platoon sergeant didn't like it either as he smoked a cigarette in the doorway, huddled into his greatcoat against the cold. He didn't like his NCOs carpeted in front of their soldiers. And he didn't like being turfed out of his dug-out at night so some jumped-up second-lieutenant could play God in the warm.

'Corporal?'

'The new men needed to see the lie of the land, sir.'

'Did you ask permission?'

'No, sir.'

'Why not?'

'I didn't see the need. No harm done sir.'

'No harm? No harm from enemy snipers? No harm in having any German look-out knowing where our support line is?'

Corporal Ross felt his face begin to glow in annoyance. 'We were under cover the whole time, sir. And as for Fritz knowing about the support line, sir, I imagine he already knows that. Just like we know where his line goes, sir.'

Tarrington glared at the man in disbelief. Seb spoke quickly.

'We asked Corporal Ross to –'

Tarrington's whip-voice cracked. 'Quiet.'

The corporal licked his lips. He knew he had offended but didn't know how. Tarrington turned to the three privates. 'You three. Outside. Wait until you're called.'

They were glad to leave. They moved quickly towards the sheet of corrugated iron that served as a door. 'And move down the trench. I don't want you listening.'

While Corporal Ross, a highly intelligent auctioneer from the market town of Wem, married with three children, was lectured on the subject of common sense and responsibility by Lionel Tarrington, who was three years younger and knew nothing, Seb, Alex and Reuben pressed together in a dark angle of the trench against the gathering rain. Reuben was alarmed. 'What does he want us for? It's not our fault. We haven't done anything wrong.'

Alex and Seb said nothing. Four minutes later the corporal stamped angrily past them without a word and the platoon sergeant whistled for them to come back. Reuben was dismissed after a simple, brief reprimand. Tarrington walked to the entrance and called the platoon sergeant. 'Sergeant? I can hear one of the pumps not working properly. Check them all, please. There's going to be a lot of water in the trenches by sunrise.'

He came back to Seb and Alex and sat on the sergeant's bunk as they stood at attention. He looked up into their faces. 'Don't expect any favours.'

In the amber glow of the candles he saw Seb's eyes fasten angrily on his face and knew he had said the wrong thing. These were not the same children he had known five months earlier. Alex seemed indifferent, watching the flickering shadows. Neither wanted or expected anything from Lionel Tarrington.

'I know all about Pavvy and the pathetic sort of place it was. Best thing that could have happened to it. Well, now you're in the proper war.'

Seb's eyes stayed intent on Tarrington but Alex slowly began to smile as he watched the shadows dance. There was no amusement in his face. Tarrington spoke sharply. 'Wipe that smirk away, Davies, or I'll do it for you.'

'No.' It was Seb's turn to use his voice like a whip. Tarrington swung to him, hardly believing his ears.

'Officers are not permitted to strike men. King's Regulations.'

'I'll do what I like.'

'No.'

Seb stopped Tarrington in his tracks. The mask of confidence he had built up so well during training with the Borderers and Salopians began to slip. He was not facing older officers impressed by his family, his accent and his daring. The schoolboy Tarrington suddenly made an unwelcome appearance. The dunce Tarrington who had to bribe cleverer boys to do his work; the Tarrington who wasn't even a house prefect and had been dropped by the Cricket XI; the Tarrington who had been bettered once before by the same two people who now stood in front of him. He gulped and fought back something that felt almost like panic. He held out a hand. 'All right. That's over and done with. School was school. A fresh start. Let bygones be bygones. What do you say?'

They said nothing and made no movement so that Tarrington felt stupid with his outstretched hand and felt his temper rising. Then Alex suddenly turned his joyless smile full upon him and he shivered. He began to speak too fast.

'The truth is, we're having a celebration on Sunday. Just before we move up into the front lines. That's the officers, of course. At Company HQ. They tell me you sang for the commander-in-chief. Is that right? Anyway, I told them I'd get you to do a bit on Sunday. All right?'

There was no reply. Alex's smile became a grin of even less joy.

'What do you say? You'll be well rewarded and looked after.'

Alex suddenly let his breath out. It could have been a laugh. It could have been a gasp of recognition – here was the old Tarrington offering money.

'What do you say? I mean, we're Old Boys of the same school. It'll be like old times again too, hearing the two of you warbling away.'

Seb was embarrassed for him and looked away. Rain flicked against the sheet of corrugated iron which rattled in a sudden breeze.

'You mustn't let me down. I've already promised Major Challenger.' He hated having to come so close to begging and looked from one to the other. Seb still kept his eyes well away but Alex's grin grew wider and again that strange gasp came from him. Seb looked across anxiously. Tarrington stood and stepped deliberately before them.

'Fight me,' he said quietly, 'and it will end the way it did before.'

Alex finally answered; his words were sad, regretful. 'I'll kill you, Tarrington. If I get the chance.'

It was clear, it was meant and it was devastating. It should have sounded ridiculous. Instead, Tarrington's heart pounded. 'Why?'

Each word of the reply was forced from deep inside Alexander Davies unwillingly. Everything hardened – his mouth, his eyes, his fists. 'You helped make me what I am.'

Seb moved nervously to his side and took his arm. 'Come on,' he said softly.

Alex snatched the arm from his friend and walked out into the night.

Seb turned to his platoon commander. 'We're not at school any more. This isn't sport; not a game.' He followed his friend. In the doorway he looked back.

'Leave us alone . . . sir.' He saluted and was gone.

Neither of them spoke during the walk back to Section Four's dug-out. As they approached the sacking across the entrance they instinctively slowed down. Everything was going wrong – first the raid, then the appearance of Tarrington and now heavy threats. Worst of all, the two friends felt the beginnings of a gulf between them. Seb reached out to lay a hand on Alex's shoulder. Alex turned. They smiled uneasily at each other. Alex put an arm across Seb's shoulders. Then they heard laughter the other side of the sack and Reuben talking about Pavé.

'It was a bad place; sloppy. No discipline. There was never any proper time when things had to happen – you know, like inspection or stand-to. Chaotic – like the people who ran it.'

For a while they couldn't go in. It would have been better to confront Reuben at once; better to put a stop to it as soon as possible. Instead they listened, bewildered

158

and aghast. They heard Reuben paint a picture of Pavé that was hardly recogniseable. He suggested that Cocky and Massey were drunkards and the latter a petty thief with his 'liberations'. He sneered at Dev as a young man out for anything he could get who was willing to keep his mouth shut about the anti-British feelings that the RSM showed.

'What about the other two? Davies and Carpenter?'

'They were always creeping round officers some-where at Mess nights or Church parades – just because they could sing a bit. There were others that could sing a bit, too, but did we get the chance? Not likely. They got all the soft jobs. They were the 'Nice Boys'. The Favourites.'

There was a brief silence. Someone asked somebody for a fill of tobacco. Conversation began to build about duties; a joke was started. Reuben pulled attention back to himself. 'I made a list – well, me and Sullivan: all the things Allcock ever said against the army and the King. We sent it to the Service Corps C.O. That's why Devereux was there the night the stormtroopers nearly got me.'

'What about the lad up at the telescope? Is it true they stripped him?'

Reuben laughed. 'Who? Ted? Ted was soft in the head. Not to speak ill of the dead but he should have been in some lunatic home – well, I suppose he was, really.' Reuben laughed again and a few of his listeners joined in. His back was towards the entrance so he had no warning until Alex clubbed him down. As he twisted to the floor Alex kicked him twice in the stomach, fast. It was all so quick that nobody realised what was happening but then the section was angry. Somebody lunged at Alex but Seb stepped in and knocked away the blow. There was much shouting. For a moment it was as if a free-for-all was about to start.

'What's going on here?'

It was the platoon sergeant, returning from checking the water pumps and in a bad mood since they had all been working perfectly. Immediately the struggling men fell back and tempers cooled. Corporal Ross stepped forward. 'Nothing, Sergeant. Difference of opinion; that's all. It's over now.' The Sergeant looked sternly at Ross and then around the crowded dug-out. 'Get your heads down,' he ordered. 'Remember where you are. Keep any "differences" for until you're away from the Front.'

He turned and moved back into the night. Alex calmly walked over to his sleeping-space and stretched out. Seb looked down at Reuben.

'You all right?'

Reuben nodded as one of the others helped him to his feet. He would not look at Seb.

'What was all that about?' demanded Ross.

'Like you said. A difference of opinion.'

The men gazed at him. He shrugged. The violent mood began to dissolve. Cigarettes were lit. Nobody understood what had happened. It was clear that Reuben was somehow in the wrong.

'That's enough then. It's forgotten,' Corporal Ross declared firmly. 'It's done with. We've got enough trouble with Fritz. We don't need this.'

There was a loud murmur of agreement and the occupants went their ways but Reuben hovered near Seb, shaking his head hopelessly.

'It's all right,' Seb said, taking the gesture as apology. 'It's a bad time.' Reuben walked away and lit a thin cigarette with a shaking hand. The flare-up was over. They were all used to nerves suddenly snapping. Every soldier in Section Four glanced secretly at Alex who lay with his hands beneath his head and his eyes closed. He did not look asleep and no one believed he had been acting from nerves. He had been as cold as ice.

11

At the Front

During the evening of 7 November, the officers enjoyed their celebration – without singers – and the next day C Company moved forward from the support trench into the reserve line to replace troops from Manchester. It was a tense time.

The complicated movement was like some gigantic puzzle but by five o'clock the silent exchange was completed. A and B Companies held the front trench; B and C Companies held the Reserve. There was extra tension at the dusk stand-to. Seb and Alex stood side by side, alert in the last of the light. They had the eerie knowledge that only one thin line of their Salopian comrades lay between them and the enemy. In four days' time they themselves would be on the firing step and there would be only No-Man's-Land and German territory in front of them.

Later, Major Challenger brought news from Battalion Headquarters which increased the tension considerably. There was to be a late offensive. Early on 13 November, a major attack was to try to take the village of Beaumont Hamel on its ground above the River Ancre. It was hoped to give the British High Command a success to carry to an important conference at Chantilly, two days later, which could be favourably compared with the French success at Verdun.

The assault on the village itself was to be made by a Highland Division; other major parts in the offensive were given to the Royal Naval Division, who were already dug in below Beaumont, and the Rifle Brigade. Beaumont Hamel lay eight kilometres west of the Salopians who had a part to play, too. It was important to keep the Germans guessing so the major brought back orders for a series of raids across No-Man's-Land which would culminate in an attack on the German front line at exactly the same time as the Scots went over the top to take Beaumont. It was believed the German Command would not know where to concentrate its defences until too late. There would be a very real chance of counter-attack. All senior officers on both sides knew that where the line was drawn on the night of 13 November was where it would stay until the Spring of 1917. The major told his tense, watchful officers that the first raiding party would be sent out the following night. Tarrington immediately volunteered to lead it and was told to report to Captain Rivett at Company HQ after evening stand-to.

Tarrington was thrilled. He had worked hard to gain a reputation for fearless daring during his training with the Archenford Militia and the Borderers. He had done his best to make sure the fame travelled with him to the Salopians. This was his chance. This would wipe the smiles from all those Archenford faces who thought him merely a fool and a bully. Lionel Tarrington intended to rewrite his personal history by burning a new and lasting image on top of the old. During stand-to in the dangerous dusk his mind raced over the possibilities. He was sure of one thing: he was not going to take some know-all sergeant who would grab all the credit.

C Company HQ was in a good, cluttered dug-out at the centre of its men. Captain Rivett took Tarrington into a cramped triangular room where the signallers were setting up field telephones and dismissed the men before calling his servant to bring them whisky. It had not rained all day – the first time for weeks – but the cold had been noticeably sharper. He advised the subaltern against polluting pure Scotch with doubtful water and wished his raid well. The fiery liquid was wonderfully strong and Tarrington watched with shining eyes as

Edward Rivett unfolded his map of the area. He pulled out a notebook and pencil; he found his seniors had more confidence in an officer who appeared to make notes.

'You'll leave the front line at midnight. They've got a sap trench heading straight out towards Fritz – a listening post. You'll follow it as far as you can and pop up well into No-Man's-Land.'

He watched approvingly as the young officer scribbled rapid notes. 'No risks, Lionel. That's an order. When you leave the listening post you'll find plenty of cover in shell-holes. I want you to go forward until you reach the enemy wire. That's your job. All right? To reach the wire and make an assessment of how strong it is. Then you come straight back. Understood?'

He leaned back and rubbed his eyes. The fumes from the oil lantern were irritating them. 'No heroics. It's the next two parties that will have to find out who Fritz has placed opposite us. I just want to know how much wire we've got to cut so they can get through.'

Tarrington felt badly let down. He had been the first to volunteer but other parties with other leaders were going to do the important, impressive work. He was going out to look at rolls of wire.

'We'll expect you back at two. Any questions?'

Tarrington bit back his disappointment.

'How many in the party, sir?'

'I'd advise four plus yourself. You'll need a good, experienced sergeant.'

Tarrington shut his notebook in what he hoped looked a bored way. 'Thank you, sir, but I don't think I do. Not for such a simple job.'

'As you like. I'll leave everything to you. Take a corporal, though. Choose who you want and rendezvous here at eleven-thirty. Good luck and cheers.' He raised his mug of Scotch to Tarrington who grinned and returned the compliment. 'Thank you, sir. Cheers.'

It turned out that the major brought other news, too, though it was much later that he remembered about it and sent a runner with a message to Seb who was busy delousing his blankets in the dug-out. Roy Brown – apprentice chef of Pavé – was officially listed as a German prisoner-of-war; he was safe and uninjured. Seb rushed out to find Alex and Reuben who were as pleased as he was. Others shared their relief.

Tarrington sent his servant to find out what the excitement was. When it was reported to him that the raiding stormtroopers had carried Roy back behind their lines, presumably, for interrogation, the officer fell quiet and thoughtful. The private ducked out of the platoon commander's dug-out, leaving Tarrington alone. He looked down again to his notebook.

Carpenter
~~Davies~~
Davies
Harvey
Cpl Martyn

He crossed out Davies again and tapped his pencil angrily on the box that served as table. He really wanted Davies there, on the raid, under his command; wanted, really wanted, to see Davies sweat, to see the cool customer scared and sweating. But he could not forget his words. 'I'll kill you, Tarrington. If I have the chance.'

He shivered and scored lead through Alex's name even more heavily. He would take Jeffery instead. It was enough this time to show plodding, sensible Carpenter how Lionel Tarrington behaved under fire. He shouted for his servant again who came at once. 'Sir?'

'More whisky. Then take this list and tell these men to meet me here after inspection tomorrow morning.'

The man splashed a generous measure into his officer's mug and collected the list. Guns began duelling

164

away to the west, heavy and sonorous. Tarrington sighed in deep contentment. Action at last. Good sport.

The platoon sergeant collected them where they waited alone and quiet in the darkest part of the reserve trench, training their eyes and ears to be sharp. 'It's time.'

The four men grinned nervously at each other and followed him along the line to where the communication trench led forward. Sentries and signallers nodded or whispered good luck as they squeezed past. Alex was on guard near their dug-out. He nodded calmly. Seb nodded back.

Captain Rivett was waiting with Tarrington at the entrance to the sap – a narrow trench which poked impudently out into No-Man's-Land for fifty yards. There was a listening post at its end.

It was an uncomfortable fifty yards. The sap was narrow and low where shell-blast had blown away the top layers of mud. They could see nothing now except the back of the man in front. Their nervous breathing rasped above the scuffling of their boots and plumed alarmingly in the crisp dry air. Suddenly the level beneath their feet sloped down and they were in a space scooped from the chalk and soaking earth. There was a signaller at the listening post and a ladder with five rungs. The signaller gave the thumbs-up signal to Captain Rivett at the head of the party: everything was quiet.

The captain took immense care in scanning the darkness through his binoculars from the top of the ladder. Meanwhile his party made a final check on bootlaces, puttees, anything that might gleam or jingle. Tarrington was the only man with a firearm – rifles were a handicap to a crawling man and certain to get clogged with mud – but Corporal Martyn had brought his fighting-knife and made sure the sheath was firmly bound to his left forearm, beneath his sleeve. Don Harvey felt in a pocket for his fishing-knife. The captain came slowly down the ladder and glanced at his watch. He tapped Tarrington on the shoulder and the raiders moved quietly up the rungs.

Seb was third, behind Jim Jeffery, and felt his knees tremble more on each rung. He hoped Don, behind, would not notice. Seb's head emerged above ground level and he gasped in a brief panic. He was out in the night, vulnerable. The sudden change from the confinement of trench life was a shock. He scrambled forward, desperate not to lose contact with JJ. The ravaged ground slowed them. They were grateful there had been no rain for two days as they stumbled on.

Although the flares were far away, Seb felt certain that the dim green light must reveal their progress to every German sentry. Tarrington obviously thought the same and passed back the signal to move close to the ground now. When one lone flare arched high above them, some minutes later, the party began a long unpleasant crawl.

They rested, aching, after only five minutes and lay clamped to the mud, panting and miserable. Their clothing was soaked and caked in the evil-smelling mud. Seb's hands were like ice. His neck muscles were already a problem. So were his shoulders and thighs. Suddenly JJ's feet jerked away and Seb hurried after. There were huge furrows to be crossed, the results of freak shelling; vast black waves which Seb flapped over like a turtle. Suddenly they were at the wire. Seb's relief was enormous.

The five men spread out as they had been ordered. Tarrington and Brian Martyn – at each end – began a slow, methodical examination of the wire while JJ, Seb and Don peered into the darkness for any sign of danger. Seb began to shiver with cold and danger. He could make out dim figures either side. He could hear Tarrington and the corporal as they explored further and further away. His teeth suddenly began chattering and he jammed his hand between them. Then his jaw cramped painfully and he took his fist out. He badly wanted to be back behind the lines.

A clatter of small-arms' fire rose below the distant thudding of heavy guns. Seb squinted into the night. It was to his left – he guessed about half a mile? Three-quarters? Then two flares washed everything green. The flares were closer and they were all shocked. Seb caught a glimpse of Tarrington at the wire before he jammed his face into the mud. Nothing happened. The spate of firing died down and the dim light halved, then vanished, as the flares burned out. Seb swore to himself. The first instant of illumination had destroyed his night-vision. When he closed his eyes he could still see the green glow. Don began moving closer to him – which meant that Brian Martyn had returned. Soon after, JJ signalled that Tarrington was back too. They all waited to be led back home. But Tarrington led them to the right, instead, along the foot of the rolls of wire. Seb began to worry. At the rear, Corporal Martyn began to worry even more. The platoon sergeant had warned him that his officer carried all the marks of a glory-hunter. Brian had no choice for the moment but to follow on.

The truth was Tarrington wanted a prisoner. The stormtroopers had taken the boy from Pavé. If they could do it, why not Lionel Tarrington? He wanted at least to be able to report the strength and extent of the wire to Captain Rivett and casually toss in a few vital facts about the German front trench on its other side. He could make out the ridge of a large depression in the earth and made for it. As he slid down into cover he could just make out Jeffery toppling over the edge after him. Tarrington jerked back and swore – the bottom of the shell crater was deep in foul freezing water. He pulled himself above it and waited until Brian Martyn at last appeared. The corporal was reassured, imagining that this was the beginning of the long crawl home.

They listened in unhappy silence as Tarrington told them his plan. The corporal spoke up at once. 'Are these Captain Rivett's instructions, sir?'

'I'm changing the instructions.'

Brian sensed the others' eyes on him, willing him to get them out of this situation. 'Our orders are to look at the wire and get straight back, sir.'

Tarrington took no notice. Fear grew. Brian Martyn tried again.

'I'm sorry, sir. We should get back.'

The whip-voice cracked. 'Are you refusing to obey an order, Corporal?'

The words were too loud, adding to the tension. No reply came from Brian Martyn. He was a good junior NCO, used to obeying. He was at a loss about how to deal with a situation like this. Tarrington ran over his vague, crazy plan once more. He had spent some time with the company map of No-Man's-Land where it approached the enemy lines. The wire had been sketched in very recently and showed a good clean gap – for which they were now to head. Very near to that gap was a trench which looked like a sap. It was worth exploration.

Tarrington checked his revolver, ignorant of the deep and uneasy silence in the crater. He was determined to carry out his plan. Tarrington was a simple soul who trusted that a wartime British map showed only the truth. He told his men to be ready and crawled up the clammy side of the slope, estimating the gap to be no more than three hundred yards away. On the spur of the moment he pulled Seb up to be second in the line. Tarrington wanted Seb to be impressed and scared; Seb was scared. They moved out.

It took much longer than Tarrington had guessed and the line of the wire seemed to be constantly bending away from them, though this was difficult to judge as they crawled along its base. The party was rapidly

becoming exhausted and one thought only filled everyone's mind – keep going. They became indifferent to the
flares and gunfire which intensified as the night wore on.

Seb crawled into Tarrington's boots. They were at the
gap.

Don was left there. Tarrington needed a marker to
guide them back through the wire in a hurry if necessary.
Tarrington whispered that this was the time to bring out
a weapon and crawled slowly and carefully towards
where he remembered the sap to be shown on the map.
Brian Martyn rolled up his left sleeve, patted Don's
shoulder reassuringly and left him on guard.

Don hated the isolation and screwed up his eyes to see
the last twitch of the last boot. There was a slight breeze
and the roll of wire rattled gently at his side with a soft
tinny clattering. Don felt in his pocket for the fishing-
knife.It had last been used on the Rea Brook, south of
Shrewsbury; he hoped like hell it would not have to be
used now. The cold was biting. His shaking fingers
began to prise the blade open but lost control and the
knife spun from his grasp. Don bent to pick it up but his
arm hit the wire and a barb tore the back of his hand. As
he jerked back and struggled to free his sleeve, the tin
cans tied to the wire began to rattle loudly and almost at
once the muffled explosion of a flare gun gave notice that
night was about to become as bright as day.

The flares were directly overhead. For a split second
everyone was frozen in their lurid gleam. Don Harvey –
one arm in the wire – gazed up, openmouthed. Brian
Martyn snatched at the sheath on his arm. JJ was on his
knees as if in prayer. Seb, propped on an elbow, astonished, stared into the night. Tarrington was on his feet,
crouching at the edge of a trench from which men were
running. Then the scene moved in slow motion. The
final running man turned and lobbed spinning sticks
through the air as Tarrington swung his revolver towards him. Seb knew he was shouting wordlessly and

getting to his feet which seemed to take a long time. The merciless, unrelenting belting of a machine gun turned time back to normal. It tore the life from Don Harvey and ripped a fast track through the mud to Brian Martyn who never had time to draw his knife. JJ was screaming and running but he missed the gap in the wire. As he capered along the rolls, the gun began to seek him out. The mud bubbled and spat near his feet as he dived in terror across the thick steel spirals. Then the line of lead found him. The wire carried him like the sea, bouncing and turning him head over heels, rocking him down into its depths before the gun released him from pain. At some point the grenades exploded. It seemed to Seb that a heavy door had been slammed on him. He didn't see Tarrington blown past his falling body.

Then the flares died. The machine gun stopped. The telltale tins on the rolling wire clattered as JJ's shredded body wallowed gently in the cold crimson tangles.

At quarter to two, Tarrington's servant put out his officer's breakfast, as he had been instructed. Whisky, coffee, army biscuit and the last of the plum jam from the Swithenbank orchard. At two, Major Challenger and Captain Rivett moved into the front trench to meet the incoming party. Since this was the first of the company raids, they had decided it deserved the congratulations of both the commanding officer and his second-in-command. At quarter past two, Alex came in from snatching a mug of tea after sentry duty. He moved into the snoring dimness and stretched out on his bedding. He decided to shoot Tarrington if he came back without Seb.

12

No-Man's-Land

Time was playing tricks again. It could have taken Seb two hours to find the shell-hole and drag Tarrington into it, or two minutes. Time became elastic – stretching, then snapping tight. For much of it, Seb was dazed with pain and fatigue. Occasionally he lost touch with it completely but was always woken by Tarrington's moaning and – once – by his delirious lashing out. There were moments when Seb's mind was suddenly crystal clear and he would make plans to tend Tarrington's wounds or work out exactly where the Salopian lines were likely to be. But then the clouds would drift across his bright thought and he would forget everything except the task in hand. Seb was glad when he was only half-awake and half in pain. His instinct would take over then as he pulled and tugged at Tarrington, moving him inch by inch. On rare occasions Tarrington seemed to sharpen and struggle to help himself; they would move faster then. Seb rolled Tarrington carefully over the edge of the shell-hole – he did not want him to slip to the bottom and have to waste time and energy hauling him back up.

'Am I alive?' Tarrington's first understandable words jolted Seb from his harvest dream of Broxwood. He slowly twisted to face Tarrington and told him he was alive and on his way back to the British lines.

Tarrington was badly hurt but the covering of filthy mud which plastered them both made it impossible to find out what his injuries were. He knew Tarrington's left leg was badly smashed – he could see the twist and angle of the knee and foot.

'My leg hurts like hell. Am I alive?'

Seb felt sick again; he supposed it was the shock. He

knew he was the lucky one of the party. He closed his eyes and wondered if it was better to stay where they were. The harvest moon shone down on the warm August night.

'Carpenter.' Tarrington was shaking him. He struggled awake. He felt better and Tarrington was conscious. Best to move. Now.

Tarrington's breakfast was cleared away at half-past three and his servant went back to sleep. At a quarter to four, Captain Rivett ducked out of B Company's HQ in the front line and wearily made for the communication trench and his bed. He had done all he could. C and A Companies would look out for Tarrington's men and send a runner if there were any news. It was not impossible that they were safe and sound somewhere and messages confirming this were already moving up and down the line. Alex, as usual, was not sleeping. His cold eyes stared into the wooden boards shoring up the dug-out roof. He knew Seb must be in trouble. There was just over an hour before they would be woken for stand-to. Alex swung his legs to the floor and stepped over the sleeping forms. Out in the night he drew the knife-cold morning air deep into his lungs and looked up at the sky over No-Man's-Land.

'Where are you, Seb?' he muttered.

Seb was dreaming he was in a miraculous trench, lined with sandbags where the flooring was firm and dry; he lay near a set of concrete steps which led invitingly down to a dark safe place. When he woke up, he was.

Seb was shivering and it took him a long time to move his limbs. His body seemed one bruising ache though his head was clear. He struggled to sit up and take stock as the danger of his situation rang like an alarm. It was light but very early. He had tatters of memory – the disaster at the wire, the shell-hole, crawling around in the mud,

172

weeping with tiredness and frustration as he forced Tarrington to use up the last of his strength to swing over the broken parapet into the trench.

He swivelled delicately to peer at Tarrington who lay propped up against the sandbags. He looked a terrifying mess, bulky with black mud, his teeth gleaming in his black face. Tarrington was sleeping or unconscious. His left leg was locked at a terrible angle. He shook in spasms. Seb decided not drag him into wakefulness. His painfilled day would be long enough.

Seb could hear only the regular sounds of life at the front. None of it was close. He twisted to examine his surroundings. It must be a German trench; he had never seen a British trench like it. The system seemed to come to an end about ten yards to his right where the wall had collapsed. He could see more to his left, but the zigzagging design carried the line round the corner where Seb hoped fervently some enemy unit was not waking late. He couldn't be sure where he and Tarrington had come into the trench but assumed it was where the collapsed end provided access. It was a cold grey morning and Seb wished Alex were with him. Keeping quiet and still to save energy, he fought the shivering and worked out what had to be done.

It took him ages to get to his feet and it was hard to stay on them. His legs were weak and there was a dull aching in his side which sharpened to a pain each time he twisted his body. He was so cased in mud he could not see if there was a wound there. He stretched gently and found it a brief luxury. It was the first time he had stood fully upright since leaving the Salopian front line.

He was twice sick on the way down the steps but blamed the smell of decay. He knew he would find dead men. In the dim light that filtered down the staircase he saw a table. On the table he found matches and a candle. The fourth match was dry enough to splutter into life and fix flame on the wick.

Three long-dead Germans sprawled over the floor. Seb was sick again and felt so faint he could only climb a few of the steps towards fresher air. Some time later, he made his way back to Tarrington. He had blankets, a towel and items of clothing he had found on a shelf. He was puzzled about the lack of other personal belongings and thought somebody had probably made an attempt to clear the bunkhouse up.

Tarrington was conscious and shivering wildly. His eyes seemed very bright against his filthy face. He stared at Seb who sat at his side and gave a brief summary of where they were and how they had come there.

Tarrington felt only despair which was an unfamiliar emotion. He knew his leg was a mess and guessed that he was smashed inside. He could not move. This was the end of everything he held important – fame, sport, power, health. It had all gone wrong. He had meant to be a hero. He felt tears smear his eyes and hoped Carpenter would not notice. There was little Seb could do for him. He dared not touch his shattered leg but managed to remove the boot and sodden sock from the other. He dried foot and leg with a blanket and wrapped another round it thickly. Tarrington said he felt better. Seb's chilled fingers slipped and stumbled at the tunic buttons but at last he got it undone. Tarrington was wearing a cricket sweater beneath but Seb was able to tear that open and do the same to the shirt and heavy vest beneath, but it all took time and energy. He tried to ease the man's arms from his uniform but they were a stiff, dead weight. Seb grew unreasonably angry. 'Can't you help me?'

The fight had left Tarrington. He could not bear the pain of movement so there was a limit to what Seb could do. Tarrington spoke softly, dully. 'It doesn't matter.'

Seb dried Tarrington's trunk as best he could, suspecting there were severe injuries to his back but there was no way of turning him to check. Seb tried again to get the tunic off and failed.

'Leave me alone. It doesn't matter.'

The words hit Seb. They reminded him of Alex's philosophy during the hopeless Archenford days. And now here was one of the main reasons for his friend's misery reduced to the same helpless thought. He shouted, 'Don't say that.'

He saw Tarrington's eyes blaze briefly. Seb swathed him in blankets and tried to scrape some of the mud from his face. He knew that he would have to be direct and tough if he were going to keep Tarrington alive. He was going to have to bully him. Seb must bully Tarrington. He could almost see Cocky's wry smile at the way it was all turning round. He asked Tarrington roughly if he was all right and forced him to state clearly that he was. He kept on talking as he managed to strip himself and rub some warmth back into his body. He was covered with cuts and livid bruises, and there was a gash in his side as he'd guessed. He hoped it was only a gash and not an entry wound; he didn't like the idea of a grenade fragment sharp and hostile deep inside him. It didn't hurt so long as he didn't twist.

The long day wore on. It must have been somewhere around noon when it began to rain. Seb put out a yellow enamel bowl he had found in the bunkroom to catch the water and, in spite of the protests, insisted on moving Tarrington to the top of the steps where he was under cover. He could not smell the death downstairs as Seb could. When Seb had done everything possible he rested at Tarrington's side and forced himself to stay sharp and alert. He decided he could not leave Tarrington unless there was a good chance of leading a rescue party back to the trench or of finding them food which they would need at some time. It became vital to discover where they were. Tarrington began to snore, Seb shook him awake. 'Don't sleep.'

'Doesn't matter.'

'Don't sleep, Tarrington. Are you listening?'

Tarrington's mouth twitched as he glared at Seb but suddenly began shivering violently and coughing sprays of bright blood. Seb wiped his face with a strip of stiff pillowcase. 'Relax. Gently. Breath softly. Don't move.'

Tarrington fought his panic and won. His breathing eased and he steadied his shivering. They sat close together, glad of each other's warmth. 'Carpenter?'

'What?'

'There's a ring. On my left hand.'

'I don't want your ring.'

'Take it. If we get clear of all this, bring it me in hospital. If you make it and I don't, take it to my father.'

Seb found his left hand and began easing the ring from the little finger. It was not easy but Seb had it at last and put it in the pocket of the German trousers he was wearing.

'If you come to me in hospital, bring Davies with you. I've done everything wrong. If I get out of this I swear I'll put it right about Davies and the God-shop.'

'You'll get your ring back tomorrow morning.'

Tarrington said nothing.

Seb put all his concentration into listening. He had decided that the afternoon barrage towards Beaumont Hamel was behind him, to his right; he wished there were some sign of sun to confirm that the trench faced south-east. He was trying to pick up any other sound – particularly sounds of men at work, or laughing – but there was nothing. He wondered why the trench had been abandoned. He had courageously explored the system as far as he dared and found nothing at all. Now he was preparing himself to take a look over the top. He leaned against the tumbled and torn sandbags. He had picked his place. There was a four-inch gap between two of them.

He moved slowly, raising his eye to the gap, straining

for any unusual sound. He peeped out. Nothing but mud. An unlucky ridge blocked his view. He would need to go higher. He took a breath and raised his head, half-inch by half-inch.

He saw a rising slope topped by a simple wire fence. To its right there was a building. He distinctly saw a horse and cart but then the sandbag at his cheek exploded. Seb fell back, stung and choking. He hit the trench floor and lay there. He raised a shaking hand to his cheek and found blood. He stared vacantly at Tarrington on the steps, as if demanding an explanation. Tarrington moved his head powerlessly and struggled to make his body obey, but it had become as much of an enemy as the sniper who had just narrowly failed to kill Seb.

Seb's brain began working again. He blinked and spat dirt. He called over to Tarrington, whose eyes were wild. 'It's all right. I'm not hit.'

There was a small explosion somewhere above them and glass tinkled as it fell. The crack of the rifle followed almost immediately. There was another smash – louder this time – and more scattered glass. Seb forced his body to stagger to the bunkhouse steps despite the sharp twisting in his side.

He was remembering what Corporal Ross had said about flasks of poison gas in abandoned trenches: 'then a sniper will smash those gas bottles and down it'll fall on to our lads'.

Seb shouted with pain as he raced down the steps to where he knew he would find one gas mask.

Tony Gould came to find Alex in mid-afternoon. 'I know you're close to Carpenter, Davies. Signals have been coming in from the Fusiliers' front line over to the east of us. There's apparently two fellows strung up on the wire facing their section. Impossible to identify what outfit they're from but since Mister Tarrington's lot were the only ones not to return last night I'm afraid we have to suspect the worst. I'm sorry.'

'Will you show me where, on your map, sir?' Alex would not permit himself to believe that Seb was one of the men on the wire.

'You don't intend anything foolish?'

'No, sir.'

So the Lieutenant took Alex to his dug-out and spent kind time with him. He personally regretted that Captain Rivett had forbidden any attempt at bringing back the bodies as far too dangerous.

'Let's hope the rest of the group have been taken prisoner.' Tarrington's servant heard the officer's voice and looked in from the kitchen area to ask if there were any news.

'I'm afraid not. Before he went out, did Mister Tarrington mention anything to you about taking a look at things further over to the east?'

The man shook his head. 'Mind you, sir, there was something on his mind. He heard about that young lad's capture over at Pavvy.' The soldier looked at Alex. 'Well, you know all about it, son. You know – the way the stormtroops took him back behind the lines.' He turned his attention back to the officer. 'He went very quiet when he heard about that, sir. Not like Mister Tarrington to go quiet all of a sudden.'

He shuffled back into the kitchen where he could be heard gloomily passing on the news to the other servants and Alex knew now what had happened. It takes a victim to know his hunter. The moment he saw, on the map, the gap where the bodies were strung up and the enticing trench behind, he knew precisely what Tarrington had intended.

Seb buried his face in the blankets and tried to breathe slowly. At his side he could hear Tarrington labouring to pull air through the gasmask. It was a chlorine mixture not that Seb knew it. He only knew he was drawing gas into his lungs, no matter how hard he tried not to. He only knew that the more scared he was the deeper he breathed and the worse it became. He felt his lungs refuse to work and began to struggle against suffocation. He coughed into the woollen fabric and struggled for breath. He knew he must control the process and fought his body, weeping with fear and anger. Brinsop and his hated breathing exercises came into his mind and he concentrated every scrap of his will-power on thinking himself back to the Song School. There were the two lines of choristers. Long, Quinn, Alex, Chatterton, Erwood, Birdy, Boliver. He crossed over. Margrave-Owen, Ruscoe, Dobbin, Matthew, himself, Edward, Tod. He swung his mind's eye to Brinsop, listened to him, obeyed his instructions, followed the exercise.

After Corporal Ross had checked Alex's work with the compass, they talked for twenty minutes and agreed to run over it all again later. Then he had to leave and organise the collection of rations and Alex studied the sketch-map. He was certain he had remembered every detail; the corporal had been impressed with the copy he had made. He practised switching the heavy compass from bearing to bearing.

Alex tried to follow Seb's reasoning after the disaster at the gap. He stared hard at the point where the patrol would have checked the strength of the wire. He stared back at the gap, so far over to the east. He drew a circle. If Seb were alive, he should be somewhere inside it. Reuben came uncertainly into the dug-out and looked at Alex nervously. 'What do you want?'

Alex raised his ice-cold glance to Reuben's eyes. He said simply, 'We're going out tonight to find Seb.'

Reuben was appalled. He licked his lips and glanced behind him, as if afraid someone might overhear.

'They'll never let you.'

'They won't know until it's too late.'

'You're mad.'

Alex considered this seriously. 'Yes,' he agreed. 'I think maybe I am. You, on the other hand, are a liar who let his mates down and can't even look me full in the face. Well, here's your chance. Tonight you can wipe the slate clean.'

He watched Reuben carefully. 'I could take somebody useful who wouldn't let me down,' he continued. 'But I'm being kind. I'm taking you.'

Reuben twisted on his feet like a small child wanting to run but unable to. Alex kept his eyes full on him. 'Your friend Sullivan would want this, so do it. Then your bad dreams will stop.'

Reuben stared directly at him for the first time.

'How do you know? About the dreams?'

Alex laughed and began explaining the plan.

The two of them huddled together beneath the mound of blankets as day slipped into night. Seb still held a pillow-case across his face. The drizzle and showers had helped disperse the chlorine gas but the sharp night air irritated his lungs. In a flicker of panic, suddenly the desperate cycle began again: the gasp and the cough and the struggle to pull air into unmoving lungs. He started to choke but Martin Cleeve shouted at him. Brinsop was furious. Alex was disappointed and shouted, too. He drew in one fifth of a breath and held it and let it go. He paused. Drew in another. Held it. Let it go. Paused. The exercises in the Song School continued. Seb could almost hear the tower bell striking. Then Tarrington's teeth began to chatter. Seb beat down the growing certainty that they would both die before morning.

Alex and Reuben slipped back into the support trench two hours before Tony Gould's raiding party was to leave the listening post. Each carried an ammunition box

180

and struggled past the sentries without incident. The boxes were realistically heavy – they contained stones and mud.

'Sooner you than me,' grinned the guard who saw them out of the system and into the open night. When they knew they were out of his sight, they dumped the boxes and began the long detour. Reuben held Corporal Ross' watch which was much admired for the dim luminous tips on its hands; Alex pulled out the compass which the corporal had set and fixed. They began the first leg of their long detour – so many minutes on such a bearing.

Their journey to the gap at the wire was swifter than Tarrington's. He had travelled two legs of a triangle to reach the point but Ross' watch, the officer's compass and Alex's sense of purpose took them there more directly. Knowing how close the enemy sap was, they took great care in their approach until they were confident it was empty. Reuben took one look at what was left of Don Harvey and refused to look again but Alex found JJ grinning and bobbing in the wire and Brian Martyn sprawled nearby. He nodded. They confirmed what he already knew: Seb and Tarrington were elsewhere. He tapped Reuben's arm and they moved quickly and skilfully back along the same bearing. They had to be careful. Alex judged the pace. After three minutes Reuben tapped his shoulder. They were there.

Alex put his lips close to Reuben's ear. 'All right?' he whispered. Reuben gasped back that he was. Alex turned and vanished into the night.

This was the part he was uncertain of. He made sure of his relation to Reuben, as far as he could, and when he was well clear, he stopped. Alex just opened himself. He knew he was mad and that people believed he was half in another world. Fine. Let the unearthly part work for him. He no longer needed sleep and was fed more by danger than food and drink. He was mad. Good. He opened his mind to whatever it could find in the ravaged landscape.

181

Seb – he thought simply. Seb – Seb – Seb – He turned half left and the picture switched. Tony Gould's map clicked up in its place. A trench section marked Abandoned. A disused enemy system close to the present enemy line. Alex snapped his mind shut like a book. He knew what to do, where to go. He bent concentration like a bow.

It happened. The familiar rush of danger rose through him as he moved. Every sense began to tighten. His nerves stretched taut as wire. His skin felt wafer-thin and as tense as a drum. The adrenalin began to pump. There was a raid somewhere over to his right and a flare blossomed into light but Alex never faltered. He held Terry's cap-badge firm in his grasp and felt totally part of that other world.

I am a spirit, he thought. I am an angel. I could fly.

Seb and Tarrington felt no terror when the figure loomed at their side. In any case, Seb was weary with his breathing practices and almost asleep, knowing if he slept he would never wake again and not much caring either way. Nevertheless, the surprise of it made him rasp and choke a little but as he tried to get back into the Song School and start the breathing exercises again, Alex knelt and rocked him in his arms. Seb worried about Brinsop's reaction to this lack of discipline but Alex seemed to be speaking and he had a vivid impression that the hallucination was true.

Alex held his friend until the grotesque breathing grew calmer. He looked at Tarrington for the first time. He saw the gasmask.

Then Seb struggled for breath and Tarrington seemed to cock his head mockingly at Alex as he clutched the mask to his face. Alex decided to kill Tarrington as he had always guessed he would. He was stretching his fingers for Tarrington's throat when he realised the man was already dead.

Reuben was relieved to see Alex and pathetically pleased to be led back to Seb. It took care and patience to bring him out in silence but they had time on their side. Out in the open air Seb revived and was able to stumble a little way with the support of Alex's arm. The watch and compass led them back to where Reuben had spent the lonely anxious hour, then they sat together in a shell-hole to wait for the Salopian raiding party to pass close by, as the map had promised.

There was some concern that Tony Gould might be disastrously fast on the trigger or that his men might be nervous enough to cut throats first and ask questions later. They hoped Seb's German tunic was not the first thing the Salopian raiders saw. Seb tried to join the conversation but choked and coughed. It was that which led Lieutenant Gould's sergeant to investigate and report back.

Seb was so used to the sense of time drifting slowly then suddenly racing, of dreams turning true and reality becoming hallucination that when he woke in a bright room between clean white sheets he was not keen to commit himself about what was really happening. Breathing was painful but he felt his chest rising and falling. That was good – even if there was something wrong. Somebody stood at the foot of his bed looking like someone he had known in a different life so he decided he was dreaming. The memory made him sad and he thought he might cry if he could spare the breath but he couldn't. He closed his eyes instead and retreated into sleep.

He looked so terrible that Winnie thought she might cry, too, but at least he was alive. An orderly came into the ward and stood quietly at her side: 'What do you think of him, Winnie?' he asked.

183

'Oh he'll live,' she said firmly. 'I can stay for a few hours, can I, Harry?'

'You know the Blatchford rules,' he replied. 'If it's good for the patient, it's allowed.'

Alex pressed back against the rubble of Beaumont Hamel and let the scare thrill through him. His breathing jerked; his stomach ached. All round him the shells snarled and whined in the dark. He shut his eyes and felt dizzy. He heard the Germans pass the broken wall – urgent whispers and boots slipping on the stones – then counted to ten and darted out: he stepped quickly from cover and ghosted to where the ground was most deeply churned. He felt safe as he paused in the shelter of a smashed gun emplacement. The dizziness had gone; he felt light-footed, light-headed. He waited briefly to catch his breath.

Two burning trucks glowed in the darkness as the man moved from shadow to shadow towards the ruined arch where the enemy section was dug in. This was the moment he longed for and feared the most. The ache and the thrill returned and he tried to force his fear into the soaring echoes of gunfire. He felt the thrill grow. Then flares hit the sky and light flooded down.

Alex was shocked. He flattened himself against the stone as a German sergeant came noisily to the other side of the arch. The flares died, returning the village to almost total blackness.

Sounds slid into the dangerous silence. From the street came the rattle of a machine gun, a man's voice screaming, pounding guns and the raucous splutter and backfire of rifle and grenade. On the village outskirts, Tony Gould blew three blasts on his whistle, the enemy sergeant limped away to rejoin his section and Lance-Corporal Davies touched Terry's battered cap-badge for luck, felt his way through the archway and shot him through the neck. He yelled he was a spirit, was an angel and could fly as he jumped towards the dug-out where the Germans screamed and scattered. His bayonet gleamed red in the flames.

PART THREE

Archenford County, England:
Winter 1916

1

A Birthday at Blatchfords

Blatchfords
Archenford
16 December 1916

Dear Alex,

I came here last week and everybody says hello and Happy Christmas. Say Happy Christmas to Section Four for me. I will write when I'm better. Still not too good. Take good care of yourself.

Your friend
Seb.

p.s. Dear Alexander – we'll look after him for you, don't you worry. Merry Christmas from Blatchfords. Your old pal Harry (Medical Orderly)

France
10 January 1917

Seb. How are you? Happy New Year – happier than 1916 I hope. Fritz frozen solid, just like us. Still, it's a rest! All the best from 4 Platoon.

Corporal Davies!!

.Blatchfords
25 January 1917

Alex hello (or *CORPORAL DAVIES*)

feeling better but got to be careful. No running about. Got to keep the lungs quiet and the breathing low. Still can't talk much. (Harry says good job!) Frank Brown came to see me with Rex Hickey. Remember? Tarrington's grandad came as well. I told him lies – better that way. Mr Cleeve is visiting Saturday. Bet Dr Brinsop and Flo don't come! Winnie comes on most days. I get

tired very easy so better stop. Everybody here says
hello and good luck for the new year and well done on
the stripe.

Seb

(Private Carpenter)

p.s. Don't catch frostbite!

Colonel Harry Tarrington awoke from a long afternoon
doze in the Swithenbank library and watched the snow
plastering the windows. As the clock struck six, Wilkins
brought his whisky and soda and pulled the curtains.

'Can't stop thinking about that poor young fellow
Carpenter.'

Wilkins crossed to make up the fire.

'My son and Mollie should go to see him. He was with
Lionel at the end, for Heaven's sake.'

'They find it hard to accept his death, Colonel. Easier
to pretend it hasn't happened.'

'He's got the ring, you know. The one Giles gave
Lionel just before he left for France. He wanted me to
take it but I said no – Lionel wanted him to hand it in
person to Giles.'

'When the weather's better perhaps Mister Carpenter
could come here.'

'Not for some time. The gas did for his breathing.
Tragic. I talked to the sister. He'll never speak above a
whisper.'

The old man stared down into the fire. Wilkins waited
politely.

'About Lionel – Carpenter's not saying what happened. And Challenger's letter is no better.'

The Colonel thanked Wilkins who withdrew, deciding
to discuss the matter with the Groom. He had a nephew
on leave who hinted that Lionel Tarrington had been
bitten by the glory bug and led his men to a tragic end. If
this were true, Swithenbank owed Seb Carpenter a huge
debt.

190

In his rooms above the Gatehouse Martin Cleeve drew the poker from his fire and plunged it hissing into Norman Wickstead's pint pot. He rammed it back among the embers.

'The life's gone from him, Norman. He gasps after every word. He daren't move for fear of losing breath. He's more an invalid than most there.'

Norman shook his head and drank his warm beer. He and Betty were to visit Seb next week, on his seventeenth birthday. Martin wanted them to be prepared.

'He's like a little old man, propped up in that bed.'

Martin reached for the poker again.

'How's his mate Alexander?' asked Norman.

The poker sizzled in the sub-organist's mug. He shrugged.

'He writes when he can. But he's got other things on his mind – like staying alive.'

Norman raised his pot.

'Here's to them both.'

Martin clinked his mug. Both men drank in silence and leaned back to remember happier days for their friends.

'We'll give Seb a good birthday,' Norman vowed.

Seb had a good birthday, as promised. His first visitor was Winnie, who brought him a box of chocolates though her greatest gift was her own cheerful presence. Her appointment to the Dormington Estate had worked wonders for her confidence and she now held the position of assistant housekeeper, though the work at Dormington had not been easy; many of the old-timers resented her youth and quick tongue. She told Seb that she would be away from Archenford for several weeks: Lord Dormington was moving to his London house and she was going with him to learn how to look after it – the present London housekeeper was about to be pensioned off. Seb was pleased for Winnie who was excited about the change and aware of the difference it could make to her ambitions. They would miss each other, though, and she promised to write often.

Martin Cleeve and the Wicksteads turned up just before noon. Martin gave Seb a book on the lives and music of the world's great composers. The assistant verger and his wife handed over a bottle of Betty's best damson wine for when he felt better. There was also a card from the choirboys – a secret, since Brinsop would have violently disapproved. Birdy Wren's talent for quick sketches had produced a wonderfully exaggerated version of 'The Great Escape' (now firmly a school legend) which all the boys had signed. Seb noted that Dobbin was head chorister and Birdy his deputy. A scribbled note on the bottom promised an expedition to see him as soon as possible. It was from James Quinn and Tim Ruscoe – no longer the youngest choristers but Corner Boys. It reminded Seb of C Company – times of war meant rapid promotion.

Seb's mother and father arrived in time to wake their son from his afternoon rest. Mrs Carpenter was tearful – two sons serving abroad and another stretched out before her, crippled for life. Why should this be? It was a question nobody could answer – certainly not Mister Carpenter who sat silent and uneasy in the unfamiliar surroundings. It was a shared sadness that all three were glad when Sister Robbins decided enough was enough and came to insist her patient had a rest.

Harry led Frank and Rex to his bedside in the early evening and they cheered Seb up tremendously. Neither had work but had come to terms with their disabilities; Rex was about to get married and promised to bring his young lady for Seb's delight and approval.

The last of the birthday visitors was Wilkins who brought a polite card from the Tarrington family and a bottle of Colonel Tarrington's finest brandy – to be sipped under medical supervision only. The butler handed over two jars of Swithenbank honey from his own hives. Wilkins sat at Seb's bedside and talked of the young man's future in a way that was kind, practical and required no tiring replies. He had been asked to limit his visit to an hour and got to his feet after precisely 59 minutes.

'May I visit you again, Mister Carpenter?'

Seb nodded, smiling.

'And do my suggestions interest you?'

There was a pause and the smile left Seb's face to be replaced by a watchful thoughtfulness. Then he looked into Wilkins' sharp intelligent eyes and gave one final emphatic nod.

Blatchfords
6 April 1917

Alex hello.

I don't know if these letters are coming through. Hope so.

Warmer here at last and big day yesterday – outside for the first time this year. Felt really strange in a wheelchair and remembered you and me pushing the Blatchford boys down to the football match nearly 12 months ago. Harry let me try walking but I over-balanced straight away. Another try later today, he says. Soon as I'm better on my pins and not gasping like a walrus (do they gasp? I bet they do!) Col Tarrington's fixing for me to visit Tarrington's mum and dad so I can give them the ring. Please write Alex. It's bad not knowing where you are or how you are. I will keep writing.

Your friend Seb.

p.s. Reuben? Cpl Ross? Lt Gould? Say hello. Winnie's working in London!

Dear Winnie,

Thank you – the letter I mean. I need to know where you and Alex are all the time. If you get any news about him please write. No answer to the last 3 letters.

Just back from Swithenbank Hall. They sent the groom for me in a carriage because Col Tarrington said it was better for me than the fumes of their Daimler car.

I gave Mr Tarrington the ring and told them all a pack of lies about his son – good officer – brave man – popular leader – that sort of stuff. I told them he was good about his wounds – and that bit is true. Mr and Mrs T didn't say much but the Col showed me round his garden. As I was getting in the carriage to come to Blatchfords a maid came running out with a sovereign for me from Mr Tarrington. I felt terrible about it after all those lies and gave it to Sister Robbins to put in the charity box.

Harry says I must rest and sends greetings. I will get him to post this now. Please write won't you. I am glad you like the London job. Do not forget us archenford bumpkins.

Your old friend
Seb

p.s. Seb's a lot better now the weather's turning warm. He can walk a bit and his breathing's really good considering. He still gets v. tired but maybe he can leave here this year.

Your old pal,
Harry

Dear Lieutenant Gould,

Do you remember me? You took me back to our lines after Mister Tarrington's raid. I have sent seven letters to Corporal Davies but got no answers. I must know if he is all right. I hope you are keeping fit.

Yours respectfully
Private S. Carpenter
12th Bat. Salopians

Giles and Mollie Tarrington had been impressed by Seb. He had spared them many of the details of Lionel's last hours and they guessed he had glossed over other aspects too hard for them to bear but they liked him all the more for that. Most important, Seb Carpenter was a link to Lionel. They had suffered together; Seb had seen him die. That night, over dinner, Mollie said as much. Giles agreed.

'Intelligent young fellow,' mused the colonel. 'Interesting background, too. Farming family, cathedral choirboy, Salopian Volunteer. Wonder what's ahead of him once he's out of hospital?'

They discussed the possibilities of Seb's future which looked bleak. The colonel signalled Wilkins over with the claret jug. 'Pity,' the Colonel commented. 'He deserves better.'

Mollie looked over the table at her husband. 'Can't we offer him something, Giles? Your father's right. He does deserve better.'

'He's a musician, of course.' The colonel nodded his thanks to Wilkins and thoughtfully swilled the wine round the elegant glass. He looked innocently up at Wilkins. 'Weren't you saying the church harmonium needs attention, Wilkins?'

195

'It does, Colonel. But so does all the church and school music since Mr Hall-Roberts left.'

Jeremy Hall-Roberts had been curate at Swithenbank. He had left to become a padre at the front. Mollie Tarrington suddenly slapped the table as an idea came to her. 'I know. Let Mister Carpenter come here. Let him help out where he can with the music. Wilkins is right. We miss Jeremy about the place. The rector's a good solid preacher but he's no musician.'

The colonel slapped the table back in admiring agreement. 'Excellent idea, Mollie my dear.'

Giles thought it over. 'He'd need somewhere to live.'

Everyone looked up at Wilkins. 'Heath Cottage is available, sir. It's small but very comfortable.'

Giles was not quite persuaded. 'But how could Carpenter manage there on his own? He's a disabled man.'

They all looked up at Wilkins again. 'It would be good experience for one of the young general maids to take responsibility for Heath Cottage, sir.'

They all kept their eyes on Wilkins. 'Diana, sir.'

'That's settled then,' beamed the Colonel.

'But will he come?' asked Mollie.

'We'll offer him a good wage for his services,' replied Giles Tarrington. 'He'll come. Where else could he go?'

Mollie and Giles smiled at each other, pleased. The colonel gave Wilkins a slow solemn wink which the butler smugly acknowledged.

2

Heath Cottage

Heath Cottage
Swithenbank
Nr Archenford
21 June 1917

Dear Winnie,

What a turn-up. I'm a teacher – well, a sort of teacher. I give singing lessons.

Heath Cottage is wonderful. First home of my own. Very old, made of stone, just outside the Hall gates on the way to the village. One of the maids – Diana, she's only 14 so I'm very kind you'll be pleased to know – keeps the place clean and tidy and gets my breakfast as well. I'm being spoiled. Every night I go down to the Hall for my supper with the butler and housekeeper. We get waited on. It's embarrassing really. I wish I could do more for myself but I can't. I'm mending the church harmonium and thinking we should have a choir – I'll be the Brinsop of Swithenbank! They pay me a good wage but I'd do it all for nothing because I love it.

If I only knew about Alex I'd be the happiest man alive. I wrote to his officer but no reply yet. Please try to find out about Alex. I hope you're safe. The newspapers are full of the airplane raids in Kent and London so keep indoors. Good news you will soon be back. I miss you. Write to me soon at my new home.

Seb

France
30 June 1917

Dear brother so I have a teacher in the family what a disgrace. You are in the best place Seb. If you read the

papers you know more about the war than we do I bet.
There was a big french defeat round Reims we are in
training for something big and new around Wipers
again. You are in the best place. I already said that.
Have you been to Broxwood? Just to show you are not
the only clever one this is from Sgt Carpenter to his
little brother. Luke.

As summer advanced Seb gratefully built himself a new
life. By July he could walk to the village and back with
only one or two rests along the way. His voice, though,
would never recover. The lungs could not push enough
breath across the vocal cords. Words emerged with effort
as harsh whispers.

He was liked by the village children. He was only the
age of their big brothers but had fought bravely in the
war. They knew he had been gassed. Their parents made
sure they behaved well to Seb and helped him whenever
they could.

The adults of the village took to the quiet young man,
too. It was well known, of course, that he had been with
Lionel Tarrington during his last hours and there were
rumours that young Tarrington's career had not been as
brilliant as they were encouraged to believe – for one
thing, they had known Lionel Tarrington from birth:
they knew what sort of officer he would be. The villagers
liked Seb's polite ways and the fact that he was not posh
gentry like the Tarringtons or superior like many of the
senior servants at the Hall. Everyone knew Seb had little
breath to spend in idle chatter and showed their friendly
concern with smiles and nods. Seb would regularly find
small gifts at Heath Cottage's backdoor – a small bunch of
wild flowers, a lettuce, a few radishes, three eggs. Seb
and Swithenbank started to become very fond of each
other. Colonel Tarrington began calling twice a week on
his evening walks. The two men would sit companion-
ably and discuss – when Seb wished – the news from

France or Palestine, or the local matters in the Archenford Gazette.

Martin Cleeve came at Seb's request to look over the work on the harmonium and one Saturday afternoon Birdy and Tim Ruscoe cycled out to see him. Sister Robbins drove over and reorganised Heath Cottage entirely – much to Diana's displeasure, who altered it all back the very next day.

Seb sat with Colonel Tarrington in the July evening sun and grinned as he watched the old man sip cautiously at a glass of potato wine, a gift from Nathan Biddle's mother. He licked his lips, and held out his glass for more. 'Not bad at all. I must have a quiet word with good Mrs Biddle.'

The news was all of the new fighting around Ypres which sounded depressingly like the old fighting on the Somme. Seb guessed that Luke would be there – and Alex if he was still alive. As Seb made to open the newspaper, the colonel laid a hand on his arm. 'Doctor Brinsop,' he said.

Seb closed the newspaper and laid it aside. He looked levelly at the colonel who reached into his jacket and drew out a letter which he handed to Seb.

From the Master of Choristers
The Close
Archenford
1 July 1917

Dear Colonel Tarrington,

It has come to my notice that Sebastian Carpenter has entered employ at Swithenbank. It is my duty to inform you of his dishonest and unreliable nature. I trust you are aware that he was instrumental in enabling a thief to escape unpunished, who not only stole from the Cathedral but also sought to defame and discredit the good name of your grandson, Lionel –

whose death we all deeply regret. The Headmaster of the School will be pleased to supply any further information concerning Sebastian Carpenter. Naturally, I shall also be pleased to make my views known.

Yours faithfully
Arnold Brinsop D.Mus, FRCO.

Seb finished the letter and laid it on the table. He looked up to the colonel's level gaze.

'I must know what this is about,' the old man said.

Seb shook his head. The Colonel smiled. 'You are neither dishonest nor unreliable. And I, in my turn, am not yet senile. I have no illusions about my grandson, Seb. Whatever you tell me will, I promise, be our secret. But you must explain.'

Seb explained. He told the wise man exactly what had happened during that final term at the Cathedral School. He was driven on by the need to keep Alex's reputation clean and the desire to keep the friendship of the family who had given him his new life. He told the whole episode as he knew it.

'Did my grandson ever mention this business when you were together in France?'

Seb dropped his eyes. Telling the story as far as the Recruiting Desk at Shrewsbury was one thing – to move to the events on the Somme was another.

'Seb,' said the Colonel softly. 'You must tell me the entire story.'

Seb's eyes rose slowly. There were very few people to whom he would ever feel able to tell the truth but this was one. He suddenly needed the relief of confession. As he whispered and gasped his way through those terrible events of the previous autumn, the darkness closed in and the air turned colder. It was an effort to force the words out. He came to the end, panting. The old man stood stiffly and laid a hand on Seb's shivering shoulders.

'This must be our secret. Lionel's parents must never know.'

'He said he'd put it right for Alex. If he got back,' Seb managed to whisper.

'I like to think he would have.' The colonel turned, picked up his stick and moved to the garden gate. He mumbled thanks as he vanished in the night, sad and dismayed but not entirely surprised.

Seb had exhausted himself. His shivering increased. He began to cough, then choke. He forced himself to be calm and moved delicately indoors.

Seb's one deep sadness was that he had lost track of Alex. Sometimes he felt his friend was dead and sank into a black mood from which none of his new friends could draw him. He wrote to Major Challenger and had a letter back, after a long delay, which told him that Colonel Challenger (everybody seemed to have been promoted) was now commanding a Training Battalion forty miles away, near Shrewsbury. A letter came from Captain Gould which wished him well but regretted being unable to help in his search for Sergeant Davies who had fought with 4 Platoon until late May. At that stage, Tony Gould had transferred to another Company and lost contact with him.

Winnie's weekly letter became all the more important to Seb and when a fortnight passed without the familiar writing on the envelope postmarked London, he put it down to extra work, perhaps, or new friends and interests. When a third week passed, and then a fourth, he wrote anxiously to Dormington Hall. A secretary replied that Winnie had asked for two weeks' holiday and was expected back at the house in Cadogan Square almost immediately.

Seb was not the only one to be worrying about Winnie. Two weeks after his letter from Dormington Hall, Seb was taking the weekly choir practice in Swithenbank Church when Hollingworth quietly pushed open the heavy door and Lady Gemma Dormington herself slipped into the back pew. It was difficult to know who was more impressed – the small choir or the newcomers who were not used to the pure, accurate sound of the Tudor anthem they heard.

Later, while Hollingworth took the boys of the choir for a spin round the country lanes in the famous Dormington Silver Ghost Rolls Royce, Gemma and Seb sat at his back door eating raspberries. They talked briefly of their different experiences in France. It was strange to think that just before Seb's arrival at Pavé, one of the Dormington ambulances had been repaired there, by Sullivan. But France had changed them both. Neither wished to recall too many memories.

'When did you come home?' whispered Seb.

'Last week – when my last ambulance was blown up.'

Gemma Dormington had come to talk about Winnie and ask Seb's advice. They were both puzzled and worried.

'She simply never came back from her holiday. We hope very much she's all right.'

They agreed this was most unlike Winnie.

'She's such a responsible woman. I sent somebody to Knighton, to see if she'd gone home for any reason but they didn't seem to know and her father didn't seem to care.'

'Have you told the police?' whispered Seb.

'Yes. They thought that a young servant on the run was no very important matter. They took down the details.'

'You'll tell me if you hear anything?'

'Of course I will.'

The Rolls Royce could be heard approaching. They got to their feet.

'Your choir is wonderful,' she said. 'I wish you would

202

come to Dormington and fashion something out of our terrible little braying donkeys.'

They laughed.

'As for your Alexander, I'll write to a few friends in high places. They may be able to find out something.'

They walked to the gate together. Gemma took Seb's hand.

'Goodbye, Sebastian. I'm sorry about Winnie and Alex. Stay hopeful.' She kissed his cheek.

Seb stood among the boys and waved as the motor roared away to the village. Seb reached for his dust-mask and pointed to the basket of fruit near his door. His boys fell on it like locusts.

When the dust and fruit had almost disappeared, Seb took up the pencil and paper at the side of his chair; he was writing a double chant for the Harvest Festival psalms. Two of the boys wandered over to watch this novelty. They were among the six village boys and girls to whom Seb gave personal singing lessons, paid for by the Tarringtons. Nathan Biddle hummed the treble line accurately. He smiled; he liked it. The other boy joined him as they sang it again. Others drifted over and muddled in, bringing confusion. Seb snapped his fingers – his way of bringing silence. He counted them in with another four fingersnaps and the Double Chant in G by Carpenter was heard for the very first time. At the end he took the pencil to make an amendment.

'You did this, did you?' accused Nathan.

Seb nodded and carried on his work as the choir watched notes dropped into place along the staves; they were impressed.

'Better'n them in the Black Book,' Nathan declared, leading the rest back to Gemma Dormington's basket.

The Black Book of Psalm Chants contained work by Sir John Goss, Doctor Wesley and Doctor Stainer, Tallis, Purcell and Beethoven. Seb saw the last of the fruit disappear. He felt a bit smug.

The sharpness of September was welcome. It had always been Seb's favourite season. A load of split logs was delivered at Heath Cottage and Diana began to light a fire. The young maid was proud and protective of Seb. She took her duties seriously and was ruthless in chasing away both dust and visitors who she thought might tire or annoy him. This was useful, for Seb was beginning to compose bigger music than psalm chants and needed time and concentration.

At first he wrote simply because the only church music he knew was impossible for his choir to perform; it was more practical to write simple pieces specially for it. Soon he realised with delight that the members were becoming capable of more complex work and that he was becoming capable of writing it. His short anthems were for unaccompanied voices – there was nobody able to play the harmonium with any degree of skill – but then Jeremy Hall-Roberts returned. He had seen enough war at first-hand and thought he would either go mad or lose his faith if he stayed to see any more. Seb and JHR liked each other at first meeting but there were other reasons why Seb was glad the curate had returned: he was a very competent organist and had recently been left a fine piano which he brought to Swithenbank.

There was another surprise visitor and the shock almost killed Seb. He was munching a sandwich while concentrating on a sheet of music before him and nearly choked when Roy Brown looked in at the window one September afternoon.

Roy stayed for two days on his way home to Bromyard just over the border in Herefordshire. He was in the first exchange of prisoners of war and had been granted three weeks' leave. Such dreadful stories of German treatment to their captives filled the newspapers that Roy was an object of awe and admiration wherever he went. The Tarringtons invited Roy and Seb to dinner and Roy spoke for the first time of his experiences.

The stormtroop attack on Pavé was intended both to find out what was going on there and to take at least one prisoner for interrogation.

'Did they give you a hard time of it, Brown?' asked the Colonel.

Roy admitted they had.

'In that case, enough said, old boy,' insisted the colonel, refilling the young man's glass.

Roy and Seb sat together and heard the church clock strike midnight. One of the candles guttered. (Seb found that the fumes from oil-lamps irritated his lungs.) Roy told Seb how well-organised the German operations seemed to be. Seb agreed, remembering the trench he and Tarrington had occupied. Roy had no news of Alex among the prisoners of war.

'I didn't get a hard time like I said at supper, Seb. Maybe I would have, but I told them everything.'

Roy stared sadly into the dying fire.

'Everything they asked. They'd seen Pavé – they knew enough anyway. There didn't seem any point in being a hero.'

Three days after Roy had left, Seb had at last a letter from Winnie.

118 Greenbury Street
Norwood
London
20 September 1917

Dear Sebastian,

You must do something for me. I cannot explain to you but *you must do it*. Send photographs of Alex to this address. It is important. I beg you – as many as you can quick as you can. Please don't come here or write. One day you will understand. *You must not tell the Dormingtons. Please.*

W. Price

Seb was upset and puzzled but wrote at once to Doctor Brinsop about the photographs hanging in the Song School and explained that the request was important. Alex would be in each yearly choristers' photograph since he joined the cathedral choir and Seb asked permission either to borrow, or to have copies made of the two most recent on which Alex featured – 1914, and 1915. He wrote an identical letter to Kemp, the Housemaster of School House. Alex would be on the House group photographs for the same years. He wrote to Martin Cleeve asking him to telephone Swithenbank Hall where Wilkins would explain. The assistant organist was a keen amateur photographer and might have photographs of Alex himself.

Finally, Seb slipped from its frame on the mantelpiece his own special photograph. It showed the two of them together, in uniform, sternly glaring at the camera. It had been taken on the day they joined up, in a studio at Shrewsbury.

He discussed the matter in confidence with Wilkins who, as ever, suggested they consult the groom but they could arrive at no conclusion. It seemed a possibility that somebody needed to identify Alex; the pictures would be proof. The need for secrecy baffled all three.

As expected, the request to Brinsop went unanswered and Kemp dismissively returned the letter. Martin Cleeve, however, not only brought Seb three from his own collection but persuaded Norman to unscrew the Choir photographs Seb had wanted from the Song School wall after morning practice and smuggle them to Goodwins, the photographer in Paternoster Road, his friend and fellow enthusiast. Ben Goodwin had copied them at once so Norman could replace them in their frames and screw them back on the wall just in time for afternoon practice.

After a simple supper, the two men sat in Heath Cottage and talked of music. Martin had been hearing good things of Saint Swithen's Choir. He had even mischievously mentioned it to the Master of the Choristers who had pretended not to hear him. Martin had no idea that Seb had begun composing and fell silent when the sheets of manuscript paper were shyly laid before him. He removed his spectacles, polished them with the corner of Seb's tablecloth and glared at Seb's music in silence for such a long time that Seb was embarrassed and moved to the kitchen to make tea. When he returned, it was to find Martin scowling fiercely. His heart dropped.

'Very good, Seb. Very fine indeed. Now sit down here – forget the tea – and let me make a suggestion or two.'

The suggestions made good sense and numbered many more than three, which meant Martin was taking his work seriously. Seb found that pleased him deeply.

Heath Cottage
Swithenbank
3 October 1917

Dear Winnie,

Here are six photographs. This is the best I can do. What is happening? Can you tell me? Is Alex missing? I would like to see you. Please write at once. Can I come and see you?

Your friend
Seb

There was no reply. The groom had a brother who was a valet in Kensington, London, and asked him to make the journey to Norwood with confidential questions. It was a waste of time. Yes, a young girl stayed at the address. No, she was not there any more and had left no new address. Yes, she had been on her own the whole time.

Accidental Death

The year began to decline. If 1916 had proved a hard year for Seb, 1917 had seen him find better health, a job, new friends, fulfilment and a home. Only the loss of his two greatest friends spoilt the year's perfection. He had still heard nothing from Winnie.

Seb and JHR joined Miss Townsend the teacher in organising a school concert which was exciting and fun. The Tarringtons attended and when the Rector closed the event with a vote of thanks and a prayer he hinted that the church carol service would be a treat not to be missed. A shower of small gifts at the backdoor began the Christmas celebrations; a rather heavier shower of snow was later welcomed even by those who had to work in it.

But Christmas fun stopped abruptly during the afternoon of Christmas Eve when the groom hurried to Heath Cottage. Seb must phone Blatchfords urgently.

It was draughty in Giles' study. Seb did his best to control his anxious breathing as he waited for Harry to be called to the phone. He was glad for the colonel in the big armchair near the fire, pretending to read the paper.

'All right, old boy?'

Seb nodded, then suddenly Harry was talking on the crackling line.

'Seb?'

'Yes.'

'Can you come?'

'Blatchfords? Now?'

'Yes. Can you come?'

'What's wrong, Harry?'

At the other end of the line Harry paused for just long enough to convince Seb he was not sure of saying the right thing. Seb's breathing began to lurch and catch.

'Harry,' he gasped. 'What is it?'

'He's here, Seb. Alex. Must see you. Can you come?'

Seb managed to rasp out that he could and hang the earpiece back before the panic started him choking. The colonel was at his side at once, calling for assistance, calming him down, telling him everything would be fine.

Harry led Seb slowly up the back staircase and he felt his spirits sink. He knew what sort of cases were cared for on the top floor of Blatchfords. He moved on a few more stairs. Then he stopped. Harry spoke softly, sensibly. 'It's just Alex. Remember that. It's still just the same old Alex. The same old friend.'

The room was almost in total darkness. A dim glow from the fireplace showed only the leg of a table or chair. Seb heard Harry creak away down the staircase. He stared round him, trying to accustom his eyes to the lack of light.

'Alex?'

'Sergeant Davies to you, Private Carpenter.'

The voice came from the darkest corner. It was not clear but it was undoubtedly Alex's voice. Waves of relief swept over Seb. It was Alex and Alex could speak, could make a joke, knew who he was. He began to feel his way towards the voice.

'No.'

Seb stopped at once. Only his harsh rasping breath broke the silence. He found a chair and sat gratefully.

'Before you ask – yes, I got your letters.'

Seb was puzzled. 'Then why? Why not –'

Alex cut into the questions. In his strange way of speaking he gave what information he was willing to give and then shut up. He had wintered at Boulogne, returned to the Somme in Spring then moved north to Flanders. When it was clear Alex was unwilling to say

209

more, Seb told him of Roy's release from German captivity. Alex gave no reaction at all. Seb asked carefully why he was here, at Blatchfords.

'Shell fragments. At Passchendaele.'

'Bad?'

'I've got my arms and legs; they all work. I've got my brain and my senses – they work too, worse luck.'

Seb was upset. 'Don't say that, Alex. Please.'

Alex laughed. 'You were always the optimistic one. The one who looks on the bright side. Look – you've even made me laugh; that's a rare event. Ask Harry.'

'How does Winnie fit into this?'

'She does. That's all.'

He would say no more. Seb asked how long he'd been in England. Alex told him he'd been back several months. Three floors below a piano began to hammer out a popular carol; voices joined in. Seb was beginning to worry. He tried to reach Alex with warm memories. 'Remember when we rowed up the Linnow to Sarson Bridge? Good times, Alex. They were good times, eh?'

Alex screamed at the top of his voice. 'No,' he shouted. 'No.'

Seb stumbled to his feet. The voice cracked across the room. 'Stay where you are.'

Seb slumped back in the chair. His lungs were pumping now, as his fear grew. He gasped and panted as Alex laughed quietly, without humour. Seb swallowed and forced himself to sit straight, to expand the last third of his lung space and be calm. His breathing levelled out. Alex's voice was soft and indistinct. 'Allcock saw through the whole messy business. Old Men killing Young Men – that's war. And do you know why we let the Old Men do it to us? Because they had us trained. That's why. They had us eager and keen.'

The voice gathered pace. It rose wildly. 'You talk of good times. The Old Men would always have stopped us if they could. They tried, remember? Kemp. Collett.

Brinsop – always Brinsop. Teaching us always to obey, ready for slaughter. It was the same in training.'

Alex spoke dreamily. His slurring was more noticeable. 'Allcock knew. He was brilliant. Massey was brilliant. That's why they killed them.'

Seb spoke gently. 'Who, Alex? Who killed them?'

'The Old Men.' The voice hardened again. 'That School. That Choir. We were used, Seb. Even our own families used us.'

There was silence. The carol came to an end in the ground-floor ward. A burst of cheering broke out. It was hard to contradict Alex. Yes, Seb's family had been only too glad to hand over one of its sons to Brinsop without even caring what sort of man he might be. One less mouth to feed at home but he was still expected to return and help the harvest. Alex's father had passed the boy to his aunt who hadn't wanted him and the choir had been an easy solution.

A new carol began, noisy and undisciplined. Seb listened to Alex damn Brinsop, Collett, Kemp for their ignorance and their bullying ways and harsh retaliations if the children in their care threatened their precious status or failed to obey their every eccentric demand.

'Don't you see, Seb? They made us ready for it – the Old Men. They forced us into thinking it's never right to question any order. They proved to us the only things that matter are the power to scare your enemies and the strength to make them suffer.'

Seb didn't know what to say. He hoped this mood would pass. Alex needed rest and care. Swithenbank would give them. Alex's voice was sly. 'Whose side is God on, Seb?'

'Both? Neither?'

'No.'

Alex was suddenly very quiet. 'God's just another excuse. The Old Men pretend they've got him on their side, German or British. *Gott Mitt Uns*. In God We

Trust. Remember the Church Parades? Remember the Sermons?'

In the silence, the carol drifted up. Seb thought he heard the stairs creak but nobody came to the door. Again, that bitter laugh.

'Now look at you. Look at me.'

Seb tried to argue against Alex's black view. He struggled to tell of his new life at Swithenbank but began to gasp and falter. Alex laughed. 'They're still using you. They give you a little house and a little girl to look after it. Don't you see, Seb? They feel guilty about you. You've come back to embarrass them with what they've done to you. They like it better if we don't come back.'

'You came back.'

Alex's voice was suddenly flat, dismissive. 'The more I killed, the more rewards I got. They liked me mad.'

'The war's marked us all, Alex.'

There was a click as Alex switched on the electric lamp on his table. Light flooded the room. Seb blinked. He stared into the corner. It was not Alex but it was like Alex.

The man in the blue suit who sat at the table in the corner was Alex in build and the way he sat but the face was like the voice: it was Alex and it was not Alex. Seb stared, shocked, trying to work it out.

'It's marked me, Seb.'

The face was a politely smiling mask. One eye was bright and sparkling but the other was red with grief. As the slit of a mouth moved it tugged at stiff smoothness all round it. Thick eyebrows – too thick. Cheekbones – too smooth. The colour – too even. Everything too smooth. Seb tried to speak but failed. The doll's face smiled politely as its owner reached for the switch and returned the room to darkness. Seb remembered Harry's words. This was Alex, his best friend who had saved his life. The same old Alex. The same old friend. Words wheezed from Seb, frightened in spite of all he could do.

He sketched out his plans. Could Alex travel? There

212

was a car outside and the driver below. By the time Christmas Day arrived Alex could be settled at the cottage – an honoured guest for as long as he wished. 'Please, Alex. I beg you come home.'

'To be Swithenbank's very own curiosity? Will the children point? Will the women look the other way?' Seb whispered he was sorry. Alex raised his voice: harsh and bitter. 'I don't want pity.'

There was silence. Seb could not help imagining the smiling doll's face in the darkness, mocking the feelings that must be moving behind it. Applause rippled from the carol concert. Seb found he was tired but calm. 'So what will you do?'

'Find the reasons.'

'How long will you stay here?'

'The rest of my life.'

Seb stood and strode to the dark corner before his friend could move to forbid him. He hit the table which fell away; the lamp crashed to the floor. Then he had Alex tight in his arms. At first Alex tried to pull away, then he put his arms round Seb and the two friends held together, trying for action when words had failed. Seb's cheek pressed to Alex's smooth cold smiling mask.

Alex finally pushed him gently away.

'Go now, Seb. How many Christmases have we seen together? Seven? Eight, is it? You'll see me again. Happy Christmas, Seb, eh?'

Winnie was waiting for him outside the door. She reached out and held him briefly, seeing his shock and dismay, before stepping into the room to check that Alex was all right. She came back out and closed the door behind her. 'You did him some good. He's quiet now.'

They went downstairs very slowly in silence. Harry had tea waiting for them in his room and left them to talk. As he left, he patted Seb's shoulder sympathetically.

The tea was a help. It was sweet and strong. Seb

sipped and listened. News of Alex's injury had come to Winnie in London by a letter, forwarded from the Dormington Estate. An orderly, removing personal possessions from the bloodsoaked uniform at Dover, had found a cap-badge and a scrap of paper bearing her name and address, part of one of her letters. It was very difficult for the doctors to make out what Alex was trying to say, in those early days, but it was clear that the badly-disfigured man desperately wanted Winnie there, at his side. She had gone at once.

She was shocked to see him, his whole head bound up, his eyes covered, but he could speak, after a fashion. For hours on end, Alex forced his ravaged mouth to confess what he had been able to discuss with nobody since the icecold surge had claimed him that terrible night on the road from Pavé.

Alex had spoken with determination; no rambling. He told her how he had gained a reputation for cruel and ruthless killing, how he was much in demand for night raiding, how even his comrades came to be uneasy in his presence and thought him mad. He told her his story and when it was over, lay back, exhausted but relieved. Later they talked of kinder times and then he slept. Winnie had felt instinctively that the worst of it was that Alex had become afraid of himself. She decided to take time from her job in Cadogan Square. Soon she realised he needed her more than anyone. Alex had nobody else. Seb was hurt.

'Why didn't you write and tell me?'

She explained Alex was ashamed of what he had become. He wanted to hide it from Seb, above all people, and she had promised not to write. Winnie told Seb quietly that if she were absent, Alex would scream for her hysterically, believing his injuries had driven her away disgusted.

"What about money? How did you live?"

'I took a morning job in a shop.'

214

Seb shook his head. Why had he known nothing? He might have helped. 'But the mask, Winnie . . .'

Alex had been lucky. The Facial Disfigurement Masks Department of Number 3 Hospital in London had decided to take him as a patient and had given them hope. The Tin Noses Shop, as it was called, had worked hard on Alex. A succession of plaster and plasticene masks had eventually led to his present electroplate face which had been modelled expertly to resemble his features.

'From photographs?'

Winnie nodded. 'It's a wonder really. The electroplating's so thin he can wear it hours at a stretch and it's painted close to his own colouring. You see the way his hair flops over on his forehead now? That's to hide where the mask fits on. And he's got glasses and a big moustache – yes, a false moustache; you'd laugh. They take the attention from the rest of his face, see. Behind it all, there's pads for comfort.'

Her energy ran out. Seb took her hand. Seb did not feel like laughing.

'What now? Alex says he'll stay here.'

She smiled. 'Does he? Tomorrow he'll say something different. I don't know, Seb. I'd like to see him settle for a bit where he's got friends.'

They looked at each other seriously. A man and a woman now. One year had changed everything.

'What about you, Winnie?'

'I stay with him. He needs me.' Her face frowned anxiously. 'He needs you too, Seb. His bitterness eats him away. And his guilt.'

Seb leaned to her and kissed her forehead gently. 'We won't let him down. Happy Christmas, Winnie. Welcome home.'

In spite of his brave words, Seb was at a loss what to do. The shock of the meeting at Blatchfords was with him continually. He backed out of dinner at the rectory and was vague and unwelcoming when Mister and Mrs Biddle turned up with Nathan and his sisters to set up a Christmas tree. He went early to bed after a strong measure of brandy and hot water, leaving JHR to conduct the choir at the midnight service. Even so his sleep was disturbed and he was awake and worrying long before Diana let herself in to light the fire and bring him a cup of tea, excited because it was Christmas Day.

He was staring into the fire when Winnie's urgent telephone message was sent up from the Hall. Alex, too, had suffered a terrible night. And now he had disappeared.

The Daimler sped through the empty roads. Muffled heavily against the cold, Seb sat next to Colonel Tarrington, numb with the certainty that something bad was about to happen. Wilkins at the wheel swung them round the top of the hill and suddenly the cathedral tower could be seen above the clutch of roofs, two miles away. The morning was icy and clear; they could have heard the bells if they had dared stop and listen. Seb was as certain where they would find Alex as his friend had been certain where he and Tarrington had waited to die.

Alex sat quietly among the rubble and tiny bones of that strange cavern between the roof and ceiling of the north transept. There were birds fluttering weakly at the dusty round windows high above but he was paying them no attention. He was there to find the reasons. He was waiting to debate with God and Brinsop about his face, about Seb's voice. He flicked dust from his uniform and waited for the bells to stop. Nobody had taken any notice of him as he made for the door in the north transept, scarf wrapped high round his neck and head down. He knew the door to the tower steps would be open for the ringers who were hard at work nearby.

Ten minutes before Matins the ringers clattered noisily down the steps into the Nave leaving the tower to

Alex. The organ began to play and Alex sharply turned his head towards the low archway that led out to the higher gallery. The organ notes bounced and detoured as they climbed echoing. Alex nodded in recognition, put Terry's cap-badge safely in his pocket and moved. It was darker inside the tower. The glow of candles from the choirstalls, two hundred feet below, barely reached him but he had no need of light. He was a man used to darkness. He sat in a corner and waited for God or Brinsop to speak.

The congregation began the first hymn. A full cathedral sang 'Christians Awake'. Alex obeyed; he had fallen into a doze. The words and music were indistinct as they slid and mingled round the ornate carvery and over the smooth stained glass. Then somebody was speaking, though the words were the thin buzzing of a fly trapped in a window. Alex dozed like a cat, ready for action the moment God was ready for him.

The morning anthem for Christmas Day was one of Doctor Brinsop's own compositions. 'The Warrior Babe – A Nativity Anthem In Time Of War.' There was a solo for Tod, at the end when Saint Matthew's words of Jesus were proclaimed: 'I come not to send peace but a sword'. Martin Cleeve in the organ loft watched Doctor Brinsop's uplifted hands reflected in the mirror. Brinsop began the beat and Martin thundered into the introduction.

Alex was on his feet in an instant, wakeful and alert. The full organ roared up to him like shells tearing through the sky. The uneven distances tugged the shape of the music into a series of dulled explosions. There was a sudden trill of ricochets. Alex smiled. God was speaking to him at last and so, in some strange way, was Brinsop. It was when the angel trumpets hit the air, snarling bugle calls, that Alex began to understand.

He nodded earnestly and shouted his army number. He looked round for the support and moved up to the parapet.

The barrage ceased as Martin lifted his hands and waited for Tod.

Alex pressed forward into the darkness and felt the scare thrill through him. Tod's voice hit top G as shrill and clear as a whistle. Alex shouted he was a spirit, he was an angel, he could fly. He climbed on the parapet, slipping his hand into his pocket for the cap-badge. Over his shoulder he could see his support arriving. Then the whistle stopped and Norman Wickstead and Wilkins just failed to grab him as Alex stepped eagerly into No-Man's-Land.

Alex was buried in February, one week after Seb's eighteenth birthday. Thanks to the evidence of Wilkins and Norman Wickstead, the Coroner passed a verdict of accidental death, and since there was no other place for him, he came to Swithenbank. Seb wrote a short anthem based on Alex's favourite hymn tune. The Wicksteads and Martin Cleeve attended, braving disapproval from the Close and there was a group from Blatchfords. It brought home to Seb the loneliness of his friend, buried by the few who had known him in a place he had never been.

4

Doctor Brinsop's Nose

Seb found it impossible to shake off his depression. He felt a numbing sense of loss. He blamed himself for not having guessed Alex's state of mind. His lessons and choir gave him no fulfilment and, accordingly, he was lacklustre and boring to his pupils. The nightmares of Pavé returned.

'So is this how you're going to spend the rest of your life, Seb Carpenter?' Winnie had borrowed a car from Dormington Hall. She had recently learned to drive and took Seb for a trip each Sunday after lunch.

He mumbled apologies and tried to explain his complicated feelings. Winnie interrupted him. 'You think I don't feel bad? I was the one who saw him at his worst and his best. If anybody should have seen what was coming, it should have been me.'

She pulled up at a high vantage point overlooking Swithenbank and turned off the engine.

'But it's like a shadow, Winnie. It won't shift, and I can't move from under it.'

Winnie got out of the car and gazed across the Spring landscape. 'You're the only one who can bring him back. You're lucky.'

'What do you mean?'

'I listened to that church anthem you did for your choir to sing at his funeral. That was Alex. You brought him back for a couple of minutes to those of us that knew him. It was like a music photograph. You know?'

Seb moved slowly to stand at her side. He took her hand. 'I still don't understand.'

She cast her eyes upwards in a show of frustration. 'Here's you supposed to be the clever one and me only a housekeeper. Write, Mister Sebastian Carpenter. Compose. Make some real music for Alex. A sort of celebration, eh? You need to be busy. Be busy for him.'

Seb kissed her. 'Winnie, you're brilliant.'

'Get off,' she said. 'There's enough rumour about you and me around that village as it is, thank you. Are we going for our walk or not?'

As ever, Winnie's instinct had been right. Seb began to do something positive about his grief and the cloud overhead started melting away. He regained his energy and purpose, much to the delight of his friends.

He needed a starting-point for the music and spent hours exploring Sir Hubert Parry's hymn tune that Alex had liked so much: 'Dear Lord and Master of Mankind'. He talked at great length to Martin Cleeve and JHR who shyly produced a notebook he had kept during his time with the army. There were poems there and vivid description; Seb had found his words and JHR began shaping them into a text for singing. Once the ideas started flooding in, there was no stopping them; Seb slept with a notebook and pencil at his side, ready for the ideas that turned up at three in the morning. There would be a march because Alex enjoyed the comradeship and the rhythm of marching – but since all marches took him closer to the explosion at Passchendaele Seb would make it a sinister march.

Seb went with JHR to a subscription concert in Archenford Town Hall and heard Elgar's 'Serenade For Strings' for the first time since it had drifted from the ruins of Pavé – Seb remembered Alex staggering down to Cocky in the shattered cellar with Massey's liberated gramophone. He was idely watching the dovecote near the Hall when he found that the birds' callings at once flashed up the memory of Ted dying with his pigeons. Recalling the terrible events of Christmas morning as he sat at his table watching Diana snooze by the fire, he knew he would be haunted all his life by Brinsop's composition – 'The Warrior Babe' – and in particular that thin cruel solo near the end 'I come not to bring peace but a sword.'

'Too much, Martin. Too much material.'

Martin Cleeve signalled to the waiter that he would enjoy another pint of beer. Seb poured water for himself and watched as Martin finished his beef.

'How's Jeremy's words?'

Seb told him, briefly. There was a fine description of a battalion on the march and a sad poem about homesickness. JHR was busy putting into verse his sharp memories of church parades. The beer arrived and the waiter removed the dishes as Seb protected the manuscript music that littered the supper table of their weekly meeting at the Castle Hotel.

'I don't think there's too much material, Seb. What you mean is that the piece is getting too big for the organ and a small choir.'

Seb agreed. That was the problem exactly. He looked up at Martin.

'What do I do?'

'You write it – write it as best you can for your choir and organ. I'll transcribe it for a small orchestra and a soloist. We'll find the musicians locally; one of the choral society women will sing your soprano solo and one of the choristers the treble. I'll conduct, while you quite fairly take all the credit. How's that?'

It sounded wonderful. Seb grinned and asked Martin to call for two glasses of port. The waiter could not hear his whisper.

Such was the drive behind the project that Seb was able to present Martin with the finished work at the beginning of May. By the last week of the month, Martin had transposed it for a small string orchestra, solo soprano and boy treble. The piece lasted twenty-five minutes and was called 'An Accidental Death; In Memory of Alexander Davies'. Martin laboured in every spare moment to make a full copy for Seb. It was because of this that the problems began.

Doctor Brinsop climbed to the organ loft to practise the voluntaries he would play during the coming week. His mouth twitched in annoyance to find – as usual – that his assistant had left the loft littered with music of his own. He shuffled it together and was about to drop it on a small table in the corner when his eye fell upon a section he knew well – it was a snatch from 'The Warrior Babe'.

He collected the manuscript together and began to read.

When Martin Cleeve returned from a piano lesson in the gatehouse there was no sign of his transcript. He rushed down to ask Gwynne who had last been in the loft. The verger smiled happily and presented him with a folded sheet of paper which demanded Mister Cleeve's presence in Doctor Brinsop's study immediately.

The two men glared at each other across Brinsop's desk. On its shiny surface lay 'An Accidental Death'. The Master of Choristers was scandalised. He could hardly spit out his words for fury. First, the work was anti-King, anti-country, anti-war and treasonable. Second, Carpenter and Davies had caused more than enough problems with their thieving, escape plots, misrepresenting the good name of himself and Mrs Brinsop – not to mention the almost blasphemous happening at Christmas Day Matins. Finally, there were clear musical references to his own work – and mocking references too.'

Brinsop picked up the manuscript with distaste. He said he intended to make quite sure that nobody with any connection to the cathedral or Archenford music would have the slightest connection with the emotional rubbish.

Martin felt heroism rush through him like a forest fire.

'And you, Mister Cleeve, you must take your choice. Assist Carpenter in this unpatriotic and ungodly work – or remain in my employ.'

Martin knew he must not do what he knew he was likely to do if the man went one step further. Doctor Brinsop raised the manuscript and tore it in half.

Martin Cleeve reached out thoughtfully and held his employer's nose as hard as he could between thumb and fingers. He began twisting and pulling down. Brinsop squawked in surprise and pain. He sank lower, trying to thrust away the hand that was causing him such pain but Martin beat away at his flapping hands. Doctor Brinsop tried to shout angry protests and cry for help but only managed to sound remarkably similar to Mister Punch. When his employer's chin touched the desk, Martin gave one final triumphant twist and let him go. He thought he had probably broken the nose.

Through appalled and watery eyes, Brinsop glared at the man in outrage. He could not believe what had just happened. 'You hab dwisted by dose,' he said with what he hoped was affronted dignity.

Martin tried not to smile.

'Id is doe laughing madder.'

Martin gave up trying not to laugh. Brinsop raised one hand to his tender nose and slapped his desk in irritation with the other.

'How dare you.'

But Martin was not listening. He was laughing with the sheer glee of somebody who had burned all his boats and discovered that he had never wanted to be a sailor anyway. He reached out again but Brinsop drew back with a nasal bleat of alarm. Martin staggered from the room helpless and hysterical with laughter and apprehension.

'Martin?' whispered Seb, pleased but surprised to see his friend so late at night. His eyes widened as a taxi driver dumped two bulging suitcases and a large box of music inside the Heath Cottage door.

'I'm a free man at last, Seb. But in need of a place to stay.'

'You've found it. What happened?'

'I've either been sacked or I've resigned.'

Seb rose and brought two bottles of beer from the kitchen. 'But what about Brinsop?' he whispered, puzzled.

'I think you could say I've managed to put his nose out of joint.'

Martin collapsed into a chair; he was laughing so

much. Seb and the car driver grinned stupidly at each other, waiting for explanation and payment.

Martin's heroic gesture was almost a disaster. Brinsop was desperate to prosecute Martin Cleeve for assault but was dissuaded by his solicitor who knew that the account, as given to a court and reported in the paper, would make Doctor Brinsop a laughing-stock. He advised the doctor to balance his certain victory before the magistrate against his dignity. After all, nobody had seen his humiliation and the nose had not been broken, only nastily tweaked. The solicitor found himself staring at the carpet under severe temptation to smile: the word 'tweaked' had been a mistake. Brinsop watched his solicitor trying not to laugh and decided to take his advice. There were other ways to attack Martin Cleeve.

The doctor wrote to the editor of the *Archenford Gazette*, the bishop, the Tarrington family and the Archenford Choral and Orchestral Societies of which he himself was President. He alerted them that an unpatriotic and blasphemous work was in danger of finding performers and a place to perform; he expressed his personal outrage and opposition. He wrote to Sir Edward Elgar informing him that a quotation – or rather a misquotation from his 'Serenade For Strings' was to be part of an amateur piece of treasonable pretensions.

His letters had their effects.

The archdeacon telephoned the Swithenbank Rector advising caution in permitting works of a possibly unchristian nature to be heard in the 'House of God'. The editor of the *Gazette* wrote a leading article condemning all those who would seek to insult the sacrifice of Archenford men who had laid down their lives in service of God and King. The secretaries of the Choral and Orchestral Societies wrote to their president assuring that no help would be given to such a despicable venture by any of their members. Letters were published in the *Gazette* damning the writing of cowardly art which sought to weaken the fighting spirit of the nation.

The dust-storm that Brinsop had blown up confused even Seb's friends. Even the Swithenbank villagers were uneasy; heated debates in the Kite's Nest Inn flared up nightly. The Tarringtons refused to commit themselves, one way or the other.

Seb found it difficult to keep his spirits up. Now the work was written he had only the responses of his friends – and enemies – to occupy him, apart from his school lessons and work with the Church Choir. He had not realised he had enemies – it was a shock to think of people he had never met feeling angry and vengeful towards him. Martin was different: the more they were attacked, the more determined he was to perform the piece Seb had written. He spent all his free time writing out copies of the piece – a long thankless task; he had only managed five so far and they would need at least twenty.

Seb saw only the impossibility of having enough scores, finding at least a dozen instrumentalists and enough singers to form a Chorus. Then there was the place to rehearse and a place for performance. There was a soloist to find – a powerful soprano voice was needed. According to the regular reports from the Kite's Nest, Seb couldn't even depend on the undivided loyalty of his choir. Winnie drove from Dormington Hall when she could, but found her friend difficult and moody. 22 June would have been Alex's eighteenth birthday. Seb had longed to give the first performance then – a birthday gift to a much-missed friend. But the local opposition produced paralysis. After two weeks of angry debate and disapproval, with friends avoiding the subject, the project ground to a halt as Brinsop had intended. Martin secretly began to regret the pulling of the nose – Seb's only regret had always been that he hadn't been there to see it.

It was Colonel Tarrington who made the break-through. He appeared in the church at the end of a Friday evening practice and asked to hear some of this music that was stirring up such nonsense. Seb sent a choirboy running to Heath Cottage for Martin Cleeve and asked Nathan Biddle to stay on, with JHR.

The three performers struggled to give a true idea of how the piece could sound. Martin did his considerable best to make the creaking harmonium sound like a small orchestra and to sing like a chorus. Nathan sight-read the easier sections and JHR filled in, singing and reading. Seb shuffled about at the back of the church in distress; it sounded terrible; it was ridiculous; he should never have even put one single note on paper.

He changed his mind at the end when, from the chaos, Nathan's clear, innocent voice drew out the Parry tune, 'Repton', quietly at first but growing, until JHR and Martin joined in, as the audience would join in, and, as Nathan sang the final verse alone without accompaniment, Seb felt excitement snatch at his heart. He knew the work was good and that Alex would have loved it – would have given anything to have the solo that Nathan had just sung. The echoes drifted along the ancient roofbeams, then there was silence. Seb found his eyes were wet and hastily reached for his handkerchief: ridiculous.

Martin at the harmonium watched the colonel. So did JHR standing with Nathan at Martin's side. Seb watched from the church door. The colonel rose. '22 June? That's when you want to do it?'

Seb stepped forward. 'Yes.'

'You want to do it here, in the church?'

'Yes.'

'Young Biddle here – he'd be the boy singer?'

226

'Yes,' shouted Nathan firmly.

'And the other soloist – the woman singer – would one of the London professionals take it on?'

Seb looked towards Martin who gulped and weakly replied. 'Yes.'

'Any other problems?'

The three men stared at each other. There were hosts of other problems. It was JHR who spoke for them. 'No.'

Martin and Seb gaped at him in horror. They switched their attention back to the colonel.

'22 June it is then. In the church – leave the rector to me. Fix up your lady singer. Send me the bills.'

Seb opened the door for him. The colonel laid a hand on his arm and moved him outside into the churchyard.

'I don't know much about music, old boy, but that made my blood run hot and cold. That's war – you've got it; you've got your friend, too, I rather think. Lionel said he wanted to make everything right if he lived. I think the Hall can do something along that line.'

He walked to the church gate, leaning heavily on his stick. Seb watched him go and then turned to where Winnie's flowers caught the bright beams of sunlight where Alex lay. His thoughts were too complicated. He turned back into the church where Nathan rushed to hug him while JHR shouted Alleluia and Martin cheered and threw the whole score fluttering into the air.

5

Turn of the Tide

Giles and Mollie Tarrington paid for a panel in the advertisement pages of the *Archenford Gazette*. The editor was not keen to accept it but business was business and it was even more important not to upset the county land-owners than people like Doctor Brinsop. It announced that Evensong at Saint Swithen's Church, Swithenbank, on Sunday 22 June 1918, was to be in memory of all local men who had lost their lives in the Great War. There would be no sermon but the service was to be followed by a performance of Sebastian Carpenter's short cantata. It concluded:

Mr and Mrs Giles Tarrington and Colonel H. Tarrington of Swithenbank Hall are pleased to be associated with Mister Carpenter's fine memorial work.

The first effect was that Joshua Beeves called in his Sunday suit at Heath Cottage to offer all possible assistance of the church choir, hay-making month or not. The second was the arrival at Swithenbank Hall of young Mister Chapman, a journalist on the *Gazette* who knew a good story when it was jumping up and down and waving. He was able to hand to his editor the story of Private Davies' search for Second-Lieutenant Lionel Tarrington and Private Carpenter in the mud of the Somme. He wrote of their discovery in the enemy trench, gassed, with the single gasmask given to the dying officer. Within three days he was further able to report to his editor that Martin Cleeve – recently Assistant to Doctor Brinsop – had secured the services of Miss Adela Edwards of the Royal Opera who would sing the soprano part in Sebastian Carpenter's work. Young Mister Chapman had telephoned Miss Edwards from the *Gazette* office for her comments and was able to report that she found the cantata 'original and moving' and felt 'honoured' to be asked to take part. She told him also that in view of the difficulties Mister Cleeve was having in finding sufficient instrumentalists she would be bringing with her to Swithenbank half the string section of the London Fidelio Players. 'We all feel strongly that this is a historic musical occasion,' Miss Edwards concluded. 'Mister Carpenter's fine work brings out the tragedy of war as well as its comradeship and glory.'

Mister Goodwin, the photographer, was the first Archenford musician to ask if he and the other members of the Paternoster Quartet, might help his friend, Mister Cleeve. The same day, Harry turned up at Swithenbank with two local wounded men from Blatchfords who had played in their regimental bands – a drummer and a trumpeter. Two copies of the score were smuggled by Norman to Dobbin and Birdy. Every senior choirboy pledged to make at least three copies each in secret.

Now the dam of resistance had crumbled, offers poured in. The Archenford Choral and Orchestral Societies were speechless with jealousy at having no place in what was fast becoming an important event, thanks to their president's narrow-minded obstinacy which had stopped them mingling on equal terms with Miss Adela Edwards and the London Fidelio. In short, everybody now wanted to get in on the act. Seb and Martin made a momentous decision. They invited Miss Edwards down to Swithenbank where she slipped quietly into the church during Evensong. As a result of what she heard, she agreed with Seb that his church choir would do very well, with rigorous training, as the chorus. When this was announced, after the service, and the famous soprano was personally introduced to each member of the choir, Mister Beeves choked with pride and emotion as he vowed that she could be sure Saint Swithen's wouldn't let her down. He would have called for three cheers if the rector hadn't been present.

Doctor Brinsop's final hope was Sir Edward Elgar. A representative of Sir Edward attended an early rehearsal of the cantata and, two days later, a letter from the great man himself arrived, not only giving full permission to use the eight bars of his music, but asking if it were possible to reserve places for himself and Lady Elgar, since they would be visiting Hereford friends at the time. The furious Brinsop was left isolated and foolish.

There was less and less for Seb to do as 22 June came closer. Martin was now the man at the centre with his boundless enthusiasm and energy. It was strongly hinted that, after the performance, he was to be asked to move to London where the Fidelio Players needed an assistant conductor. Adela Edwards came, with her French maid, to take up residence at the Hall. Three days later, the Fidelio Players were met at Archenford station by a variety of vehicles. They were housed, according to their orchestral status, at the Hall, the Rectory or the Kite's Nest – those lucky enough to lodge in the latter never forgot the experience (and neither did the Kite's Nest).

Winnie made a point of seeing as much of Seb as possible during these hectic days when the man who had made it all possible seemed to be shuffling about on the edge of things. They would drive into the country or stroll through Swithenbank estate where they would not be in danger of meeting performers or organisers rushing about in a panic. They talked much of Alex. Often it seemed as he were as solid a companion to them as he had been on the river trip. They often drove to Sarson Bridge and waited for a train to go over.

Winnie had driven back to Dormington Hall one day and left Seb to stroll home alongside the lake when he met Colonel Tarrington sat on the grass enjoying the sun.

'Hello old boy. How's our famous composer?'

Seb smiled and sat at the old man's side. They watched the breeze rippling across the water. The colonel confessed he was a refugee from the excitement and hullabaloo at the Hall.

'Did you expect all this, Seb?'

'I wanted it more personal – just Alex and me.'

The colonel nodded understandingly. They both clambered to their feet.

'Two old crocks – that's us,' chuckled the colonel.

They set off slowly towards Heath Cottage.

'It will be a great occasion, Seb.'

'Thanks to you.'

'Thanks to us all. We're a clever lot at Swithenbank, one way and another.'

He asked if it were true that Martin had decided to leave for London immediately after the great day. Seb replied that it was. 'And you? You don't intend to leave us, I hope?'

'No, Colonel. I've found my real place.'

The old man was pleased. They came through a small gate, on to the road. 'The next thing, in that case,' he said slyly, 'will be to find you a wife.'

Seb looked across at him. 'I'm not much of a catch, Colonel. An old crock, as you said.'

'What about that young lady of yours from Dormington Hall?'

'Winnie? She's like Martin. She's got higher ambitions.'

The two long sentences had tripped up Seb's regular breathing. The two men stopped for a while.

'We must have a word with Wilkins,' declared Colonel Tarrington. 'That man can arrange anything.'

6

Eighteenth Birthday at Swithenbank

It was, as the colonel had foretold, a great occasion. The village street was packed with carriages and cars; some had travelled a great distance. The crush in Saint

231

Swithen's was so heavy that worshippers filled the porch and spilled out into the churchyard. The day was sunny and warm so the church doors were opened wide.

Evensong itself was simple; Seb had chosen plainsong for most of the music, saving his singers' voices. The rector and Colonel Tarrington read the lessons and the anthem was a simple chorale by Bach.

Quiet anticipation began to settle among the congregation as soon as the rector and choir had moved away into the vestry. Immaculate in morning dress, the dozen members of the Fidelio Players filed in as Wilkins and a team of helpers swiftly set up music-stands and seating for the performers. The two Blatchford men came awkwardly forward, one on sticks, in their blue suits, white shirts and red ties. Mister Goodwin nervously led the Paternoster Quartet to its place while JHR slipped unnoticed onto the harmonium stool. The sense of excitement grew as the orchestra began tuning up and the choir returned, no longer in cassock and surplice but Sunday best. Adela Edwards followed them, serene and elegant in black, resting a reassuring hand on Nathan's shoulder whose expression was grimly set in determination to sing better than he had ever done. Martin Cleeve left the vestry, feeling ill at ease in the morning suit borrowed from Giles Tarrington; he threaded his way through the crowded performers and stood on the wooden platform that the Estate woodworkers had made especially for the occasion. He faced outwards, away from his chorus, orchestra and soloists. The rector was the last to leave the vestry. In a solemn voice, loud enough to overcome the buzz of excitement, he asked the congregation to stand.

Gently, the rector recited the names of local men whom the Great War had killed. Men from parishes neighbouring Swithenbank – Treestone, Willowsmill, Saint Ann's, Linford, Cumberly. The Swithenbank men came last, Alex among them. 'Evan Stock, Timothy Packman, Lionel Tarrington, Alexander Davies.'

Winnie's hand tightened on Seb's. The rector sat. The twenty-four names were known to most of the congregation. They brought a sad and sombre atmosphere.

Martin raised his head to meet Seb's steady gaze. The two men held their eyes together for perhaps ten seconds but much passed between them. The look was one of gratitude and friendship. It remembered cold practices in the Song School; interventions in Collett's classroom; a missed entry in Stanford's Magnificat. It remembered a frantic and barely believable escape – where both men suddenly smiled. The look spoke of a room in Blatchfords where Alex and Seb had decided to become soldiers. That was as far as Martin was able to go. He suddenly became brisk and professional. He eased his jacket across his shoulders and glanced once more at Seb. This time the conductor was asking the composer if he were ready to hear his music. Seb nodded.

Martin swung around to face the performers and raised his hands. In the silence a cough was muffled as Martin swept his hands down, in memory of Alex Davies, 1899 to 1917.

The opening was quiet. The quartet played a tune full of sweetness and nostalgia, recalling the 'Serenade'. There were high notes on a cello which suggested birdsong. Adela Edwards stepped forward to recite JHR's words about a country boy in battle remembering home.

The march followed. At first it was jaunty, swaggering – full of hope and glory – but after a while, without any of the hearers knowing exactly how, it became a funeral march, slow and sombre. Then it was not even that, and the instruments fell silent one by one, until only the drummer was left. Now his rhythm faltered and his beats became confused, quieter and quieter like a blind man wandering into the distance.

Miss Edwards sang her first song magnificently. Chorus and orchestra combined in a solid, respectable patriotic song. She sang with the trebles, stirringly, until the other voices fell silent and she took up the solo. Seb had written her a high line which moved higher and higher until it became a meaningless cry, level and desperate.

The high level note was obliterated by a series of trumpet calls – reveille, mealtime, fall in, dismiss – which heralded the movement entitled 'Pavé'. It was deeply private to Seb and perhaps only people who had known Pavé could appreciate it. It caught the quirky eccentricity of Cocky and Massey, the clockwork efficiency, the relaxations and alarms. A sudden furious discordant destruction shocked the listeners. Children put hands to their ears – though those who had been to war, the Blatchfords people and the Dormington Ambulance Girls, closed their eyes or nodded in recognition. Then there was silence, broken only by low cello trills which sounded like pigeons to Nathan – pigeons asking questions (but that was daft, he thought). The cello died away and, without any accompaniment, Adela Edwards sang a sweet song, to an Archenford folk-tune, about a shy farm lad.

The harmonium wailed into the silence at full volume. A hymn about the army of God was bawled hatefully by the chorus. There were three desperate verses, followed by a shouted 'Amen' – a shock.

Almost as soon as the Quartet began to play, Winnie caught her breath and squeezed Seb's hand. Seb was conjuring Alex into the Church. The music was friendly, quiet, cheeky. Almost everyone in the building who had known Alex found him in their minds' eye without knowing why. It was the Alex they knew. But then the poise of the music started to slip; the rhythm faltered and lost control as Alex became the man known only to Winnie and guessed at by Seb. The disintegration moved on unstoppable – until the frightening, long-drawn-out discord of the Passchendaele explosion crashed through the Church.

From underneath this terrifying noise crept 'The Warrior Babe', more aggressive every second, until Adela Edwards hit her highest note on the words 'Not peace but a sword'. She sang it over and over again. Harsh and compromising. The orchestra softened and died away, leaving her voice crying alone. Suddenly, in mid-sentence, she stopped and the harsh, adult voice gave way to Nathan as he began Alex's favourite hymn, alone, without accompaniment.

> Dear Lord and Father of Mankind,
> Forgive our foolish ways . . .

The quartet crept softly in behind the child's steady treble and stayed there gently during the first of three verses.

Martin suddenly swung to face the congregation and raised his baton to lead them all into their verse. Orchestra and harmonium thrilled into the air with chorus and soloists together. The congregation inside and outside, took up the words.

> Drop Thy still dews of quietness
> Till all our strivings cease . . .

Everyone sung, needing to sing, needing to share the tensions and the heartache. Voices were rough, out of time or tone-deaf; it did not matter. Nothing mattered but to be part of the extraordinary moment. Gemma Dormington and her Girls sang. The Blatchfords group sang. The families and friends of the dead men sang. Mollie and Giles and the colonel sang, remembering Lionel. Tears streamed from Winnie as she heard Seb rasping and gasping the words as best he could:

Take from our souls
The strain and stress,
And let our ordered lives confess
The beauty of Thy peace . . .

Then Martin turned from the congregation back to Nathan who concluded the hymn alone:

Breathe through the heats of our desire
Thy coolness and Thy balm.
Let sense be dumb,
Let flesh retire.
Speak through the earthquake, wind and fire,
O still, small voice of calm . . .
O still, small voice of calm.

The quartet echoed his pure last line and one violin echoed the quartet. On the final note, all strings came in, low, sad throbbing, while the rector read again the Roll of Honour, slow and unhurried:

'. . . Timothy Packman. Lionel Tarrington. Alexander Davies.'

The strings vibrated in the evening air for perhaps another twenty seconds, before they died away, merging, like the dead, into silence.
Silence.
Martin gently lowered his arms and Seb whispered inside his head, 'Happy Birthday, Alex.'
Nobody moved. Seb turned as a hand rested on his shoulder. Sir Edward Elgar, behind him, nodded slowly. Winnie at last let go his hand and Seb saw that Diana, near the back of the church, was crying. He always told their children that was why he married her.

Gillian Rubinstein

BEYOND THE LABYRINTH

Growing up seems difficult enough for Brenton. He can't get on with his parents, his younger brother is taller than he is and seems to be overtaking him in every way, and his mother has invited 12-year-old Victoria Hare to live with them as her parents are overseas. Life becomes even more complicated when an alien anthropologist arrives to study an ancient Aboriginal tribe who once lived in the area round his home. . . .

Robert Westall

THE KINGDOM BY THE SEA

Bombs were falling on Tyneside. Harry began to count. If you were still counting at ten, the bombs missed you . . . The last thing he remembered was saying 'seven'.

Harry survives but his parents, his home, are gone. He can't bear to be fussed over so he goes away, where nobody knows him.

So begins an incredible journey. Harry is alone except for Don, the dog, bombed-out like Harry, whom he finds on the beach. Harry is a survivor, but there is one last battle he is unprepared for . . .

Winner of the Guardian Children's Fiction Award and shortlisted for the Carnegie Medal.

A Selected List of Fiction from Mammoth

While every effort is made to keep prices low, it is sometimes necessary to increase prices at short notice. Mammoth Books reserves the right to show new retail prices on covers which may differ from those previously advertised in the text or elsewhere.

The prices shown below were correct at the time of going to press.

☐	416 13972 8	**Why the Whales Came**	Michael Morpurgo	£2.50
☐	7497 0034 3	**My Friend Walter**	Michael Morpurgo	£2.50
☐	7497 0035 1	**The Animals of Farthing Wood**	Colin Dann	£2.99
☐	7497 0136 6	**I Am David**	Anne Holm	£2.50
☐	7497 0139 0	**Snow Spider**	Jenny Nimmo	£2.50
☐	7497 0140 4	**Emlyn's Moon**	Jenny Nimmo	£2.25
☐	7497 0344 X	**The Haunting**	Margaret Mahy	£2.25
☐	416 96850 3	**Catalogue of the Universe**	Margaret Mahy	£1.95
☐	7497 0051 3	**My Friend Flicka**	Mary O'Hara	£2.99
☐	7497 0079 3	**Thunderhead**	Mary O'Hara	£2.99
☐	7497 0219 2	**Green Grass of Wyoming**	Mary O'Hara	£2.99
☐	416 13722 9	**Rival Games**	Michael Hardcastle	£1.99
☐	416 13212 X	**Mascot**	Michael Hardcastle	£1.99
☐	7497 0126 9	**Half a Team**	Michael Hardcastle	£1.99
☐	416 08812 0	**The Whipping Boy**	Sid Fleischman	£1.99
☐	7497 0033 5	**The Lives of Christopher Chant**	Diana Wynne-Jones	£2.50
☐	7497 0164 1	**A Visit to Folly Castle**	Nina Beachcroft	£2.25

All these books are available at your bookshop or newsagent, or can be ordered direct from the publisher. Just tick the titles you want and fill in the form below.

Mandarin Paperbacks, Cash Sales Department, PO Box 11, Falmouth, Cornwall TR10 9EN.

Please send cheque or postal order, no currency, for purchase price quoted and allow the following for postage and packing:

UK	80p for the first book, 20p for each additional book ordered to a maximum charge of £2.00.
BFPO	80p for the first book, 20p for each additional book.
Overseas including Eire	£1.50 for the first book, £1.00 for the second and 30p for each additional book thereafter.

NAME (Block letters) ....

ADDRESS ....

....

....